DARK REBEL'S FORTUNE

THE CHILDREN OF THE GODS
BOOK NINETY-FOUR

I. T. LUCAS

Published by Evening Star Press, LLC.

EveningStarPress.com

ISBN: 978-1-962067-72-0

CONTENTS

KYRA

K yra woke before dawn, her body instantly alert despite having slept only a few hours. The weight of Max's arm draped across her waist was both comforting and unfamiliar.

His steady breathing warmed the back of her neck, and for a moment, she allowed herself to savor the closeness.

No wonder she'd had such a good night's sleep.

She felt safe for the first time in forever.

So much had changed since her rescue from that hellhole in Tahav. She'd gone from being a prisoner with no known family other than her rebel crew, to being set free and discovering she had a grown daughter, four nieces who needed her protection, and possibly four sisters and their families waiting to be saved. Not to mention whatever was developing between her and Max—this connection that had sparked instantly and burned with an intensity that thrilled her but also scared her a little.

She didn't know how to do this or be a part of a couple, and she was winging it, hoping that staying true to herself would be enough. Heck, she couldn't be anything else even if she tried. But it was okay. Max was like her, and he understood her—the same way she understood him.

For better or for worse, they were warriors, both dealing with the ugly side of humanity—him fighting traffickers and pedophiles in addition to Doomers and her fighting a fanatical regime that had stripped Iranian women of fundamental human rights and financed terror globally.

She and Max were comrades in arms, and even though it seemed like they were fighting different battles, it looked like their enemies were working together.

Carefully, she slipped from under his arm and exited the bed. Max stirred but didn't wake. He must feel safe with her to sleep so peacefully.

She allowed herself a moment to study him—the strong line of his jaw, the slight furrow between his brows, the way his blond hair fell across his forehead. It was hard to reconcile his youthful, almost boyish appearance with his age, and that was coming from her, an immortal who was nearly fifty years old. Still, he'd lived for half a millennium, and compared to that, she was a baby immortal.

Max had seen empires rise and fall.

His eyes suddenly fluttered open. "Time to go?" he murmured, his voice husky with sleep.

"Not yet." She cupped one cheek and leaned to kiss the other. "But soon."

Smiling, he reached up to tuck a strand of hair behind her ear, his fingertips brushing over her cheek. "I should head downstairs to my apartment to get ready."

"We can have breakfast when you return."

"Sounds like a plan." He slipped out of bed, pushed his feet into his boots, and, after a quick peck on her cheek, exited the master suite, closing the door silently behind him.

If he encountered anyone on the way out, they would assume that she and Max had shared a night of passion. No one would believe that they had just slept in each other's arms, finding comfort and strength in the closeness, in the connection.

Let them believe what they would.

Kyra didn't care.

After a quick shower, she dressed in her new tactical gear, appreciating how perfectly everything fit. The cargo pants with multiple pockets, the light-weight top that wouldn't restrict her movement, the boots that felt as if they'd been made specifically for her feet and weighed next to nothing.

She strapped her pendant around her neck, then slid the two rings Jasmine had given her onto her fingers. They felt foreign on her hand—relics from a life she couldn't remember. But perhaps her sisters would recognize them, and that recognition might help her prove to them that she was indeed their sibling despite not having aged much since they had parted decades ago. Her sisters had been so young then that they might not remember what she had looked like.

She was zipping up her bag when she heard a soft knock on her door.

"Come in," she called, expecting Max, but instead Jasmine poked her head in.

"The girls are up," she said. "They want to see you before you go."

"I was hoping to let them sleep." Kyra shouldered her pack.

Jasmine shook her head. "Not a chance. I think they have barely slept, waiting for you to get up, and they would never forgive you if you tried to sneak out without giving them one last hug."

Jasmine's comment warmed Kyra's heart. Her nieces had barely gotten to know her, but they were already attached to her and she to them.

As she and Jasmine passed by the door to Arezoo and Laleh's room, it flew open, and Arezoo stood in the doorway with her hands on her hips.

"You weren't going to leave without saying good-bye, were you?"

"Of course not," Kyra said. "I was just coming to wake you."

The other three girls appeared behind Arezoo,

looking sleepy and determined at the same time. Laleh, the youngest, rubbed her eyes.

It seemed that the four girls had all slept in one bedroom, which was kind of sweet. It made perfect sense that they would feel safer together.

"We want to make you breakfast," Arezoo announced.

"That's really not—" Kyra began, but Arezoo cut her off with a gesture that was so like Kyra's own that Jasmine laughed.

"Nonnegotiable," Arezoo said. "Donya makes excellent eggs, and I can handle the coffee. Azadeh, go get the fruit from the refrigerator."

Watching the girls mobilize with military precision, Kyra felt a swell of pride. Despite everything they'd endured, they retained a resilience that was nothing short of remarkable.

They were survivors, just like her.

"You might as well surrender," Jasmine murmured. "When Arezoo makes up her mind, there's no changing it. I wonder where she gets that from?" There was a teasing lilt to her voice as she cast a sideways glance at Kyra.

While the girls got busy in the kitchen, Kyra and Jasmine sat at the bar and watched.

Jasmine leaned toward her. "You've left one rebel group only to lead another, but I have a feeling that Arezoo will fight you over leadership."

Kyra nodded. "She reminds me a lot of myself. I

guess it is true what they say about blood being thicker than water."

"Yeah." Jasmine winced. "The problem is that we carry some nasty genes in addition to the good ones. I don't like what your father did to you. He wasn't a good person."

"No, he wasn't," Kyra agreed.

She would have liked to believe that her father had had her best interests at heart when he'd stolen her from her husband and daughter and asked Durhad to make her forget about them, but now she had to accept that this was not true. Based on the information that she had pieced together from what she'd learned, it had become obvious that his career and his reputation were the only reasons he hadn't killed her but instead had her committed to an insane asylum for reprogramming. He'd hoped no one would ever find out her so-called transgression, and so his honor would remain intact.

When the doorbell rang, Ell-rom walked over to the door and opened the way for Max.

He was dressed in tactical gear similar to hers, and a duffel bag was slung over his shoulder.

His face brightened when he saw the scene in the kitchen. "Something smells amazing," he said, setting his bag down.

"Breakfast is almost ready," Arezoo said. "You all need to move to the dining room. There are not enough seats next to the counter."

As they headed to where Arezoo wanted them,

the doorbell rang, and Jasmine went to answer it, returning with Fenella in tow.

"I smell coffee," Fenella said, sliding into a seat on Max's other side.

She looked good in a pair of black leggings and an oversized blue top. Some color had returned to her cheeks, and her smile looked more genuine, but even though Fenella was healing and her natural beauty was emerging, Kyra was no longer jealous of her.

Last night's episode was one big misunderstanding, and Kyra was now secure in the knowledge that Max was interested only in her, and Fenella was just a friend to him.

Arezoo brought the coffee pot to the table, pouring for everyone with the gravitas of someone performing a sacred ritual. Donya followed with a large platter of eggs, Azadeh with another one of cut fruit, and Laleh with a basket of toasted sliced bread.

"Thank you," Max said, helping himself to some eggs. "This looks very nice and much better than anything I make."

"Do you cook often?" Donya asked him.

Max laughed. "Let's just say my culinary skills peaked sometime during the Renaissance, and I haven't bothered updating them since. I can build a decent cooking fire, though."

Kyra stifled a laugh. He was exaggerating and clowning around to put the girls at ease.

"Renaissance?" Laleh's brow furrowed. "That was hundreds of years ago."

"It was," Max agreed. "I'm that old." He winked.

Laleh giggled. "You're joking. Right?"

"Not at all. I'm over five hundred years old."

Kyra enjoyed watching the easy way he interacted with her nieces, drawing out smiles and questions even from Azadeh, who was the least talkative of the four. His ability to put people at ease and make them feel safe around him was endearing, even though he sometimes overdid it. She could see how some could interpret his teasing as offensive.

Not her, though, and not her smart nieces, who got his dry humor.

The conversation flowed around Kyra as they ate and drank coffee and chatted as if they'd been a family for years instead of just days.

Max glanced at his watch. "We should be heading out. Traffic in LA is unpredictable, and we don't want the others to have to wait for us."

A heavy silence fell over the table, and then Arezoo stood up, coming around to wrap her arms around Kyra's neck. "Bring our mothers, aunts, and cousins," she whispered fiercely.

"I will," Kyra promised, holding her niece tightly.

One by one, the other girls came to embrace her while Max stood a couple of feet away, giving them space for their goodbyes.

When the girls were finally done, he touched her elbow. "We should go."

Kyra hugged Jasmine, Fenella, and Ell-rom next,

and then she and Max gathered their belongings and headed for the elevator.

"Hold on," Jasmine called after them. "I almost forgot." She produced a familiar velvet pouch from her pocket. "For luck." She handed it to Kyra.

"Your tarot cards?" Kyra asked. "But last night you said—"

"I know what I said," Jasmine interrupted. "But I want you to take them. You left them for me to guide me through some dark times, but now you need them more than I do. It's just a loan." Jasmine pressed the pouch into Kyra's hands. "You'll have to return them to me. I consider it insurance that you'll come back."

Kyra's throat tightened with emotion as her fingers closed around the pouch, feeling the well-worn velvet between her fingers. "I promise to bring them back."

Jasmine pulled her into a fierce embrace, and Kyra held her daughter close, memorizing the feel of her, the scent of her hair. Twenty-three years had been stolen from them. After the completion of this mission, she vowed not to allow anything to take even one more day.

"I love you, Mom," Jasmine whispered, the words nearly undoing Kyra completely.

"I love you too, sweetie," she murmured.

2

MAX

The Audi R8 purred beneath Max and Kyra as he guided it along the highway. The car was pure indulgence, a low-slung beast that could hit sixty miles per hour in 3.2 seconds. Not that Max needed such speed for daily life, but five centuries of existence had taught him to appreciate life's pleasures when he had the opportunity.

It had taken some maneuvering to get a car that was not the standard issue most clan members had been given, and then having it modded with the custom self-driving and specialty windows required of all village vehicles for security reasons. Luckily, Toven had paved the way by getting two specialty vehicles first, so there was a precedent, and then Kalugal followed, getting himself a Mercedes-AMG S63 sedan. Once the floodgates had opened, many more village residents ordered fancy rides and the necessary custom modifications for them.

Kyra hadn't seemed to notice, though, and she hadn't commented on the superb vehicle, which was disappointing. After all, what was the point of having a luxury car if it didn't impress the ladies, right?

Instead, she was busy scanning their surroundings.

"Not many people on the road this early," she observed, her voice cutting through the comfortable silence that had settled between them.

"One of the few perks of leaving early," he said, downshifting as they rounded a curve. "But that will change as soon as we hit the freeway. Fortunately, we are going in the opposite direction of the morning rush-hour traffic, so perhaps it's not going to be that bad."

She nodded, her fingers touching her amber pendant. "I've never been to Los Angeles before," she said after a moment. "Or at least, not that I can recall. It's different from what I expected."

"How so?"

She gestured toward the sprawling cityscape stretching inland. "It's more vertical than I imagined. All those buildings clustered together in the center, reaching upward."

Kyra had only been to downtown Los Angeles, so she thought that the rest of the city was like that as well, but most of it was spread out horizontally rather than vertically.

"I'll give you a proper tour when we get back," he said.

Her lips curved into a small smile. "I'd like that."

Max navigated the car onto the highway that would take them inland toward the foothills. Nestled among them was the airstrip that the clan maintained for their private use.

"Nice car," Kyra finally commented, her hand running appreciatively over the leather dashboard. "Not exactly inconspicuous, though."

Max chuckled. "I'm not a spy, and I don't use it on missions. It's for my private use." He cast her a side-long glance. "What's the point of accumulating wealth if not to spend at least some of it on indulgences?"

"I wouldn't know." She looked out the window. "I've never had much."

That made him feel like a spoiled brat, and that was not how he wanted her to see him. "There's something to be said for driving a vehicle that can outrun almost anything on the road."

There. A legitimate excuse for spending an insane amount on a car.

"Planning on making a getaway?" Kyra teased, one eyebrow arched.

He shrugged. "One never knows. Five centuries of fighting has taught me that every advantage, be it a better weapon or a better escape vehicle, can mean the difference between victory and failure, life and death."

She laughed—a sound he was finding increasingly addictive. The way it transformed her face, softening her hard edges, made his chest inflate with an emotion he was still getting used to.

"That's an awesome excuse to get a fancy toy, Max. But I get it. You've earned it. Enjoy."

They fell back into comfortable silence, and as the scenery changed into a boring urban sprawl, Max let his mind drift to the previous night.

After Kyra had fallen asleep, lulled by his singing, he'd spent nearly an hour just watching her, marveling at how peaceful she looked in slumber, how the fierce warrior façade dissolved into something softer, more vulnerable.

It had been intimate in a way that transcended physical connection.

Sex was easy. Max had centuries of experience in that department, but this was new territory for him. The fact that she'd asked him to stay, to simply hold her through the night, meant more to him than if she'd wanted him for sex.

Fates knew he'd had enough of those kind of nights and not enough of what he'd shared with Kyra last night.

"You're smiling," she said.

"Am I?" He glanced at her, not bothering to hide his grin.

"What were you thinking about?"

"Last night," he admitted. "Holding you while you slept."

She held his gaze. "It has been a long time since I've slept so soundly. Usually, I keep one eye open, so to speak." She paused, then added, "I don't remember ever feeling so safe."

Coming from Kyra, who had survived two decades as a resistance fighter in one of the world's most dangerous regions, the admission felt monumental.

Max reached across the console to take her hand, squeezing it gently. "I'm glad that I make you feel safe."

Her fingers intertwined with his. "Yeah, me too. It was nice knowing that someone I trusted was watching my back. Literally."

When he turned into the unmarked dirt road that seemed to lead nowhere, Max slowed, carefully navigating the luxury sports car over the rough terrain.

"This vehicle is not exactly designed for off-roading," Kyra noted, bracing her hand on the dashboard as they bounced along.

"Don't worry, it's only about half a mile of this, and then we hit the paved section. This is just to confuse the enemy, so no one suspects it actually leads anywhere." Max patted the dashboard apologetically. "Sorry, baby."

Kyra snorted. "Do you always talk to your car like it's your girlfriend?"

He grinned. "Guilty. I get lonely sometimes, and Melinda here is a good listener."

"Right." Kyra rolled her eyes, but the amusement in her voice was unmistakable.

They soon reached the paved section of the road

as it wound through a stand of trees, eventually opening up to reveal the airstrip and the large hangar in the back.

Despite them arriving almost half an hour early, the jet was already on the tarmac, and its engines were running.

Max pulled the car into a parking area, where two other vehicles were already parked—a van and a car probably belonging to the pilot. He would need to arrange for someone to pick up his baby and bring her to the parking garage either in the keep or the village. He wasn't leaving her out in the open.

After grabbing their bags from the trunk, they walked toward Yamanu, who was waving them over.

"About time," he said by way of greeting, though his tone was light. "I was beginning to think you'd decided to skip the mission and elope instead."

"Careful," Max warned, though no real heat was behind it. "I'd hate to have to kick your ass in front of everyone this early in the morning."

"You can try, buddy." Yamanu laughed, then turned to Kyra. "I have a gift for you." He pulled a package out of his duffle bag. "A new clan sat phone, pre-loaded with all the contacts you'll need."

"Thank you." Kyra took it, examining the sleek device. "Is it secure?"

Yamanu grinned. "It's encrypted six ways from Sunday, according to William. You can even call your rebel friends."

"I wouldn't. Not directly."

"Max can show you how it works. And now, for the big gift." He handed her a large shopping bag. "Compliments of Eva, our master of disguises."

It was heavy, and as Kyra unzipped the bag, she found a folded black abaya and niqab and then another garment that looked like the torso of a fat woman with large breasts. "What is that?"

"That's a fat suit," Yamanu said. "You wear it under your clothing to change the shape of your body. Eva used to do undercover detective work before she joined the clan. She's still in that business, but she mostly manages it these days. Now that she's a mother, she has a crew of young immortals doing the fieldwork for her. Mey called her yesterday about Iranian traditional clothing, and she suggested pairing it with this. You can hide a lot of weapons under these fake boobs and that belly, or anything else you might need to conceal, for that matter. It can't fool a scanner, but it can pass a pat-down."

A slow smile spread across Kyra's face as she examined the garment more closely. "That's ingenious," she said. "No one looks twice at a heavyset woman in conservative clothing. This is perfect camouflage. And you are right. I can hide all sorts of weapons under it."

"That was Eva's thinking," Yamanu agreed. "She says it gets a little sweaty inside, so take that into consideration."

"Tell her I said thank you." Kyra put the items

back in the bag. "This will make things much easier for me."

"You can tell her yourself." Yamanu pointed at the phone. "Eva said to call her if you have any questions about how to strap it on or anything else you need. She has a lot of experience working undercover."

"I will. Thank you."

"And this one is for you." Yamanu handed Max a small bundle. "You'll need a little makeup if you don't want to draw attention to yourself."

Max frowned at the package. "Is that what's in here? Makeup?"

Yamanu laughed. "It wouldn't do the trick without the proper clothing, right? We are going all out."

"Don't tell me that I need to wear a caftan. How am I supposed to run or fight in that?"

Kyra chuckled. "If I can do all that in an abaya, niqab, and a fat suit, you can do it in a caftan."

Max groaned. "You're right, but I don't have to like it." He put the bundle inside his duffel bag and zipped it up.

They followed Yamanu to the jet, where the rest of the team was gathered. Jade stood with the two pureblooded Kra-ell females, Rishba and Asuka, and the hybrid males, Dima and Anton.

As they approached, Jade turned to them. "Good morning."

Kyra handed the bag with her new disguise to Max and stepped forward. "I want to thank all of you for doing this. I know you're risking a lot to help rescue my family, and I'm grateful."

Jade waved away her thanks with a dismissive gesture. "We're doing this for fun," she said, and though her tone was flat, there was a gleam in her large, dark eyes. "And for the clan. We owe them a great deal."

"Still, thank you," Kyra insisted.

"Okay, people," Yamanu said. "We can continue chatting on board."

As the team began boarding, each carrying their personal gear, Max hung back with Kyra, allowing the others to go ahead.

"Nervous?" he asked quietly.

"Yes, but not about the mission per se," she said. "I've done extractions before, which were much more complicated than getting civilians out of their homes. Also, we have a good team with extraordinary abilities in addition to good intelligence." She paused, her fingers unconsciously reaching for her pendant again. "I'm more concerned about my sisters' reactions and whether they'll come with us willingly or fight us so we don't take the rest of the children."

"We'll cross that bridge when we come to it," Max said. "There is no point in speculating about the unknown, right?"

"I know it's pointless, but I can't help it." Kyra started up the stairs.

Max followed her into the jet's spacious cabin.

It wasn't nearly as luxurious as Kalugal's, but it was still quite nice compared to a commercial aircraft. The clan's private jet was configured for both comfort and functionality, with seating arranged in conversational groupings and side panels that could be pulled out and turned into tables or desks.

Max led Kyra to a pair of seats near the middle of the cabin. "These are the most comfortable," he explained, stowing their bags in the overhead compartment. "And they can recline fully if you want to get some rest during the flight."

"How long until we reach Tehran?" she asked, buckling herself in.

"About fifteen hours, give or take." Max settled into the seat beside her. "We'll make one refueling stop where the clan has arrangements." He gave her a sidelong glance. "You should try to get some sleep during the flight so you'll be sharp and ready when we land."

"I doubt I could sleep," Kyra admitted. "I'm pumped with too much adrenaline."

"I could sing to you again," he offered with a half-smile. "Or we can do it together." He pulled out his phone. "I have a karaoke playlist we can sing along to."

"Maybe later." She adjusted her seatbelt and reclined her seat by a few degrees.

The engines increased in pitch as the pilot prepared for takeoff.

"Have you ever flown before?" Max asked. "I mean before we rescued you and the others?"

Kyra shook her head. "Not that I remember, but I had to, if you think about it. I didn't swim to America when I came to study here, right? And I didn't swim back to Iran." She gazed out the window as the jet began to taxi. "It's strange, having this big gap in my life. Sometimes I feel like I'm living someone else's story."

The raw honesty in her voice touched Max. He reached over for her hand, rubbing his thumb over her knuckles. "You're living your story now," he said. "And from where I'm sitting, it's a pretty amazing one."

She turned to him, her amber-gold eyes meeting his, and for a moment, everything else faded away— the mission, the jet, the team. There was only Kyra, with her quiet strength and fierce determination, looking at him as if he might hold answers to questions she hadn't even formed yet.

"You're good at that, you know," she said finally.

"At what?"

"Saying the right things." She squeezed his hand. "It's annoying, actually. Makes you irresistible."

Max laughed. "I'd say that it was five centuries of practice and my natural charm, but the truth is that I'm like that only around you."

"Don't push it with fishing for compliments," she warned, but there was humor in her eyes.

"It's true," he insisted. "Ask Yamanu. He'll tell you how much of an ass I am."

She patted his hand. "I doubt that."

The jet accelerated down the runway, the force of takeoff pressing them back into their seats. Kyra's grip on his hand tightened slightly, but her expression remained calm as the ground fell away beneath them.

As they climbed into the sky, Max studied Kyra's profile—the proud line of her jaw, the slight furrow between her brows, the subtle curve of her lips. He was struck again by how quickly and completely she had inserted herself into his life, as if the Fates had carved out a Kyra-shaped space that had just been waiting there all along for her to fill it.

He'd lived long enough to recognize when something significant was happening, and this thing growing between them was monumental. It wasn't just physical attraction, though there was plenty of that. And it wasn't the shared adrenaline rush of going together on a mission, though that certainly strengthened their connection.

This was something deeper, something he'd observed in other couples of the clan but had never expected to experience himself. That cosmic connection that Jasmine and Ell-rom shared, that Kian and Syssi had found, and now it was his turn.

The Fates had opened a door, just as he'd told Kyra the night before. And he'd walked through it willingly and eagerly.

"You're staring," Kyra noted without turning from the window.

"Can you blame me? You are stunning."

As she turned to him, he expected a rebuttal, a tease, but not the vulnerability in her expression. "This is all new to me, Max. Not just us but all of it. Having a daughter, nieces, a family. Confirming my immortality and finding out how it happened. Fighting for something personal instead of a cause. I'm trying to wrap my head around it, but it almost seems like I'm inside a drug-induced hallucination. Like there is no way all of this can be true."

"It's a lot to take in," Max acknowledged.

"And yet it feels right, somehow. Like pieces of a puzzle finally fitting together."

As the jet leveled off at cruising altitude, the clouds spreading out beneath them like a vast sea of puffed-up cotton, Max turned to Kyra, reaching for the phone Yamanu had given her. "Let me show you how this works. It's fairly straightforward, but there are a few features you should know about."

He guided her through the basics, and Kyra picked up everything quickly.

"This is much more advanced than anything I've used before," she commented, scrolling through the contact list. "I've usually had only burner phones."

Max smiled. "William is a genius, and he has an entire team of brainiacs working with him. The phone is just the tip of the iceberg. When you come to the village, I'll show you some of his other inventions."

"I'd like that." She leaned back. "Anything else that I need to know?"

"I've pre-loaded the maps of Tehran with the locations of your sisters' homes marked," Yamanu added, walking over and leaning down to show her.

Kyra studied the map intently, her eyes narrowing as she processed the information. Max could almost see her mind working, plotting routes, identifying potential extraction points, and assessing risks.

Why did he find this so incredibly sexy?

Well, that was obvious. His mate was a warrior queen, and he had won the mating lottery.

Was he jumping the gun?

Probably. But he knew what he knew, and he had no doubts.

"This will help," Kyra said finally, slipping the phone into one of the many pockets of her tactical pants. "Thank you."

Yamanu took a seat across from them. "We should go over the plan," he said. "Turner sent over some updated intelligence this morning."

Max reluctantly released Kyra's hand, shifting into mission mode. "What's changed?"

"Security has been tightened at all four residences," Yamanu reported, pulling out a tablet. "Soraya's husband has called in some high-level favors. There are now four armed guards posted at the houses of those with children and one guard attached to each of the sisters whose daughters were taken. They work in three eight-hour shifts, so the family is watched around the clock."

Kyra frowned. "That complicates things, but it doesn't change our approach. I still believe my best chance is to make contact as a distant relative coming to offer support during their time of distress. The traditional clothing and padding will help."

"Don't forget that you have me." Yamanu spread his arms. "I'm like a genie full of wonders."

Kyra sighed. "I wish I could see what you can do, but Max explained that your mind tricks don't work on immortals."

"Regrettably, they don't," Yamanu said. "But your disguise does, even on immortals."

"That fat suit is something else." She smiled. "What's our timeline once we reach Tehran?"

"Forty-eight hours," Max said. "Any longer, and we risk being detected, but we have the option to extend if needed."

"The safe house is ready," Yamanu added. "It's a small apartment building that has enough room to accommodate all the families temporarily, and it's in a secure location."

3

FENELLA

Fenella stood by the penthouse windows, gazing at the sprawling cityscape of Los Angeles. In fifty years of wandering the globe, she'd somehow never made it to this city of Angels and Hollywood stars.

"Penny for your thoughts?" Jasmine appeared at her side with two mugs of coffee.

Fenella accepted the offered mug with a grateful nod. "I was just thinking about how bloody strange life is. A week ago, I was chained up in that hellhole, and now I'm standing in a luxury penthouse drinking fancy coffee." She took a sip, savoring the rich flavor. "And contemplating babysitting duty."

Jasmine laughed. "The girls are not babies. Besides, they adore you."

"God knows why," Fenella muttered, though secretly she was touched by the girls' affection, which defied logic, but then teenagers weren't the most logical of creatures.

"We need to keep them busy today." Jasmine leaned against the glass. "Otherwise, they'll just sit around like zombies in front of the screen, worrying about their families."

Fenella nodded. Distraction was a powerful tool against anxiety—something she'd learned through decades of her own struggles. "What did you have in mind? Shopping? Though I suppose they've got enough new clothes to last them a while."

"I was thinking something more touristy," Jasmine said. "Show them a bit of the city. Hollywood, maybe? Santa Monica Pier?"

"I heard that the Hollywood Walk of Fame is rather underwhelming." Fenella took another sip of the fabulous coffee. "It's just a bunch of stars on the pavement with names they probably won't recognize. Santa Monica could be nice, though. Beach, board-walk, that giant Ferris wheel..."

"It's called the Pacific Wheel," Jasmine corrected.

"Whatever." Fenella waved her hand dismissively. "The point is, it might be nice." She looked at the four girls huddled on the couch and watching cartoons, or anime as it was called these days.

Not that Fenella knew the difference. Perhaps it was about the emo-looking characters with hair blocking one eye?

Kids these days were weird.

"Let's ask them what they want to do," Jasmine

suggested. "After all, they are young ladies, not babies."

"Sure thing," Fenella waved a hand. "After you."

Jasmine walked over to where the girls were sitting and sat on the enormous coffee table, facing them. "Fenella and I were just discussing plans for today," she said. "Would you like a tour of Los Angeles?"

The suggestion brought a spark of interest to the girls' eyes.

"Where would we go?" Donya asked.

"Hollywood, maybe," Jasmine suggested. "Or Santa Monica—there's a beautiful beach and a pier with rides."

"What about Disneyland?" Laleh asked, her eyes sparkling. "I've heard it's magical."

Fenella blinked in surprise. The request seemed so normal. So innocently childlike. At sixteen, Laleh was not a child, but perhaps because she was the youngest, the others treated her as one, and she was comfortable with that.

"Disneyland is a bit far," Jasmine said. "It's about an hour and a half drive from here, depending on traffic."

Laleh's face fell, but she nodded in reluctant acceptance.

"I've never been there either," Fenella admitted, trying to soften the disappointment. "I heard about it, of course. Giant mouse, overpriced everything, and loads of screaming children." She grinned to show that she was being deliberately flippant.

"We could go to Universal Studios instead," Jasmine suggested. "It's closer, and they have the Wizarding World of Harry Potter. Have you heard of Harry Potter?"

The effect of those words was immediate and electrifying. All four girls straightened up, their eyes widening with excitement.

"Harry Potter?" Azadeh repeated, speaking up for the first time that morning. "They have a Harry Potter movie set?"

"Well, yeah." Jasmine looked surprised by their enthusiastic response. "Have you read the books?"

"All of them," Arezoo said with unexpected passion. "Twice."

"There is a Persian translation of Harry Potter?" Jasmine asked.

"Of course," Arezoo said. "We also saw the movies."

Fenella didn't ask whether those were pirated or legit. She doubted the movie version had been approved by the regime. The book translations could have been modified to appease the censors, but it was more difficult to do with movies.

"So, Universal Studios?" Jasmine asked. "We could go today if you like. Ell-rom has never been either, so it will be new for him too."

"Yes!" Laleh exclaimed, then immediately looked embarrassed by her own enthusiasm. "I mean, if it's not too much trouble."

"No trouble at all," Jasmine assured her. "Why don't you all get dressed? We can leave in about an hour, and we can have lunch in the park."

As the girls hurried back to their rooms, chattering excitedly about Hogwarts and wands and something called butterbeer, Fenella shook her head in amazement.

"Harry bloody Potter," she muttered. "Who would have thought?"

"It's perfect, actually," Jasmine said, her voice low enough that only Fenella could hear her. "Give them something magical to focus on, something that represents good triumphing over evil. They need that right now."

"Don't we all." Fenella wondered whether her brother and his children were safe.

She hadn't kept in touch because she'd gotten tired of having to invent excuses for why she couldn't visit, but that didn't mean she'd forgotten about Walter or had stopped caring.

It suddenly occurred to her that Din had no way to contact her. She didn't have a phone, and there were no landlines in either of the penthouses.

Bloody Din.

How the hell had he expected her to know he was pining after her?

Fifty years ago, she'd barely noticed him—Max's quiet, intense friend who always seemed to be lurking in the shadowy parts of the pub she'd bartended in. She'd been attracted to Max's easy charm, his obvious and intense pursuit of her, never even realizing that Din had been hanging around the pub because he fancied her.

Still, the fact that the guy had harbored feelings for her for five decades was kind of touching.

When Jasmine's phone rang, Fenella tensed, expecting bad news for some reason.

Jasmine checked the screen and frowned.

"That's odd," she said. "It's a Scottish number, and there is no caller ID. I don't know anyone in Scotland."

A jolt of adrenaline shot through Fenella. "Answer it," she urged. "It might be Din."

Jasmine accepted the call and held the phone to her ear. "Hello?"

Fenella could hear only faintly what was being said on the other side, but it was a male voice.

"Yes, she's right here." Jasmine lowered the phone and held it out to Fenella. "It's for you. It's Din."

Fenella took it, suddenly aware of her sweaty palms and the nervous energy thrumming through her body. "Hello?" she said, aiming for casual and missing by a mile.

"Fenella." His voice was exactly as she remembered it—deep and soft at the same time. Velvety.

He'd barely spoken a few words to her in the bar, and it had been over five decades ago, and yet she remembered.

"Din," she said, going for casual and indifferent.

"It's good to hear your voice," he said.

"Yeah, yours too. Do you have news about my brother?"

"I do. I just got back from Invery, in fact. Walter's doing well—retired now, living in the same house. His hair's gone white, what's left of it, but he still has that same laugh."

The mention of her brother's laugh hit Fenella unexpectedly hard. Walter had been just a teenager when she'd left—gangly, full of mischief, with dreams of becoming a footballer. Now, he was an old man, while she remained exactly as she'd been the day she walked away.

"What about his children?" she asked.

"All grown with families of their own. The eldest, Michael, moved to New York some years back. Works in finance, according to your brother. The other two are still in Scotland."

"Are they safe?"

"According to Walter, they are," he assured her. "I've had a couple of my friends check on the two that stayed in Scotland, and they reported nothing out of the ordinary. I doubt anyone went looking for Michael in New York."

Relief washed over her. At least, that was one less thing to worry about. "Thank you. How did you even find all this out?"

There was a chuckle on the other end of the line. "I used my municipal inspector disguise," Din said. "Clipboard, official-looking badge, high-visibility vest—works every time. Told him I was checking the water lines in the neighborhood. Walter invited me in for tea and started chatting away. He's a friendly sort, your brother."

"That's very ingenious," Fenella said.

Din hadn't impressed her as being particularly cunning or resourceful during their brief acquaintance fifty years ago. Clearly, there was more to him than she'd realized.

"Long life gives you plenty of time to perfect your cons," he said. "I've got a few different identities I can slip into when needed."

"Sounds like you are leading an interesting life."

"I have my moments," Din admitted. "Though I suspect mine is not as colorful as yours, from what Max has hinted at."

"Ah, so he's been telling tales, has he?" Fenella rolled her eyes, though Din couldn't see it. "Don't believe half of what that pain in the arse says."

Din laughed, the sound rich and unexpectedly affecting. "I've known Max long enough to separate fact from his particular brand of fiction."

There was a brief pause, filled with unspoken questions and five decades of distance, and Fenella found herself uncharacteristically uncertain about what to say next.

Din broke the silence first. "I'd love to talk more, but I need to finish packing. My flight leaves in three hours, and I still need to get to the airport."

"I'm surprised, I have to admit. I mean, are you flying over just because of me?"

"I blew my chance once. I'm not going to blow it again."

The directness of his statement left her momentarily speechless. In her experience, men were rarely so forthright about their feelings—especially not Scottish men, who tended to guard their emotions as fiercely as their whiskey.

"Safe travels, then," she managed finally. "I'm looking forward to seeing you again." She snorted. "Not that either of us have changed much since we last saw each other. Not physically, anyway."

He was quiet for a moment. "I'll see you soon, Fenella." The promise in his voice sent another flutter through her chest. "Take care of yourself."

"I always do," she replied automatically.

After he ended the call, she stood staring at the phone for a long moment, trying to process the conversation and the unexpected emotions it had stirred in her.

"So?" Jasmine prompted. "How did it go?"

Fenella handed the phone back, struggling to regain her composure. "Fine," she said. "My brother's well. No sign of trouble there."

Jasmine raised an eyebrow, not buying the casual act. "How is Din?"

"Still interested."

Jasmine grinned. "That's so romantic."

Fenella shrugged. "I barely know the man. We

exchanged no more than twenty words fifty years ago."

"But he's harbored these feelings for you through all this time," Jasmine insisted. "That's incredibly romantic."

"Or incredibly pathetic," Fenella muttered, though without real conviction.

"Don't be so cynical," Jasmine said. "It's okay to admit you're a little excited."

Fenella shot her a glare that held no real heat. "I'm not completely opposed to seeing him," she conceded grudgingly. "But I'm not planning our everlasting, immortal future together either."

Jasmine grinned. "Of course not. Not yet."

4

KYRA

Kyra pressed her forehead against the cool glass of the airplane window, watching as the landscape below transformed from the azure blue of the Mediterranean to the rugged, mountainous terrain of western Iran. Patches of green dotted the otherwise arid landscape, villages and small cities clustered in the vast expanse.

Her pendant felt warm and alive against her skin, a near-constant sensation since they'd crossed into Iranian airspace. Was it warning her of danger she was unaware of? After two decades of relying on its guidance she'd learned to interpret its subtle communications, but this steady warmth was new.

"Excited to be back?" Yamanu asked, glancing out the window.

"Yes." She cast him a smile. "I'm excited to see my sisters."

Her only memory of Tehran was of the asylum

and her escape from it, but those memories were vague. She'd been so heavily drugged back then that she had a hard time forming coherent memories. Still, the fragmented visual clips stored in her mind were enough to guess what had been done to her, and she was grateful for not remembering more.

Jasmine had said something about the Clan Mother's ability to retrieve her memories, but unless the goddess could do so selectively and retrieve only the memories before the asylum, Kyra preferred not to remember anything rather than remembering that dark time. If she was unable to process those memories, they might break her, and she needed to be as whole as she could be for her family.

Yamanu nodded, his pale eyes showing a depth of understanding. "Home soil has a way of stirring things up, even when the memories aren't always welcome."

The Guardian somehow grasped the strange duality of returning to a place that should feel like home but instead felt like enemy territory. Had he been through something similar?

She wanted to ask, but that type of conversation required privacy.

Instead, her mind drifted to the cover story Onegus had supplied them with.

"You'll be traveling as the Al-Nouri family," the chief had explained, distributing passports and identification papers. "A wealthy merchant from Tabriz, his wife, his brother and sister-in-law, plus bodyguards and servants. The documentation should pass scrutiny, with or without Yamanu's shrouding."

The forged documents were impeccable and indistinguishable from legitimate government-issued IDs. The clan's resources were impressive.

"We'll start our descent in about half an hour," the pilot announced.

Max pushed to his feet. "We should change into our disguises."

Around the cabin, team members began pulling duffel bags from overhead compartments and extracting folded garments.

Max handed Kyra her bag—the one Eva had prepared with the specially modified traditional clothing and fat suit.

Jade and the two pureblooded Kra-ell females, Rishba and Asuka, withdrew similar garments from their bags, as did the men, pulling out long caftans and small, simple turbans.

"Eva's been busy," Kyra remarked, running her hand over the fabric of the abaya.

Yamanu's lips quirked into a small smile. "These aren't from Eva. Jade and one of the Guardians went shopping for the rest of the stuff. Only yours has the special modifications."

Jade nodded from across the aisle, where she was already unfolding a plain black abaya. "Standard stuff is easy enough to find," she said.

Kyra lifted the fat suit and examined the various

straps. "I can't put it on out here. I'm going to the bathroom."

"Need help?" Max asked, his lips quirking up in a suggestive smile.

"I think I can manage," Kyra said dryly but returned his smile.

His consistent good humor was both ridiculous and endearing. It was also enviable, and she wondered if she could learn to be more like Max. It seemed like a more fun way to live, even if it was sometimes forced.

Kyra knew better than most what it was like to fake it until you made it. Except, in her case, it was pretending to be brave when she'd been scared, and confident when she'd been anything but.

The airplane's bathroom was cramped, barely large enough for Kyra alone, let alone with the bulky garments. She maneuvered awkwardly, shedding her tactical jacket and pants, and wondered whether she should put the fat suit over her T-shirt or her bare skin.

Eva had warned that it would be hot in the suit, and the T-shirt might add to that, but on the other hand, it would absorb sweat, so it was hard to decide.

The suit was an engineering marvel, with inner slots sized perfectly for knives along the ribs, a larger pocket across the belly that could hold a handgun, and even thin channels running down the thighs where smaller weapons could be concealed.

As she strapped herself into the contraption, Kyra

admired Eva's ingenuity. The padding distributed the weight evenly, making the arsenal she was now carrying surprisingly comfortable. There were even small hooks to hang ammunition pouches. The problem would be accessing her arsenal. The disguise was effective for smuggling weapons but not for actual combat.

Once the suit was secured, Kyra draped the abaya over her body and added the niqab to cover her head and face. The black fabric fell from her head to her feet, concealing not just her padded figure but every aspect of her identity. There was a slit for her eyes, and they were distinctive, but she could wear sunglasses to conceal their unique color.

For a moment, she stood still, confronting her reflection in the small mirror. The woman—if one could even tell it was a woman—staring back at her was a featureless black shape devoid of identity, of humanity. The sight stirred something uncomfortable in her.

She felt erased.

Over the years with the Kurdish resistance, Kyra had seen the traditional clothing used as both a tool of oppression and, paradoxically, of freedom. For some women it was forced upon them, a physical manifestation of their society's determination to render them invisible. For others, particularly female resistance fighters, it provided anonymity, a way to move undetected through hostile territory.

Kyra had never worn one herself, preferring the

moderate hijab that allowed her greater mobility during operations. Standing here now, completely encased in black, she forced herself to focus on the benefits of anonymity and invisibility rather than the erasure of her personhood.

How could this modern era be the worst time in human history for women in these parts of the world?

How had humanity allowed that to happen?

When she finally emerged from the bathroom, the cabin had transformed. Instead of two Guardians and five Kra-ell warriors, she was greeted by three females in traditional garb, two rich-looking Iranian males in caftans and elaborate turbans, and two in simpler clothing but still in caftans and turbans.

Max had undergone the greater transformation, with his eyebrows and hair darkened with what she assumed was hair powder, and a fake beard to complete the look. He still looked too European, but many Iranians had some Russian heritage, so it wasn't unusual to see lighter-skinned people like him.

Max walked up to her, the disguise doing nothing to diminish his swagger. If anything, it was more pronounced than usual because he was leaning into the role he was playing.

The problem was that he didn't know that, given her background, it rubbed Kyra the wrong way. She didn't say anything, because he was nothing like those males who used their masculinity to intimidate women instead of offering safety and protection.

"Must be stifling in there." He reached for her hand, the only part of her other than her eyes that was exposed.

"It is, in more ways than one," Kyra admitted. "I try to think of this as my invisibility cloak, but I can't ignore the fact that while I can take it off, others can't. My heart bleeds for them."

"They should rebel," Jade said. "No one should live like that." She tugged at her head covering. "This is not nearly as bad as yours, but I hate it with a vengeance. A warrior's hair shouldn't be covered." She turned to the other four Kra-ell, who all had long hair gathered either in a ponytail or a braid, including the males. "Am I right?"

"It's an affront to the Mother of All Life," Dima said. "But at least we don't have to cover our faces. It's disgraceful for a warrior to kill an enemy with a concealed face."

Kyra found it fascinating how different cultures had different traditions that stood in direct opposition to one another, but there was something to what Dima had said about killing with a covered face like an assassin. She'd done it, and it had never sat well with her.

Max squeezed her hand. "You are still beautiful to me, even with the fat suit on."

"How would you know?" She pulled her hand out of his. "I'm covered from head to toe."

Max tapped his temple with one finger, a lopsided smile playing across his lips. "I see you in here, and you are perfect."

"How about me?" Anton strutted down the aisle, exaggerating the swish of his caftan and striking ridiculous poses. "Am I beautiful?"

"Dashing," Kyra said. "Absolutely dashing."

Not to be outdone, Dima followed his friend's example. "How about me? Am I dashing as well?"

"Very much so," Kyra said.

"The hair covering sucks, but I love the dress." Anton spun in a circle, making his garment billow out around him. "I've never felt so free. The ventilation is refreshing."

Yamanu adjusted his fancy turban and struck a pose. "I'm ready for my big break in the next *Aladdin* remake."

"Only if they're casting for the comic relief side-kick," Jade said in her usual dry voice, though there was a hint of amusement in her usually impassive features.

Max arched a brow. "And how would the fearless Kra-ell leader know about comic relief and sidekicks in movies?"

She looked at him down her nose. "I've seen every Disney movie ever made. I used to get them for the kids in my compound, and after Igor enslaved me along with all the other females of my tribe, I convinced him to continue purchasing the movies for the kids so they could learn English."

Kyra's gut twisted. "You were enslaved?"

She couldn't imagine the proud warrior being anyone's slave.

Jade nodded. "It's a long story, and one day, I will tell you about it over a bottle of vodka. But not today. Today, I need to erase it from my mind so I can do what needs to be done."

Kyra understood that better than most.

"I don't understand why women accept these," Rishba said, fingering the edge of her own head covering. "To be erased like this, made into a ghost."

"Not everyone is a rebel and a warrior." Kyra reached out to adjust the female's niqab. "For most, it's what they know and what their families expect. They don't have a choice, even if they hate it. Resistance will get them beaten and sometimes even executed. Sometimes, it's just easier to accept the dogma and believe that they are following divine commands and will go to hell if they don't obey."

Jade adjusted her own garment the way Kyra had demonstrated on Rishba. "It serves our purpose today. No one will suspect that beneath these symbols of female oppression are warriors capable of eliminating them with their bare fangs."

"Please take your seats," the pilot announced over the intercom. "We're starting our descent."

Kyra sat down and watched Tehran coming into view through the window—a sprawling metropolis nestled against the Alborz Mountains.

Somewhere in the vast city were the missing

43

pieces of her past, her sisters, nieces, and nephews that had been stolen from her. But lurking out there were also the Doomers who sought to enslave her family, even though the fake doctor was no longer issuing orders.

There might be others who knew about her family's godly genes and were planning to exploit them.

5

MAX

As the plane touched down with a gentle bump, Max tightened his grip on Kyra's hand. It was supposed to be a gentle gesture of reassurance, but the surge of adrenaline he always experienced before the start of a mission made him squeeze a little too hard.

"Sorry." He brought her hand to his lips for a kiss.

"I'm not fragile despite what I look like now," she reminded him. "I'm an immortal warrior. I'm resilient and strong."

"Yes, you are." He kissed her knuckles.

It was Max's first time at Tehran International Airport, and it surprised him how small it was for a country of nearly ninety million people. In the US, an airport this size would serve a community of two to three million at the most.

Apparently, Iranians didn't do much international travel.

He touched the teardrop hanging on a short string around his neck. None of them other than Kyra spoke Farsi, and he hoped the teardrops would do a decent job of translating for them.

He and Yamanu were supposed to be Iranian businessmen returning from a trip to Turkey. Kyra and Jade were their wives, the two Kra-ell females their servants, and Dima and Anton their body-guards. Yamanu's shrouding and thralling would do the heavy lifting of getting them through the check-points, so he didn't worry too much about the teardrops doing a convincing job, but it was still the trickiest part of their mission.

Eric, who was scheduled to arrive later that day with the second jet, wouldn't have the benefit of a master shrouder and would have to rely on the forged documentation and bribes that had been paid to airport personnel. Hopefully, that would be enough. They needed the extra space in his jet in case they were going to return with all of Kyra's family members.

"How exactly does the blanket thralling and shrouding work?" Kyra asked Yamanu. "Do you plant thoughts in their heads or just confuse them and make them think of something else?"

Yamanu tilted his head. "I make a mental sugges-tion for them to see what I want them to see and what they expect, and I also discourage curiosity by making them feel bored. It's like creating a subtle pressure that guides attention away from us."

As the jet came to a final stop, Max rose to his feet and retrieved his and Kyra's bags from the overhead compartment.

As they disembarked, he positioned himself in front of Kyra, which for him was a protective instinct but would seem perfectly natural in this culture, where women trailed behind their men.

Yamanu was at the head of the procession, his mind tricks making the process entirely frictionless. Max kept his movements relaxed, but his senses were on high alert, cataloging exits, security personnel positions, and potential choke points.

The officer who took his passport barely glanced at it, his eyes unfocused as he stamped the document and handed it back without a single question.

A tense moment came when a uniformed guard approached their group, his hand resting casually on his holstered sidearm. Max maintained his outward composure while readying for potential trouble. The guard's eyes passed over them, and then he simply nodded and continued on his patrol.

They cleared customs with surprising speed, emerging into the arrivals hall where dozens of people were waiting with signs bearing the names of those they were meeting. Max scanned the crowd, looking for their contact.

"There," Kyra murmured beside him, her voice muffled by the fabric covering her face. She subtly nodded toward an older man holding a sign in Farsi script.

"What does it say?" Max asked quietly.

"Yamanu's fake name," she replied. "That's our contact."

The man spotted their group, smiled, and dipped his head. He looked to be in his early sixties, with a neatly trimmed white beard and the weathered face of someone who had spent much of his life outdoors.

As they walked over to him, he inclined his head again. "*Salam*," he greeted, his voice low and gravelly. "My name is Nadim. I'm your driver."

He'd said all that in Persian, but Max's earpieces translated his words to English.

"This way, please," Nadim said, motioning for them to follow him.

He led them through the terminal and out to the parking area, where three nondescript vans waited. They were older models that looked well maintained but not flashy.

"I will drive the first vehicle," Nadim said, switching to English even though they all had translating earpieces and teardrops to translate their speech to Farsi. "You will follow in the others."

"Kyra and I will ride with you," Max said, glancing at Yamanu for approval.

The head Guardian nodded in agreement. "I'll take the second van with Dima and Anton. Jade, you take the third."

"It's about forty minutes from here, depending on traffic," Nadim said, handing keys to Yamanu and

Jade. "If we get separated, continue to the address programmed in the GPS units."

Max had questions—dozens of them—about local conditions, security situations, and the intel Nadim and his team had gathered on Kyra's sisters, but they could wait until they reached the safe house and could talk privately.

He helped Kyra into the middle seat of the first van, then climbed in beside her while Nadim took the driver's seat.

Tehran sprawled across a vast plain at the foot of the Alborz Mountains, whose snow-capped peaks were visible in the distance through the haze of pollution that hung over the city. The contrast between old and new was striking—ancient architectural elements juxtaposed against glass-and-steel high-rises, traditional markets alongside modern shopping centers.

Traffic moved chaotically with cars weaving between lanes with barely inches to spare and motorcycles darting through dangerously narrow gaps.

"First time in Tehran?" Nadim asked.

"Yes," Max said. "I'm surprised at how vibrant it is."

Nadim nodded appreciatively at the assessment. "Western media often portrays us as a joyless, oppressed people. The reality is that even though we are not as free as we want to be, we still laugh and find things worthy of celebration."

The van turned onto a wide boulevard lined with trees, whose canopies provided shade for the throngs of pedestrians milling about. Shops and cafés dotted the street level of buildings, while apartments rose several stories above. Women in various styles of hijab walked alongside men in both Western and traditional clothing, the diversity of dress more varied than Max had expected.

Nadim turned to look at Kyra. "The security around your sisters' homes has increased in recent days."

"We've heard," Max said. "Has anything changed since the last report?"

"Not really," Nadim said. "The two older sisters, those whose daughters were taken, have one guard each posted near their homes. Private security was hired after the girls' disappearance. The other two sisters have four guards each, and no one leaves the house without an escort. The guards even accompany the children to school."

Max exchanged a glance with Kyra. "They are afraid for your other nieces and nephews."

"Is the security provided by the Revolutionary Guard?" Kyra asked.

Nadim nodded. "Not in an official capacity, but they look well trained."

With Yamanu's shrouding, there could be twenty guards stationed at the house and it wouldn't make a difference. What Max was more worried about was the surveillance equipment and who was watching the feed. Yamanu's mind tricks didn't work on electronics, and if the observer was far away, Yamanu's influence wouldn't reach him.

"We got all the equipment Turner requested," Nadim continued. "Weapons, communications gear, surveillance equipment, C4, remote detonators, and timers."

Kyra looked impressed. "I bet it wasn't easy to get everything on that list."

"We have our sources." Nadim smiled, looking smug.

As they drove deeper into the city, the character of the neighborhoods shifted, the buildings becoming less imposing, the streets narrowing. They were entering a lower-middle-class residential area, where multi-story apartment buildings lined the streets, and small shops and food vendors operated from ground-level floors.

Nadim navigated the van through a series of turns, occasionally checking the rearview mirror to ensure the other two vehicles were still following. Finally, he pulled into a covered parking area behind a three-story apartment building that was indistinguishable from its neighbors.

"We have arrived," he announced, killing the engine. "The entire building is secure. I'll show you in through the back entrance."

They waited for the other two vans to park, and

then their group followed Nadim inside through a service door and up a narrow staircase to the second floor.

The apartment was modest, but spacious and well appointed, with multiple bedrooms, a large living area, and a kitchen that had seen better days but was clean and serviceable. The furnishings were worn out but looked comfortable, and everything smelled of cleaning solution and air freshener.

"Let's sweep the place," Yamanu said. "I want to be certain it's clean."

"I assure you that it is," Nadim said. "But I understand if you want to double-check."

Yamanu pulled out the portable scanner William had designed just for such a purpose and did a walkabout, checking every room and closet. "All clear," he announced once he was satisfied that there were no bugs. "Go ahead and get rid of those outfits."

"Thank God," Kyra said as she ducked into one of the bedrooms.

"Do you need help?" Max called after her.

"Thank you, but I'll manage."

Nadim walked into the kitchen and pulled out the refrigerator, which slid out of its place with surprising ease. "This is where we hide the arsenal." He tapped the wall behind the refrigerator, and a panel popped free, revealing a large niche behind it.

"As requested," Nadim said, stepping aside so Yamanu and Max could inspect the contents.

The weapons cache included several handguns

with silencers, assault rifles broken down into easily concealed components, ammunition, and various tactical gear. On the bottom shelf, securely packed in cushioned cases, were the explosives—enough C4 to create several diversions or, if necessary, bring down a medium-sized building.

"Good job." Yamanu clapped the guy on his back. "Thank you."

"You are most welcome." Nadim smiled. "I'm handsomely paid for my services, but I'm glad to help regardless of pay."

"What about the neighbors?" Max pointed at the side wall. "What if they hear something?"

"The entire building is yours, and sound doesn't carry to the neighboring houses unless you are very loud."

"Excellent," Yamanu said. "Do you have any other intelligence for us?"

Nadim closed the panel and pushed the refrigerator back with ease as if it was gliding on wheels, which it probably was.

He moved to the kitchen table where a worn leather satchel sat. From it, he withdrew a collection of maps, photographs, and documents. "Detailed layouts of the neighborhoods where each sister lives. Building floor plans where available. And surveillance photos of the sisters themselves, taken over the past week."

Max lifted his head as Kyra entered the kitchen

sans the fat suit and traditional clothing. "You will want to be here for this."

She nodded, her eyes scanning the photographs.

They showed four women of varying ages, all bearing a striking resemblance to Kyra and Jasmine—the same high cheekbones, the same graceful necks, the same amber-brown eyes. They were dressed in traditional attire, their heads covered with headscarves, but their faces were visible—a sign that they weren't as strictly religious as the ultraconservative elements who insisted women cover every inch of their skin.

Kyra lifted her hand to her pendant, her eyes wide as she gazed upon the faces of siblings she didn't remember.

"Soraya," she whispered, touching one photograph. "Rana. Yasmin. Parisa." She turned to Nadim. "Did I guess correctly?"

The guy nodded. "Indeed."

Max looked at the pictures, trying to see if Kyra could have guessed who was who by their ages, but it was hard to tell who was the oldest and who was the youngest. "I guess that the heart remembers what the mind forgets," he murmured. "They look like you. Same eyes."

She picked up a photo of the eldest sister—Soraya, the mother of Arezoo, Donya, and Laleh. The woman was perhaps in her mid-forties, lines of care etching her face, but still beautiful. In the image, she stood in a market, examining produce with a distracted air, unaware of being photographed. A single guard could be seen in the background, not even attempting to be inconspicuous.

"We need to get to her first," Kyra said. "I have notes from each of her three daughters, so she will believe me, and she's the eldest, the others will listen to her."

6

FENELLA

The morning sun beat down on Fenella as she stood in line along with Jasmine and her cousins at the entrance to Universal Studios.

She shifted impatiently from foot to foot, adjusting the borrowed sunglasses perched on her nose. After fifty years of wandering the globe, she'd somehow never made it to a theme park, and now she wasn't sure it had been a wise idea to let Jasmine convince her to come.

Most of those standing in line were Americans, some speaking English, some Spanish, and here and there, she could spot German, French, and Italian. Everyone looked ridiculously excited about parting with a large chunk of their money for the dubious privilege of baking in the hot California sun and trudging from one silly attraction to the other.

Fenella would have much preferred staying in the

penthouse and lounging by the pool with a fruity cocktail in hand.

"How much longer?" she muttered to Jasmine, who was consulting a map of the park while the four girls huddled together, whispering excitedly in rapid-fire Farsi that Fenella couldn't follow even with her translation earpieces.

"It won't be long now." Jasmine folded the map and tucked it inside her oversized satchel. "They're moving the line pretty quickly."

Fenella had to grudgingly admit that Americans were very efficient when it came to moving crowds along. Everything was also clean, which was quite an achievement given how many people passed through these grounds each day.

What made the whole thing worth the trouble was watching the girls bounce with excitement. They didn't look traumatized or scared while standing in line to get in. They looked thrilled, like other young people their age, eager for the fun that awaited them beyond the gate.

Arezoo tried to maintain a veneer of sophisticated disinterest, but Fenella caught the way the girl's eyes darted around, taking in every detail. It was an act Fenella recognized all too well—the careful pretense of being above it all.

Ell-rom stood slightly apart from their group, his tall frame and otherworldly beauty drawing curious glances from passersby, which was obviously making him uncomfortable.

"Don't worry about it." She sidled up to him. "This is Universal Studios Hollywood. They think you are an actor, just another prop as fake as everything else here. Plastic plants, painted concrete made to look like stone, and a man who is too pretty to be real."

He frowned. "Was that a compliment? Should I thank you? Or should I be offended that you compared me to a plastic plant?"

Jasmine laughed. "From her? It's a compliment." She wrapped her arm around Ell-rom's middle and smiled at Fenella. "You're not fooling anyone with your indifferent, snooty act either, you know. For someone who claims to be unimpressed, you've been rubber-necking worse than a first-time visitor to Times Square."

Fenella opened her mouth to deliver a retort, then closed it with a huff when she realized she had indeed been craning her neck to see over the crowd ahead of them. "I'm merely assessing my surroundings. It's an old habit. Always know your terrain."

"Of course," Jasmine agreed, her tone making it clear she wasn't buying it.

"I don't understand the purpose of this place," Ell-rom admitted. "Why are people so excited to visit these structures?"

The poor prince was even more out of his element than she was. Seven millennia in stasis followed by a crash course in modern life on Earth was not the best way to prepare him for a visit to a theme park. Naturally, it would be bewildering.

"It's about the movies," she said. "Did they have those where you come from?"

He nodded. "I wasn't privy to them, but I knew of their existence. I've also watched a lot of television since arriving here, so I know what movies are."

"Good. That makes it easier to explain. So, Universal Studios makes films, and to make even more money from them, they build attractions in this park based on their most successful movies, so people can enjoy feeling like they are inside their favorite stories."

Ell-rom frowned. "So, it's like a physical manifestation of storytelling?"

"Something like that," Fenella agreed, though she suspected he didn't fully understand yet.

"Next!" called an attendant, and suddenly, they were at the front of the queue. Jasmine handed over the tickets she'd purchased online, and moments later, they were through the turnstiles and into the park proper.

The main plaza was ringed with shops, restaurants, and entrances to various themed areas. Music played from hidden speakers while costumed characters posed for photos with excited children.

"Where to first?" Jasmine asked, consulting her map again.

"Harry Potter!" Laleh nearly yelled, then immediately looked embarrassed by her outburst.

"Definitely Harry Potter." Donya seconded her

sister's choice, putting a supportive arm around Laleh.

Jasmine smiled. "The Wizarding World it is. This way."

As they made their way through the park, Fenella was constantly distracted by the sights—enormous, detailed re-creations of movie sets and iconic locations, improbably cheerful employees, and masses of people who seemed thrilled to be spending exorbitant amounts of money on overpriced concessions and souvenirs.

It was ridiculous. It was garish. But if she was being honest with herself, which she rarely was, she had to admit that it was fun.

"Here we are," Jasmine announced as they rounded a corner, and the Wizarding World of Harry Potter came into view.

Fenella stopped in her tracks, momentarily speechless. Before them stood what appeared to be an entire village plucked straight from the films—crooked buildings with snow-capped roofs, cobblestone streets, and at its center, the imposing silhouette of Hogwarts Castle perched atop a rocky crag.

The scale was nothing like the movie, which was understandable, but it was still breathtaking.

"Bloody hell," she muttered. "Now I'm really impressed."

The girls' reactions were even more dramatic. Laleh gasped, her hands flying to her mouth. Donya let out a squeal of delight that she quickly tried to convert into a more dignified sound. Azadeh's eyes widened to an almost comical degree, and even Arezoo abandoned her pretense of sophistication and grinned.

"It's exactly like in the books and the movies!" Laleh whispered with reverence in her voice.

Every shopfront, every sign, every costume worn by park employees was meticulously designed to create the illusion that they had stepped into the fictional world of the Harry Potter series. Fenella had watched a few of the movies years ago in a rundown cinema in Budapest, but she had never read the books. Still, even she could appreciate the craftsmanship involved.

"I'm a Ravenclaw," Arezoo said decisively as they paused before a store window displaying school uniforms. "Intelligence and wisdom are the most important qualities."

"You're totally a Slytherin," Donya countered. "Ambitious and cunning."

Arezoo looked momentarily offended before conceding with a shrug. "There are some Slytherin qualities I can admit to."

"I'm definitely Hufflepuff," Azadeh said. "Loyalty and patience."

"What about you, Laleh?" Jasmine asked the youngest.

Laleh hesitated, chewing her lower lip in thought. "I think... Gryffindor. Not because I'm brave now, but because I will be one day."

The simple honesty of the statement caught Fenella off guard, a lump forming in her throat. These girls had endured horrors that would break many adults, yet here they were, braving a trip into a fantasy world.

"Let's go in," Jasmine suggested. "We should all get properly outfitted."

Inside the shop, Jasmine began selecting items—skirts, shirts, and ties in the colors of the various houses. The girls reverently held on to each piece, parading in front of the mirror and debating which combinations looked best.

Within minutes, Jasmine had amassed a sizable pile of merchandise on the counter, and Fenella's eyebrows rose higher with each item added to the growing stack.

"Who's paying for all this?" she asked in an undertone as Jasmine pulled out a credit card.

"Kian gave me a clan card a while ago and never asked me to return it." Jasmine looked the card over sheepishly. "I'm still using it, and I hope that's okay. I haven't had time to talk to him about money yet and how much I'm allowed to spend."

"That's one hell of a sweet arrangement," Fenella murmured, watching as the cashier rang up a total that made her wince. Living on her own for decades had made her acutely conscious of money—where it came from and how quickly it could disappear. "Must be nice to have all your expenses covered like that."

"You'll get a card too." Jasmine signed the receipt.

"All clan members receive an allowance, and housing is provided free of charge."

"I'm not a clan member," Fenella pointed out.

Jasmine laughed, gathering up the shopping bags. "Not yet, but soon. You'll find a nice guy to settle down with. Maybe Din, maybe someone else."

The mention of Din sent an unexpected thrill through Fenella, which she firmly ignored. "Let's not get ahead of ourselves."

But the idea wasn't entirely unappealing. After fifty years of wandering the world like a nomad, never staying anywhere long enough to form real connections, always looking over her shoulder for danger—the thought of having stability, security, and people who had her back was more tempting than she cared to admit.

The girls changed into their new Hogwarts attire, complete with house-appropriate ties. They left the store, each carrying a shopping bag with her clothes and a matching Hogwarts sweater, which was too warm to wear right now.

"What about you?" Jasmine asked. "Didn't you want a Hogwarts uniform? It's not too late."

Fenella chuckled. "You keep forgetting how old I really am."

"I don't," Jasmine insisted. "But you are never too old to have fun."

The truth was that Fenella couldn't remember the last time she'd done something purely for fun. Her existence for the past half-century had been focused on survival, on staying one step ahead of trouble, on earning enough to eat, and on finding safe places to sleep. There had been moments of pleasure, certainly, breathtaking vistas witnessed from mountain trails, the satisfaction of a well-played poker hand, and the occasional physical connection with a stranger who asked no questions and expected no commitment.

But this—wandering through a fantasy land with no purpose beyond enjoyment, surrounded by people she considered friends—was new and far more enjoyable than she wanted to acknowledge.

It was also insanely frivolous.

"Can we go to the Three Broomsticks for lunch?" Laleh asked as midday approached.

"Excellent idea," Jasmine agreed. "I'm starving."

The Three Broomsticks restaurant was designed to look like the pub from the novels and films, complete with exposed wooden beams, long communal tables, and servers in period costumes. The girls examined every detail, talking among themselves about elements they recognized from the books.

"They even have butterbeer," Donya noted as they examined the menus.

"What the hell is butterbeer?" Fenella asked.

"It's a special drink from the books," Arezoo explained. "Non-alcoholic, of course."

"I know what it is in the movies. I just want to know what it is made from."

No one knew how to answer her.

"We should all try it and find out," Ell-rom suggested.

When their drinks arrived—frothy concoctions topped with whipped cream—Fenella eyed hers suspiciously. "It looks like bath water with foam on top."

"Just try it." Jasmine took a sip of her own.

Fenella cautiously raised the mug to her lips and took a tentative taste. The flavor burst was intense— sweet, butterscotch-like, with hints of vanilla. It was ridiculously sugary, completely indulgent, and utterly delicious.

"Well?" Jasmine prompted.

"It's not terrible," Fenella conceded, taking another, larger sip.

Ell-rom's reaction was more dramatic. His eyes widened with surprised pleasure, and he stared at the mug as if it contained some profound revelation. "This is remarkable," he declared.

The girls giggled at his reaction, and even Fenella had to smile at his childlike wonder. It was easy to forget that beneath his regal bearing and alien heritage, Ell-rom was experiencing many elements of human culture for the first time.

As their lunch arrived and the girls chatted about their favorite scenes from the books, comparing them to the same scenes in the movies and complaining about everything that hadn't been done right, Fenella was content to just observe, to be part of this improvised family unit without needing to maintain her usual walls and defenses.

It was a strange feeling—unfamiliar—but not unwelcome.

After lunch, they continued exploring the park, eventually making their way to a shop selling replica wands from the Harry Potter series.

"Each wand is unique," a shop employee explained with practiced enthusiasm. "Just like in the books, the wand chooses the wizard—or witch."

The girls took this ritual very seriously, handling different wands until they found ones that 'felt right.'

"You should get one, too," Jasmine told Fenella, holding out an intricately carved wand.

"Don't be ridiculous," Fenella scoffed. "I'm not a child."

"Neither am I," Jasmine countered, "but I want one for a souvenir. Come on, admit that you want one, too. Don't you want to pretend that you are a witch? When was the last time you let loose and allowed yourself to play? And I don't mean poker to swindle unsuspecting guys out of their money."

"Fine," Fenella relented, accepting the wand. "But only because I have an idea for a wand game to play with the girls when we get home and because you are paying for it. I would never waste my own hard-earned money on a plastic stick."

By mid-afternoon, they were all in need of a break. They found a café with outdoor seating where they could rest tired feet while enjoying cold drinks.

The girls were comparing their souvenirs, still buzzing with excitement despite hours of walking.

Fenella kicked her shoes off under the table and sipped her iced coffee, when the harsh ring of Jasmine's phone cut through the ambient noise of the park.

Jasmine pulled it from her purse, glancing at the screen with a frown. "Unknown number again," she murmured, then answered cautiously. "Hello?"

Her expression cleared almost immediately. "Oh! Yes, she's right here." She held out the phone to Fenella. "It's Din."

Fenella took the phone, trying to appear casual despite the sudden dryness in her mouth. "Din? What's up?"

"Fenella. How's your day going, lass?" It seemed just a bit strange for Din to call again so soon.

"Fine," she replied, turning slightly away from the table to create at least the illusion of privacy. "Jasmine's taken us to Universal Studios. It's all very..." She searched for a suitably dismissive description, then settled on "American."

Din chuckled. "Aye, I imagine it would be. Having fun despite yourself, are you?"

Fenella bristled at being so easily read, even from thousands of miles away. "It's entertaining enough," she allowed. "Why are you calling? Aren't you supposed to be in the air on your way over?"

"Ah, well, that's the unfortunate part," Din said, his tone shifting to apologetic. "There's been a bit of a setback. Massive traffic accident on the way to the airport—lorry overturned, blocking all lanes. By the time they cleared it, I'd missed my flight."

Disappointment hit her with unexpected force, followed immediately by a creeping sense of unease. "So, you're not coming?" she asked, hating the hint of vulnerability in her voice.

"Not today," Din clarified quickly. "I've rebooked for tomorrow's flight. Just a twenty-four-hour delay, that's all."

A superstitious chill ran down Fenella's spine. In her experience, delays and obstacles were rarely coincidental—they were warnings, signs from a universe that had saved her skin many times by creating roadblocks when danger lay ahead.

"Maybe it's for the best," she said. "Perhaps you shouldn't come at all."

"What?" Din sounded confused and offended. "Why would you say that?"

"Things like this happen for a reason," Fenella explained, lowering her voice further. "It could be a bad omen."

"An omen?" Din repeated, sounding amused. "I didn't take you for the superstitious type, Fenella."

"I've learned to pay attention to signs," she said defensively. "It's kept me alive this long."

There was a brief pause, then Din's voice returned gentler now. "It's not an omen, lass. It's just a traffic accident. These things happen all the time. Planes get delayed, and roads get blocked. Doesn't mean anything beyond the fact that some poor driver is having an even worse day than me."

His pragmatic response should have reassured her, but the uneasiness lingered. Not just about Din's journey now but about Max and Kyra's mission as well. What if the universe was trying to warn them all of an impending disaster?

"Still there?" Din prompted when her silence stretched too long.

"Yes," she sighed. "I suppose you're right. It's just a delay."

"Indeed," he agreed, sounding relieved that she wasn't going to argue any further. "I'll be there tomorrow, barring any more unexpected calamities. Just wanted to let you know so you won't be waiting at the airport for me."

"I wasn't planning to go to the airport," Fenella admitted, perhaps a bit too quickly. "I don't have a car or money to pay for a cab," she explained.

Din chuckled again, the sound sending another unwelcome flutter through her chest. "Of course not. I wasn't really expecting you to come. Well, enjoy your day at the park. I look forward to seeing you tomorrow."

After he ended the call, she handed the phone back to Jasmine, aware of the curious gazes of the girls fixed on her.

"Din missed his flight," she explained, aiming for casual indifference. "Traffic accident on the way to the airport. He'll be arriving tomorrow instead."

"That must be disappointing." Jasmine's expression was sympathetic.

"Not really." Fenella took another sip of the overly sweet drink. "It's just a delay."

Despite her dismissive words, though, the sense of foreboding refused to dissipate. She should have been more insistent and convinced Din to cancel his plans. Heck, she could have told him that she would come to him instead. Anything to keep him from boarding the next flight.

Perhaps she should call him back.

Except, she had a feeling that the stubborn ox wouldn't listen to reason.

7

KYRA

The team was gathered around the dining room table, an array of enlarged maps of Tehran neighborhoods that were relevant to their mission spread out, along with surveillance photos and building schematics. It was a mosaic of vital intelligence for their mission, but Kyra was paying little attention to anything other than the photographs of her sisters.

When Nadim's cousin entered with a tray of steaming plates, Max collected the strewn papers into a neat pile to clear the table, and Kyra helped her set out lunch.

Nadim had vouched for Fatima, claiming that she'd been part of the underground network that he had worked for many years and that he trusted her with his life. Max had peeked into her head just as he'd peeked into Nadim's before, making sure that she was legit, and had approved her presence.

Given her apparent culinary skills, the woman was certainly a great addition to the team. A well-fed warrior was more effective than a hungry one.

After they were done with the first course, Yamanu wiped his mouth and turned to Kyra. "We need to decide how to approach each target and in what order. I understand your argument about approaching the older sister first so she can help convince the others, but operationally, we may need to choose differently."

Kyra had suspected as much, and the truth was that her younger sisters were more vulnerable and should be prioritized because they still had their children with them, and that's who the Doomers were mainly after.

The older women were less of a priority.

Still, she'd rather start with Soraya because she could help with the others.

"Soraya and Rana have the least security," Max said, echoing Kyra's opinion. "They each have just one guard, but even though they might be easier to extract, we need to get those with children out first."

Traitor. Still, he and Yamanu might be right.

Kyra was too close to the targets to think objectively, and she should leave those decisions to Max and Yamanu, who were no less experienced than she was and knew how to handle situations like that.

In fact, they were better equipped than she was because they'd dealt with Doomers many times before, while Kyra's experience with them had been anecdotal.

"I suggest we get Parisa first," Yamanu suggested. "Since she's a widow, there is no husband to consider. She's alone with her sons."

Jade shook her head. "They're more heavily guarded precisely because their children haven't been taken."

"They still don't know why the girls were kidnapped," Nadim said. "The missing girls' fathers suspect someone wants something from them because of their military connections—perhaps to release prisoners or to extract ransoms. But since no demands have come, they're half-mad with worry."

Kyra felt a pang of sympathy. These men had lost their daughters, not knowing they were safe across the world. But that sympathy was tempered by the knowledge that at least one of the husbands—Fareed, Soraya's husband—was a commander in the Revolutionary Guard and was possibly working with the Doomers, either knowingly or unknowingly.

"I still think that we should prioritize approaching Soraya," Kyra said. "Firstly, because she's not heavily guarded, and secondly, because I can easily convince her to help us by showing her the notes from her daughters. Also, Arezoo told me that her mother had mentioned me, saying that she missed me. This suggests that she might draw parallels between what happened to me and her daughters, and she will consider the possibility that her daughters will never be heard from again, much like what happened with me."

Max frowned. "She's also the riskiest because her husband and the girls' father is a high-ranking commander in the Revolutionary Guard, who could have direct connections to the Brotherhood."

"Which is precisely why we need to get Soraya away from him," Kyra countered.

"I still think that the widow would be the safer first approach," Max persisted. "No husband to complicate things, and according to our intelligence, she's struggling financially. She might be most receptive to an offer of a better future for her and her sons."

As the team looked between them, waiting for a resolution to their tactical disagreement, Kyra felt the weight of their gazes, but she'd learned a long time ago to listen to her gut and stand strong on her opinions even when her team disagreed with her.

Her fingers moved to her pendant, seeking its guidance.

The stone was warm against her skin, a sensation that had become more pronounced since they'd arrived in Iran. It wasn't a warning signal, though, but rather a reassurance that she was on the right path.

"Soraya has to be first," Kyra said. "It's my gut feeling, and it rarely steers me wrong."

Max held her gaze for a long moment, then

nodded. "We'll do it your way." He glanced to Yamanu for confirmation, and when the head Guardian nodded, Max turned to the others. "Kyra will make first contact while we maintain positions nearby, ready to move in if needed."

8

MAX

Max stood in the doorway of their bedroom, watching as Kyra laid the abaya, the niqab, the fat suit, and loose pants and shirt on the bed, but he wasn't looking at the black fabric or the nude-color padded suit. He was looking at the woman who had captured his heart and was now standing in a pair of modest panties and a tank top, looking sexier than any lingerie model on the cover of a fancy magazine.

"I wish this was a vacation, and we didn't need to leave." He closed the door behind him and walked over to her. "Seeing you like this gives me all kinds of ideas." He pulled her into his arms.

Her body was rigid with tension, but when he started kissing her, she melted against him, getting lost in the kiss and the intimacy of the moment.

When they had to come up for air, she leaned

away, placing her hands on his chest. "I need to get ready."

He nodded, reluctantly letting go of her.

She picked up the suit. "It's truly ingenious, now that I've had the time and space to properly inspect it." She strapped it around her waist and thighs, and Max stepped forward to help with the adjustments.

He tried to be professional as he helped her hide several items inside the enormous fake breasts, but he couldn't help brushing his fingers against her own flesh through the thin fabric of her tank top.

Talk about a trigger. For both of them.

It was a reminder that despite the night they had spent in each other's arms, nothing had happened, and now they were going to share a bedroom for the duration of this mission, and Max couldn't help hoping that there would be more.

"Can you fit my backup piece in there?" Kyra asked, breaking the sudden tension between them.

Max snorted. "I could fit two handguns and a couple of grenades in each."

Kyra looked down at herself and burst out laughing. "Not exactly how I imagined the first contact between your hands and my breasts."

And…the tension was back in full force.

"I assure you that in my fantasies, there's considerably less padding involved." He sounded husky.

Their eyes met, and for a moment, it seemed like Kyra was ready to drop the suit and tackle him down to the bed, but then a knock sounded on the door.

"Are you about ready?" Yamanu asked.

"Almost there," Max called back. He cleared his throat and took a step back. "You probably want to finish this by yourself."

Kyra nodded and quickly finished adjusting the padding before reaching for the pants and shirt that went over the suit and under the abaya. "This makes me swear that I will never gain this much weight," she said as she struggled to bend down to put the pants on.

"You're immortal. Unless you force yourself to eat cheesecakes all day long, your body is not going to change significantly even if you overeat."

She looked at him with an unreadable expression on her face. "If I ever get pregnant again, it will be just as difficult, but it would be worth it."

Max swallowed and nodded, not knowing how else to react. Did she mean that she wanted to have a child with him, or just in general?

"How do I look?" she asked after pulling on the abaya and niqab.

"Like a perfectly unremarkable matron," Max said. "No one would suspect you're carrying enough fire-power to take down a small army."

He couldn't see her smiling, but he could practically feel it.

"Remember, we'll be listening the entire time," he said. "If anything goes wrong, we'll be there in seconds. Did you figure out what you are going to do?"

Kyra shrugged. "I'll knock on the door. If the guard answers, I'll tell him that I'm an old friend from Soraya's high school, and if she answers, I'll tell her that I have news of her daughters." She took a breath. "After that, I'll have to improvise based on her reaction."

"What if she doesn't let you in?" Max asked.

"She will," Kyra said. "She's desperate for news of her girls. If she's anything like me, she will want to hear it even if she doesn't think what I'm going to say is true."

"There are listening devices inside the house, so don't say anything that will give you away. Just show her the notes or maybe lift your face-covering and put a finger to your lips to let her know that she shouldn't say anything."

"Right." She smoothed a hand over the black fabric. "Thank you for pointing that out to me. I'm not thinking strategically like I normally would because it's my family."

"It's perfectly understandable." He took her hand and kissed the back of it. "That's why doctors don't treat their family members and certainly don't operate on them."

She chuckled. "That's counterintuitive. If I were a physician, I would want to take care of my family, and unless I personally knew a better physician, I wouldn't want anyone else taking care of them."

9

KYRA

Kyra turned around and crouched next to her open duffle bag, reaching for the small velvet pouch containing Jasmine's tarot cards.

"What are you going to do with these?" Max asked. "Are you planning on showing them to Soraya?"

She straightened and put the pouch in the pocket of her pants under the abaya. "Jasmine believes that I got them in America, so they will mean nothing to my sister. It's just for good luck." She patted her side where the cards were. "It's a talisman of sorts, a connection to the daughter I found and the family I hope to reunite."

She lifted her hand, showing him the two rings Jasmine had given her. "I hope Soraya will recognize these. Jasmine doesn't know if I had them with me when I arrived in America or bought them later. I'll just make sure that Soraya notices them, and I'll watch her response."

He gently gripped her fingertips and lifted her hand to his lips. "They look—" Max began but was cut off by the sound of the safe house door banging open.

They exchanged a quick look before rushing out to the main room.

"There's been an attack on Yasmin's home," Nadim announced without preamble. "It's happening right now."

Kyra felt ice flood her veins. "What do you mean, an attack?"

"Our watcher just reported in," Nadim said, his words clipped. "Armed men stormed the house. The guards are down—likely dead. At least two men entered the residence."

Kyra clutched her pendant. How could she have been so wrong? Why hadn't it given her a warning?

Perhaps getting in contact with Durhad's evil body had contaminated it.

"The enemy has made its move," Max said.

He had to remember not to mention Doomers in front of Nadim. The guy knew that the bad guys who had taken the daughters of two families were involved with the Revolutionary Guard, and that was enough for him. He knew not to ask too many questions.

"How many people are in the house?" Yamanu asked, holstering his guns.

"Yasmin, her husband, and their five children," Nadim said.

Five children. Kyra's nieces and nephews, blood of her blood, were now in the hands of the same creatures who had tortured her, Fenella, and her four nieces. The thought sent a wave of rage through her so potent that it momentarily stole her breath away. She thought of the cruelty which the Doomers had exhibited in the past and all the horrible things they had done that Max had told her about.

That same soulless cruelty would be turned against Yasmin's children now.

"We move," Yamanu said. "We won't get there in time to prevent them from being taken, but we might be able to follow their trail and retrieve them."

His words gave Kyra hope. Perhaps the situation was still salvageable.

The team sprang into action, the careful plan they'd spent hours crafting discarded in an instant, replaced by the urgent need to intercept the Doomers before they could disappear with Yasmin and her children.

"I'll drive the lead van," Nadim said, keys already in hand. "I know the fastest routes."

Within minutes, they were loading into the three vans they'd arrived in. Kyra considered shedding the traditional clothing. They were going in hot, ready for combat, so she wouldn't need to blend in, but she needed to leave the fat suit on because her weapons were in there, and she didn't have time to take it off and put her hidden arsenal in holsters. She could feel the dull press of her knives, guns, and gear through the padding, and it was a strange comfort amid the chaos.

As she and Max got into the van with Yamanu and Nadim, Kyra felt the pendant grow almost painfully hot against her skin, and the sensation only further fueled her anger. The heat seared into her sternum as if chiding her for not sensing the ambush coming. She balled her free hand into a fist, knuckles whitening.

Now you are warning me? When the danger is obvious?

You're useless.

"We'll get to them." Max took her hand, reading the fear and fury in her expression. "We're not too late."

Kyra wished she could believe him. Questions assaulted her thoughts in rapid fire. Had they taken Yasmin's husband alive or gunned him down for interference? They weren't human, so they could've just snapped his neck and done that right in front of his children. She could practically hear the terrified cries that must be echoing in that house right now.

As the vans pulled away from the safe house and accelerated through the streets, her mind raced with horrific scenarios. What if they arrived only to find the entire family already gone? What if the Doomers had killed the parents and taken the kids?

Hang on, she directed the sentiment toward a

sister she couldn't remember and children she'd never met. *I'm coming for you.*

The van swerved around a corner, horn blaring to clear pedestrians from its path. Through the windshield, Kyra could see the traffic parting before them, startled faces turning to watch them speeding away. She felt the adrenaline spike flowing through her veins, every sense sharpened as her body prepared for the imminent fight.

Drawing on years of combat experience, she steeled herself for what they might find and pushed down the personal terror threatening to overwhelm her focus. One way or another, the Doomers would learn they had made a grave mistake—and Kyra vowed she would not let them slip away unscathed.

10

MAX

As the van careened around a corner, tires screeching in protest, Max braced himself against the door. Through the windshield, Tehran's afternoon traffic parted like the Red Sea before Moses—drivers swerving frantically to avoid the three-vehicle convoy barreling through the streets with total disregard for traffic laws.

This would draw a lot of attention, but Yamanu couldn't shroud them when they needed people to get out of their way.

Centuries of combat experience had taught Max to use the moments before engagement to center himself and find that cold, clear focus that had kept him alive through countless battles, but this time it was personal, and getting into the zone was impossible.

Kyra was radiating barely contained waves of fury and fear that were impossible to block. They were affecting him as if he were connected to her with wires.

"Two minutes to target," Nadim said with a calmness that would have been enviable if it weren't fake.

Even without smelling the human's fear, Max could see the guy's white-knuckled grip on the steering wheel.

Yamanu activated his earpieces, linking with the teams in the other vans. "Listen up. We're approaching Yasmin's house. At least two hostiles were seen entering the house, but there could be more, and they are likely enhanced soldiers."

Nadim had no idea that the people he was dealing with were not human, so enhanced was the code word for Doomers. Still, he might notice things he shouldn't know about, so after the mission they would in any case need to scrub some of his memories.

"Remember, our priority is the safety of Yasmin and her children," Yamanu said. "Jade, you go in from the back with Dima and Anton. Rishba and Asuka, you protect our flank. Max, Kyra, you are with me through the front door. Nadim, you stay with the vans."

A chorus of acknowledgments came through the earpieces.

"I see smoke," Kyra said suddenly, leaning forward between the front seats and pointing toward a dark column rising in the distance.

Max's jaw tightened. Smoke could mean many

things, none of them good. "Faster," he instructed Nadim, who nodded and floored the accelerator.

As they turned onto the street where Yasmin's house stood, Max caught movement at the far end of the road—two black SUVs speeding away.

"They are moving north," he called. "At least two vehicles, high speed."

Jade's voice crackled back immediately. "We see them. Permission to pursue?"

Yamanu's reply was immediate. "Affirmative. Jade, you follow these vehicles but do not engage unless absolutely necessary. Track and report position."

"Understood," came the terse reply, followed by the sound of an engine revving as the second van broke formation to chase the fleeing SUVs.

Nadim pulled their van to an abrupt stop half a block away from Yasmin's house—close enough for a rapid response but far enough to avoid a potential ambush. The second van, carrying Dima and Anton, stopped behind them.

"Dima, secure the vans," Yamanu said. "Anton, go around the back. Max and Kyra, let's go!" he said, weapon already in hand.

Regrettably, Yamanu's shrouding was useless against Doomers, and it didn't make sense for him to waste his energy on the humans.

The four of them moved fast while maintaining partial cover behind the cars parked along the curb. The neighborhood was eerily quiet—no pedestrians and no curious onlookers despite the smoke. People here knew to mind their own business or risk ending up in prison, or worse, at the end of a noose.

The city's modern appearance misled outsiders into thinking that the place was home to a contemporary society where people enjoyed human rights, but nothing could be further from the truth with the medieval regime in power that operated according to barbaric rules that hadn't been modified for modern times. If anything, they'd become worse.

The front gate of Yasmin's home was open, and so was the door to the house itself.

They walked through the gate, Yamanu taking the lead with his weapon drawn. The small front garden showed signs of struggle—overturned planters, a child's bicycle knocked on its side, and drops of what was unmistakably blood darkening the stone path.

That shouldn't have happened if the perpetrators were Doomers unless someone in that household was immune to their mind control. Then again, some Doomers were so inept at thralling that they couldn't take the family without using force. There was also a very high likelihood that they just enjoyed terrorizing humans.

As they reached the open front door, Yamanu moved to one side of the opening while Max took the other with Kyra. Extending his senses, Max detected no sounds of movement inside the house, only the faint crackle of flames from somewhere deeper within, explaining the smoke they'd seen rising from the structure.

He nodded to Yamanu, who nodded back, signaling for him to go in and for Kyra to stay put.

She didn't like that, but neither of them was going to argue with Yamanu, who as Head Guardian was the senior officer on this mission.

As he entered with his gun leading the way, the interior of the house revealed the grim story. The air hung heavy with the acrid smell of gunpowder and the coppery tang of fresh blood, and the entry hall and living room beyond had been trashed—overturned furniture, vases shattered, and walls that were pockmarked with bullet holes. A fierce battle had taken place there, and someone had paid with their lives for the brave defense of the family because it sure as hell wasn't the Doomers who had been left to bleed out on the floor.

As Yamanu and Kyra entered behind Max, he extended his arm to block them from going ahead of him.

The pair of legs sticking out from behind the overturned couch looked like they belonged to a man, but just in case he was wrong about it, Max didn't want Kyra to see her sister like this.

"We are going to secure the rest of the house," Yamanu said quietly behind him.

Max nodded and waited until he was sure that Kyra had followed Yamanu before moving forward to examine the owner of the legs.

The man, probably Yasmin's husband, had died fighting. A pistol lay beside his outstretched hand, its magazine empty. Multiple bullet wounds marked his chest and abdomen, the pattern suggesting he'd faced his attackers head-on.

"He tried to protect them," Max said, respect coloring his tone despite not knowing the man. "He fought until his last breath."

Kyra and Yamanu returned from inspecting the rest of the house and walked over to him.

Max could smell her tears even though she didn't let them fall.

"Is it only my impression or are the good ones always the first to die?" she murmured.

Yamanu draped a comforting arm around her shoulders. "If you asked Jade that question, she would have said that dying heroically in battle was the ultimate reward."

"Death is death." Kyra knelt beside the body, murmuring something in Farsi—a prayer, perhaps, or simply an acknowledgment of the man's sacrifice. "May his soul know peace in the presence of the Almighty."

Max wasn't familiar with that prayer or invocation or whatever that was, and whether the Almighty was the creator of the universe or the Fates, he had no problem echoing the sentiment.

"The house is secured," Yamanu said. "There are no other victims and no booby-traps, and it's safe to assume that Yasmin and her children were taken alive."

Max's earpieces crackled a split second before

Jade's voice came through. "We've got a problem. Lost visual on the targets."

Max swore under his breath. "What happened?"

"They went into a tunnel," Jade said, sounding irritated. "We followed, but when we emerged on the other side, the vehicles were gone."

"Where was this tunnel?" Yamanu asked.

"Northern outskirts, heading toward the mountains."

That narrowed it down somewhat but still left hundreds of square kilometers of potential territory to search. They needed more information and fast.

"Return to the safe house," Yamanu instructed. "We'll regroup and—"

"Wait," Nadim's voice interrupted through the comms. "I may know where they're headed. There's a facility in that area, officially a military research station, but my network has reported special units activity there for months. Some of the soldiers seemed foreign and enhanced."

Hope flared in Max's chest.

"Send the coordinates to everyone's phone," Yamanu instructed.

Kyra shook her head vehemently. "We don't have time for that. We need to follow them now."

"We rushed in here with minimal preparation, and they still escaped with your sister and her children," Yamanu countered, keeping his voice steady. "If we go after them ill-prepared as we are, we'll just get ourselves killed and help no one."

"Every minute we delay—"

"I know," Max jumped in, cutting her off. "But I am with Yamanu on this. We need to regroup and rearm. We also need to find more details about that facility, or at least its layout."

"What if they don't go to the facility?" Kyra said. "What if they are heading to the airport? We will never find them."

"That's not likely," Yamanu said. "Possible, but I bet Nadim is right. The enhanced soldiers are physically powerful, but they are not great independent thinkers. They do what they are told, and it makes sense that they were told to bring your sister to a nearby facility before she and her children were to be sent someplace else."

11

KYRA

Kyra struggled to reconcile her warrior side, which was calculating their odds of success, with that of the worried sister who was desperate to rescue her family.

Finally, she nodded.

"You are right about making a plan instead of rushing in unprepared, but we need to secure Parisa. They might go after her next."

Yamanu looked conflicted. "I can ask Nadim to send more people to watch her house, but there isn't much they can do against enhanced soldiers."

His comm was closed, so he didn't need to talk in code, but it was better to keep doing that than let things slip within Nadim's hearing.

"I can call her and pretend to be a government official, telling her that Yasmin was taken and to go to Soraya's house. It might slow down the enemy."

"Good thinking," Yamanu said. "But I'll get Nadim to do that. He knows all the official lingo."

When Kyra nodded, Yamanu activated the comm and gave Nadim the instructions.

"We should move out," Max said. "The authorities will be here any moment now."

"Right." Yamanu strode out of the house.

Kyra looked one last time at the brother-in-law she'd never gotten to know and prayed again for his soul to ascend to heaven.

He'd been a good, loving husband to her sister and a good, loving father to her nephews and nieces. He'd died protecting his family. He deserved the highest honor heaven could give a man.

Max took her hand. "The Kra-ell believe that warriors who fall in battle get to spend eternity in the Fields of the Brave, which is their concept of heaven. They are not afraid to die."

"I pray it is true, but since no one returns to tell us what's on the other side, this is just wishful thinking for people who are afraid of death."

As they got in the van and Nadim pulled out into the street, Kyra wondered why the police hadn't shown up yet. Had the Doomers arranged for that?

It was possible.

"Chief," Yamanu said, talking into his comm. "The enemy took Yasmin and her kids. Jade followed them and lost them, but Nadim thinks he knows where they are taking them, and we are going back to the safe house to regroup and rearm. It would be extremely helpful if you could get us satellite imaging of the facility and its area. I'll have Nadim send you the coordinates."

"I'll get on it right away," Onegus said. "Did they take her husband as well?"

Yamanu cast a sad look at Kyra. "The husband fought bravely to protect them and fell in battle."

"That's sad news," Onegus said. "Send me the coordinates as soon as you can."

"Will do, chief." Yamanu ended the call.

"Why kill him?" Kyra asked quietly so Nadim couldn't hear her. "Couldn't they have just thralled everyone to leave without a fight?"

They were sitting in the back of the van this time, and Nadim was busy navigating the busy city streets.

"There could be several possibilities," Max said just as quietly. "He might have seen them taking down the guards, opened fire, and they shot back. Thrall requires focus and direct eye contact, which is difficult to maintain in an active firefight, even for someone who is good at it. Another is that they were really bad at it. Some Doomers can't thrall at all."

She had a feeling that he wanted to say more but stopped himself, and she could guess what that was. The Doomers might have shot and killed Javad with the intention of inflicting more trauma on his family.

Max had forgotten that for the past two decades, she'd lived and fought in these parts of the world, where savagery and cruelty were celebrated and encouraged. She was no stranger to either.

That was what she'd been fighting, what the rebels were trying to end.

Their slogan was Woman, Life, Freedom, which was in direct opposition to everything the Iranian regime was about.

The drive back passed in tense silence, with Kyra staring out the window, her hand continually going to her pendant as she thought through tactical scenarios in her mind.

A fortified facility, an unknown number of hostiles, six hostages, five of them kids. It would be challenging under the best circumstances, but with the emotional component added in, it got exponentially more complex.

While they were heading back, Nadim mobilized his network, sending operatives to Parisa's home while others gathered whatever intelligence they could on the facility where they believed Yasmin and her children had been taken to.

When they arrived, Max and Yamanu headed straight for the weapons cabinet, and Kyra followed right behind them.

"I want you in battle-ready full tactical gear," Yamanu instructed, lifting out a case of explosives.

Jade and her team arrived minutes later, her frustration at losing the Doomers evident in her tight lips and rigid posture.

"They knew exactly what they were doing," Jade reported, going into the cabinet for weapons and a Kevlar vest. "The tunnel was a planned escape route. They must have had vehicles waiting on the other side. The question is how did they know we were coming?"

"They didn't," Yamanu said. "They prepared for being chased by police or the Iranian army. I assume they don't have friends in every department."

Once everyone was armed, Max turned to the Kra-ell warriors. "Remember that the safety of the hostages is our absolute priority." He fixed his gaze particularly on the Kra-ell females for some reason. "Don't take unnecessary risks, no heroics, and no wild charges into unknown situations."

Maybe they were more savage than the males?

They certainly looked ready to tear the Doomers limb from limb, and Kyra was glad that both their hosts were in another part of the apartment and couldn't see the red glowing eyes and elongated fangs.

"We get it," Jade said, her large dark eyes blazing red. "The children are a priority. We will get them out alive."

"My sister, too," Kyra said.

Jade nodded. "We will do our best."

Kyra hoped that they were disciplined enough not to succumb to their savage urges and to think ratio-nally despite their blood lust. Rescuing hostages was

97

not the same as storming an enemy post and inflicting maximum damage.

Then again, they had done remarkably well rescuing her, Fenella, and the girls from the facility in Tahav, so she had to trust that they knew what they were doing.

After removing the fat suit and getting dressed for battle, Kyra returned to the living room, but then it occurred to her that she might need the disguise, so she went back to retrieve the suit and the traditional clothing.

Max arched a brow when she tucked both into a shopping bag.

"It's just in case I need them. If I don't, I'll leave the bag in the van."

"How are you holding up?" he asked quietly, keeping his voice low enough that only she could hear.

"I'm fine."

"Kyra." It was just her name, but the sound was loaded with meaning.

She looked up, her eyes meeting his. "What do you want me to say, Max? That I'm terrified? That I'm imagining what those monsters might be doing to my sister and her children right now? That I'm furious with myself for not moving faster, for not getting to them in time?"

"You did everything you could, but if you need to vent, go ahead. It's better than to keep it bottled up inside."

Kyra's fingers tightened around the bag handles. "I can't afford to feel anything much right now. I need to stay focused. I need to remember all the things I've learned over the years and utilize them to save my family. I need a cool head."

"I understand," Max said. "I understand compartmentalization. But ignoring those emotions doesn't make them go away. They'll still affect your judgment, your reactions."

"What's your point?" she asked, an edge creeping into her voice.

"My point is that you should acknowledge them first and then put them aside. Another point is that you don't have to carry this alone." He reached out, not quite touching her but close enough that she could feel his presence. "I'm here. The whole team is here. We're going to get your family back."

She nodded, swallowing the lump in her throat that had started in her sister's house and had kept growing as time went on.

"Thank you." She leaned over and kissed Max's cheek.

Something had shifted between them—a deepening of the already profound connection that had been developing since their first meeting.

"Five minutes," Yamanu called to the team, checking his watch. "Finish gearing up and move out."

Kyra checked her weapons one last time, ensuring each was loaded and secured properly. The weight of them was familiar, comforting in its way—tools of her trade, extensions of her will. But more comforting was the knowledge that she wouldn't be facing this battle alone. She had a team she trusted and Max at her side.

KYRA

The sun was setting as the team got in position around the Doomers' compound. Kyra lay flat on her stomach at the crest of a low ridge, high-powered binoculars pressed to her eyes as she studied the facility below. The wind carried dust that gritted between her teeth, but she barely noticed it.

"Two guard towers on the north perimeter, another on the east," she murmured into her comms unit. "The main entrance has a checkpoint with at least four armed personnel. Vehicles moving in and out through the south gate—looks like less security there."

The compound sprawled across several acres of land, surrounded by a concrete wall topped with razor wire. Inside the perimeter stood several buildings—a central structure that looked like a warehouse, two smaller rectangular buildings that could be barracks or prisoner facilities, and a fortified administrative building with satellite dishes on its roof.

"I've just gotten the satellite imagery," Yamanu said in her earpieces. "It confirms your assessment."

"South gate shows regular vehicle traffic with minimal inspection protocols," Max said.

Something about the compound's layout tugged at her memory—the arrangement of buildings, the positioning of guard posts, and the strong lighting that was designed to eliminate blind spots. It reminded her of something, something that made her heart rate quicken and her palms dampen with sweat.

Then, it hit her with the force of a physical blow. The facility's design was eerily similar to the compound where she had been held twenty-some years ago, the place she'd awakened with no memories of her life before, only to find herself a prisoner.

The same cold grip of fear she'd felt then threatened to close around her throat now. For a moment, she was back there—disoriented, terrified, watching guards drag screaming women through the corridor.

Except, that facility was inside Tehran, not outside of it. She hazily remembered running through the streets with fellow liberated prisoners and people running interference for them, blocking the pursuers' path, seemingly unintentionally.

Then again, her memories of that day were so

fuzzy that her mind had probably made up most of the details to fill in the gaps. Perhaps the facility had not been in Tehran. Perhaps she and the other escapees had taken a vehicle and driven it to Tehran, ditching it somewhere, and continuing on foot to disappear among the crowds.

Had it been some kind of holiday that so many people were on the streets? Perhaps it was a protest?

When she returned to America with her sisters and her nephews and nieces, she would put some effort into researching what had happened to her, but now she had a mission to focus on. Her family depended on her, and she couldn't afford distractions.

Kyra forced herself to take a deep breath, then another, and one more. That was then. This was now. She was no longer a prisoner but a warrior, and she was no longer alone. She had a team of superheroes with her. Yamanu, the incredible shrouder and thraller, and the Kra-ell, who were warriors on a whole different level.

Max had told her how they'd plowed through the guards at the compound in Tahav, human and immortal alike.

Then there was Max, who was not going to let her down if it was the last thing he did.

Her pendant pulsed against her skin, warmer than usual but not with the burning heat that signaled immediate danger.

Except, she no longer trusted its input.

It had betrayed her, had sent her on the wrong path, and hadn't warned her that she was making a mistake. Max had tried to convince her to go for Parisa and her children first, but she'd insisted that her gut was telling her to start with Soraya.

Then the Doomers had moved against Yasmin.

But the truth was that even if she had listened to Max instead of the stupid pendant, they might not have gotten there in time to prevent Javad's senseless death.

As she swept her binoculars across the compound once more, the pendant's warmth intensified when she focused on one particular building that she'd originally thought was barracks, but upon closer inspection, the bunker-like structure looked more like a holding facility than housing for soldiers.

Was the pendant trying to compensate for its previous failure? Or maybe it was good for some things and not others. Or maybe she should stop relying on it altogether.

"The northeastern building," she said into the comm. "I think that's where they're holding them."

"Why do you think that?" Jade asked through the comms.

Kyra hesitated, unsure how to explain her gut feeling. "It's the same size as the one on the other side of the administrative building, but it's built like a bunker and has more guards than all the others. To me, it looks like a classic prisoner containment setup."

"That's our target," Max said.

"Agreed," Yamanu confirmed. "Jade, Rishba, and Asuka. You create a diversion. When security responds, Kyra, Max, Dima, Anton, and I will infiltrate from the south and make our way to the building. We secure the family and extract them via the route we discussed. Is everyone clear on the plan?"

After a chorus of acknowledgments came through the comms, Kyra slid backward from her position until she was safely below the ridge line, then rose to a crouch and moved toward where Max and Yamanu waited with the rest of the team.

The sun had nearly set now, the mountains to the west silhouetted against a sky painted in violent shades of orange and crimson. Appropriate, given what was about to happen.

"We are in position," Jade reported through the comms. "Ready on your mark."

Yamanu checked his watch. "Five minutes. Final equipment check, everyone."

Max reached out to briefly squeeze her shoulder —a small gesture of support that carried more weight than words could have. "Just remember, we do this together. No lone wolf heroics."

He sounded like her teammates back in the rebel camp, but the situation was a lot different now. Back then, she was the strongest warrior in their organization, and she had taken on more risks because she knew she was immortal while her teammates were human and fragile in comparison. Now, every member of her team was stronger and better trained than she was. For best results, she should let them take the lead and follow their commands.

"Don't worry." She squeezed his hand. "For a change, I'm the weakest link in the operation, and I'm going to do my best not to do anything that might impede our superhero team. That being said, this is my family, and I will do whatever is necessary to save them, including risking my life."

Max nodded. "Thanks for the honest reply. Just don't die on me because I don't think I could ever recover from that."

His words touched her more than he could have imagined, and she leaned over to plant a quick kiss on his cheek. "You're not getting rid of me that easily. I don't plan on dying today."

He grinned. "That's the right answer."

"Time," Yamanu announced. "Jade, you're on."

The plan was for Jade's team to approach the main gate in one of the vans, with Jade driving and Rishba and Asuka crouching, hidden from view in the back. As the van neared the checkpoint, explosives set in a fuel depot, which was some fifty meters away, would provide a calculated distraction that would draw attention and resources without arousing suspicion of a coordinated attack.

Right on time, there was a sudden flash, followed by a rolling boom that shook the earth beneath Kyra's feet. Immediately, alarms blared across the compound, and guards began rushing toward the site of the explosion, exactly as planned.

"Move now," Yamanu ordered, and their team sprinted from cover, using the lengthening shadows to approach the southern perimeter where security would be the thinnest.

Kyra's body remembered the countless missions she'd led with the resistance, and she settled into the familiar rhythm, entering the zone. The weight of her weapons was reassuring—the primary firearm strapped across her chest, the blades secured at her thigh and ankle, and the backup pistol holstered at the small of her back.

She'd fought her way out of situations worse than this.

She would get her family out.

They reached the perimeter wall without incident, taking advantage of the chaos unfolding on the other side of the compound. Yamanu produced grappling hooks, and within moments, they had scaled the wall and dropped into the compound proper.

"Two guards approaching from the west," Yamanu whispered, detecting them before the rest of them did. "Don't engage unless necessary."

As the five of them pressed themselves into the shadows between two storage containers, Kyra controlled her breathing, making herself as still and silent as the night itself. If these guards were Doomers, they would be able to hear her and her companions' heartbeats, so she prayed that they were human.

The two men hurried past, speaking about the explosion and speculating whether it had been sabotage.

Once they had passed, Kyra followed Max and Yamanu to the northeastern building, with Dima and Anton guarding their rear. They were using the structures and vehicles on their way for cover, which slowed them down, but the longer they remained undetected, the better.

Her pendant continued to pulse warmly against her skin, seeming to confirm they were on the right track, but she no longer trusted it and remained hyper-vigilant.

As they neared their target, a pair of guards appeared unexpectedly around a corner, spotting them immediately.

There was no time for stealth, and as they reached for their weapons and opened their mouths to shout an alarm, she unsheathed her daggers, ready to throw them at her targets, but Anton and Dima reacted faster than anything Kyra had thought possible. Before the guards could utter a sound, the two Kra-ell closed the distance, their blades finding the guards' throats with synchronized precision.

She was still in a state of awe and shock as they dragged the bodies behind a utility shed.

After they returned, the entire team continued toward the bunker-like building, and Kyra felt the familiar combat calm settle over her—the hyper-focused state where everything slowed down and where every movement became deliberate and precise. Yet beneath that professional exterior, fear still churned, not for herself, but for her sister and the children.

What if they were too late?

What if the Doomers had already begun whatever procedures they had planned?

What if they had already sent her family to their vile island of depravity?

No time for that now. Focus on the mission. She cut off the spiral of dread.

At the rear entrance, two more guards stood watch. They were alert but not alarmed, still unaware of the intruders concealed in the shadows.

"They are human. I'll take them," Yamanu whispered.

He didn't seem to be doing anything, but the guards froze in place, their expressions going blank.

If anyone were to look at them from some distance, they would seem to be perfectly fine, doing their job and guarding the building. No one would suspect that they were under a powerful immortal's thrall.

"Inside," Yamanu commanded softly.

Max moved first, with Kyra close behind him. They entered the building, finding themselves in a dimly lit corridor with numbered doors running its length. The interior was sterile, institutional—more like a medical facility than a prison, which made it more disturbing.

At the end of the corridor was a security station, but Yamanu took control of the guard's mind the same way he had done to the two outside.

"You don't leave any fun for us," Anton complained.

Kyra ignored him. "We need to check the monitors," she said as she scanned the displays for a sign of her family.

The security station provided views from cameras throughout the facility, but the images were black and white and grainy. "There!" She grabbed Max's arm, pointing at one screen.

Even though the image was blurry, it was easy to see that the cell contained several occupants—a woman sitting on a bench with five children of varying ages clustered around her.

"Room twelve," Max said, checking the monitor label. "Now, isn't that serendipitous?"

Fenella had been locked in cell number twelve, and now Kyra's sister and her sister's children were locked in a cell with the same number.

As they rushed down the corridor, Kyra's heart hammered in her chest, adrenaline and anticipation making her hyperaware of every sound, every shadow. Her pendant grew warmer with each step, confirming they were getting closer.

They encountered two more guards en route, dispatching them quickly and silently. The lack of general alarm suggested their infiltration remained undetected and that the compound's security forces were still focused on the distraction at the main gate.

When they reached the door marked Twelve, Max took position on one side, rifle angled low, while Kyra mirrored him on the other. Yamanu stood back, eyes fixed ahead, ready to thrall anyone inside who might raise the alarm.

Kyra gave a nod.

Max tried the handle, then shook his head. "It's locked. I need to breach it, but the charge won't be subtle. I need the people inside well clear of the blast zone, and I'm not sure they can hear us through the thick door."

"I'll handle it," Yamanu said. His voice had that distant edge he got when he was focusing. "Give me a second."

He closed his eyes. A beat passed.

"They're moving back," he confirmed. "They won't come forward unless someone screams."

Max gave a quick nod and pulled a small, clay-colored charge from his vest. "Mini C4 satchel—shaped for directional force. Won't blow the door off the hinges, just crack the lock." He pressed it into place just above the latch, flattening it with nimble fingers.

He attached a remote detonator and then looked over his shoulder. "Back up. Stay tight to the wall."

Dima and Anton ducked across the corridor to

get a view of the breach while the rest of the team retreated several doors down.

The blast was sharp but surprisingly contained—a low, concussive thump followed by the soft clatter of warped metal. Kyra blinked. She'd expected something louder.

"Good stuff," Max muttered. "Precision compound. Focused yield."

13

KYRA

When the dust settled, the door stood slightly open, and as Max pushed it in all the way, Kyra and Yamanu swept into the room, covering all corners with their weapons.

The scene inside seared itself into Kyra's memory.

Yasmin was huddling with the children in the back of the cell. Her body curved protectively around the three smallest ones. A little girl, no more than six years old, clung to her mother, her face buried against her chest. The two older ones, about fourteen and fifteen, flanked their mother, hugging her from both ends.

Yasmin looked up with wary defiance in her tear-stricken eyes, one arm tightening around her youngest while the other moved subtly to push the older children behind her. Even in captivity, even in fear, she was protecting her children with a fierceness that made Kyra's chest ache with pride.

"Who are you?" Yasmin demanded. "What do you want with us?" Her voice was steady despite the tremor visible in her hands.

Kyra lowered her weapon, keeping it ready at her side but trying to appear less threatening.

"We're here to free you."

Suspicion flickered across Yasmin's face. "You're not with them?"

"No," Kyra assured her. "We're with the Kurdish resistance. We learned of your capture and came to free you."

The lie was an easier and faster explanation. The truth could wait for when they were not in immediate danger.

Yasmin's eyes narrowed, studying Kyra's face with a scrutiny that seemed to pierce through flesh and bone. "You look familiar."

Something twisted in Kyra's chest—hope, perhaps, that her sister might recognize her despite the years and the impossibility of her youthful appearance. But there was no time for revelations now.

"We can talk later," she said. "Right now, we need to move. Quickly and quietly."

Yasmin hesitated only a moment before nodding. She rose from the bench, gathering the youngest child into her arms. "Do exactly as she says," she told the other children.

They nodded, wide-eyed but obedient. The oldest boy, who looked to be about fifteen, moved to help the younger ones.

"Max, take point," Kyra instructed. "Yamanu, rear guard. I'll stay with the family."

She was taking command from Yamanu, but he seemed okay with that. Later, she would apologize, but right now she needed to be in charge of the operation.

Kyra turned to Yasmin. "Stay close to me. If I say drop, you all get down immediately. No questions and no hesitation. Your lives depend on your quick responses."

Yasmin nodded again, her lips tight with determination. The initial shock was wearing off, replaced by the strong will of a mother intent on getting her children to safety.

Max checked the corridor before motioning them forward.

They moved as one, with Dima and Anton going first, Kyra positioned between Max and her family, and Yamanu bringing up the rear. The youngest child whimpered softly in her mother's arms, but the others maintained a disciplined silence, or maybe a terrified one.

They had made it halfway back to their entry point when a shrill alarm sounded throughout the facility. Red emergency lights flashed, bathing the corridors in an eerie, pulsating glow.

"They discovered the breach," Yamanu said. "We need to move faster."

"This way," Max urged, leading them down a side corridor. "I see a sign for an exit."

The sound of running footsteps and shouted commands echoed from ahead just as their group detoured into the side corridor.

Anton ran ahead while Dima joined Yamanu to bring up the rear.

Yasmin clutched the little girl tighter while the other children moved closer together, their faces pale with fear.

"It's going to be okay," Kyra assured them in a whisper. "Just stay close to me."

They turned another corner and found themselves facing three armed guards. There was no time for stealth, no opportunity for careful planning. The guards shouted in alarm, raising their weapons.

Kyra reacted on pure instinct. She pushed Yasmin and the children back around the corner, providing them cover with her body, then spun back to face the threat. Anton had already dispatched two of the guards, but the third managed to shoot, hitting the hybrid in the back, where a Kevlar vest protected him.

Kyra's weapon came up smoothly, but Max beat her to it, firing at the third guard.

The guy went down, and Anton straightened, patting his front and back as if surprised that he was unharmed.

"Let's go!" Kyra urged the family, shepherding them past the fallen guards. "We're almost there."

They increased their pace, the children running to keep up. Yasmin stumbled once, weighted down by the child in her arms, and Kyra instinctively reached out to steady her. Their eyes met briefly, and something passed between them—not recognition, exactly, but a connection that transcended their current circumstances.

The exit was just ahead, a service door that would lead them back to the compound's southern perimeter, where they had entered.

Freedom was tantalizingly close.

Then Kyra's pendant suddenly flared with heat so intense she nearly gasped aloud. Without conscious thought, she spun around, her weapon already tracking toward a new threat she hadn't yet seen.

A soldier had appeared from a side passage, his weapon aimed directly at Yasmin's back. In the split second before he fired, Kyra lunged forward, knocking her sister aside with one hand while firing with the other. Her bullet caught the guy in the shoulder, spinning him around but not dropping him.

The oldest boy reacted with surprising speed, pulling his younger siblings down to the floor just as Max turned and emptied three rounds into the soldier's chest. When the guy staggered but didn't go down, Kyra realized that he was either an immortal or was wearing a Kevlar vest, but her gut told her that he was a Doomer and not an ordinary soldier.

Ordinary bullets could slow him down, but they wouldn't kill him.

Yamanu stepped forward, lifted his gun, and fired at the Doomer's head. "Regenerate from that, asshole."

Kyra felt bile rising in her throat, and she could only imagine how traumatic it was for the children.

"Move!" Max shouted. "Now!"

They didn't need to be told twice. Yasmin gathered her little girl closer and ran for the exit, her other children following close behind. Kyra remained between them and the fallen Doomer, her weapon trained on him just in case he regenerated from the deadly wound.

"Go," Yamanu told her. "He's not going to be able to fix that."

Kyra nodded once and followed her family through the exit. Outside, the compound was in chaos. The distraction at the main gate had escalated into a full-blown firefight, with Jade and her warriors engaging a large contingent of forces. The sound of gunfire and explosions filled the air, along with shouts and curses.

Dima and Anton leaped over the wall to check that it was safe before signaling for the rest of them to follow. Max helped Yasmin over the wall, and Dima helped her on the other side. The youngest girl was hoisted up next.

The oldest boy turned back, his eyes finding Kyra's. "What about my father?" he asked.

The question hit Kyra like a punch to the stomach. In all the rush, she hadn't had time to prepare for this inevitable question.

"I'm sorry," she said, the words inadequate but necessary. "He didn't make it."

The boy's face crumpled for an instant before hardening into a mask of control beyond his years. He gave a single, sharp nod, then turned to help his siblings over the wall.

Kyra followed, her heart heavy with the weight of everything this family had lost and everything they still had to face.

But they were alive, they were together, and they would overcome.

14

MAX

"Stay alive," Kyra said in Max's earpieces. "And leave some scum for me to finish. I'll be back as soon as my family is safe in the vans."

Max calculated the odds of finishing the job before Kyra managed to come back. It was a twenty-minute trek at a human walking pace to where they'd left the vans, then a few minutes to settle her family, and an additional few minutes for Kyra to run back. It wasn't enough time to clean up the compound before her return.

"Stay with them," he said. "We can handle this."

"Not a chance. You can't take the entire compound down with five people. Dima and Anton will keep my family safe."

"Stay in the van, Kyra," Yamanu's voice sounded on the comm. "That's an order."

There was a long moment of silence and then a terse, "Yes, sir."

Max had a feeling that Kyra wasn't going to obey Yamanu's order. She wasn't a Guardian, and although she'd agreed to Yamanu leading the extraction, she was not duty-bound to do that, and she was a rebel.

Max let out a breath.

It was time to finish the job and ensure not only their safe escape, but also the rescue of Kyra's other sisters. That meant killing everyone in this installation and, most importantly, all the Doomers.

It seemed ludicrous to attempt that with the limited resources at their disposal, but with Yamanu's thralling and the incredible power of Jade's female crew, it might be possible. He wished Dima and Anton could fight as well, but it was more important for them to safeguard Kyra and her family.

Backtracking, Max placed explosives at key structural points throughout the building, not enough to bring it down but sufficient to create a distraction. After all, there might be more prisoners behind the closed doors who didn't deserve to die tonight.

A Doomer appeared at the end of the corridor, his inhuman speed marking him an immortal. He wasn't pointing a gun, but his fangs were fully elongated, and the half-crazed, determined look in his eyes was one that Max had seen in countless others over the centuries. The fanatical devotion of these brainwashed monsters and their religious fervor for their twisted ideology made them dangerous beyond their immortal physical capabilities.

Capture was not an option for Doomers. They fought to the death.

Max was happy to oblige, and as the thirst for Doomer blood clouded his senses, he charged instead of first aiming at the Doomer's head, which was one of the few ways of killing an immortal. The problem was that it was a nearly impossible shot to make at a moving target, and hitting him anywhere else on the body would only slow the Doomer down but not kill him.

The immortal's body would fix the damage in minutes, and he would be back to hunt them and Kyra's family. Besides, if he managed to subdue the Doomer, he could get him to reveal how many other members of the Brotherhood were in the compound and what their plans were for Kyra's other sisters.

As Max collided with the Doomer, the force of that collision would have shattered human bones. They grappled, a brutal dance of strength against strength. The Doomer's fully extended fangs sought vulnerable flesh, but so did Max's, and long decades of superior combat training gave him an edge over the enemy.

With a move that combined leverage and raw power, Max forced the Doomer against the wall, pinning him with one arm while placing his free hand over the immortal's heart.

"How many of you bastards are in this compound?" he commanded an answer.

The Doomer struggled and kept his mouth shut, his eyes blazing with hatred rather than fear.

Max punched through his chest and wrapped his hand around the Doomer's heart. A normal human would already be dead from such an assault, but immortals were much harder to kill.

"How many?" he repeated his question.

Instead of answering, the Doomer spat in his face in defiance.

"Wrong answer." Max closed his hand around the beating heart and ripped it out.

The body crumpled to the ground.

He wiped his bloody hand on the Doomer's shirt and moved to his next position.

Max pressed the trigger on the detonator, and a heartbeat later, the night split open with a thunderous boom. The ground shook beneath his feet as a section of the building's outer wall collapsed in a cloud of dust and debris.

With the wall out of the way, Max caught glimpses of the battle unfolding across the compound. Jade and the two Kra-ell females had engaged a group of Doomers near the main gate, the confrontation having evolved from a mere distraction into a full-fledged assault.

The Kra-ell were magnificent in combat, their physiology giving them advantages even against immortals. Rishba and Asuka moved with a lethal grace that was almost hypnotic, their slender bodies belying their incredible strength.

Jade fought with a ferocity that bordered on artistry, her movements so fast they blurred even to Max's enhanced vision. She had already downed three Doomers, their bodies lying in unnatural postures around her as she engaged a fourth.

Yamanu's blanket thralling had taken care of all the human guards, paralyzing them on the spot, so the only ones still resisting were the Doomers and perhaps the odd human or two who were immune to thralling.

Two Doomers rushed from the neighboring building with automatic weapons in hand, and Max took cover behind the fallen wall debris as they opened fire, their bullets chewing into the concrete barrier.

Max drew his own weapon and returned fire.

One of the Doomers staggered as Max's shots found their mark, giving Max the split second he needed. He vaulted over the barrier, closing the distance between them. The second Doomer swung his weapon around, but he was too slow. Max was already inside his guard, one hand seizing the rifle and wrenching it away while the other delivered a blow to the Doomer's throat that would have decapitated a human.

The Doomer fell back, temporarily disabled but far from defeated. His companion had recovered enough to re-enter the fight, and Max found himself engaged with both simultaneously in a deadly ballet of strikes, blocks, and countermoves.

In his earpiece, Kyra's voice cut through the din of battle. "I'm coming back—"

"Negative," Max barked, ducking under a Doomer's swing and delivering a devastating counter that shattered the immortal's knee. "Stay put. We are almost done here."

That was a big-ass exaggeration.

He dispatched the first Doomer with a blade through the heart that should keep him down long enough for Max to finish his comrade. The second proved more resilient, landing a blow that sent Max crashing into a wall with enough force to crack the concrete.

Max shook off the impact, a savage grin spreading across his face. A part of him reveled in the pure, unfiltered violence of immortal against immortal. The Guardian Force had given him a purpose and a moral code, but it had also given him a sanctioned outlet for the predatory instincts that were inherent in all immortals.

Killing monstrous Doomers was the most satisfying channel for those instincts, and Max had no compunctions about indulging them to their fullest.

He re-engaged the enemy, their impact sending them crashing through the wall into a room that must have served as a clinic or laboratory. Max pinned his opponent against a steel table, one hand crushing the Doomer's throat while the other drove his blade through the immortal's chest with enough force to pierce the metal surface beneath.

The next part was gruesome but necessary. He removed the beating hearts from both Doomers.

More explosives sounded from the other buildings, the work of Yamanu, Jade, Asuka and Rishba.

Max made one more run through the building to verify that there were no more Doomers left and then went to locate the security hub of the compound. They needed to eliminate all recorded evidence of what took place here. The existence of the Kra-ell must remain hidden from the Doomers, and the existence of vampire-like immortals must remain a secret from humans.

Finding a thralled soldier, it was easy to find the information he needed. With his remaining explosives set, Max withdrew from the structure and detonated, eliminating all possible evidence of tonight's battle.

Max then rushed to see if his team needed his help.

He made his way through the compound, encountering no further resistance. The battle had shifted to the administrative building, where Jade and her team were still engaged with what remained of the Doomer force.

The Kra-ell warriors had the upper hand, dispatching their opponents with savage efficiency.

Outside, the night was only illuminated by the fires burning throughout the compound and the harsh beams of searchlights sweeping across the grounds. Max kept to the shadows, making his way toward the breached section of the perimeter wall.

He found Kyra waiting just beyond the breach, her weapon ready, her posture betraying her tension despite her outward calm.

"I told you to stay with the hostages," Max said, checking over his shoulder for pursuit.

"And I decided that was a stupid order," she replied with a ghost of a smile. "Dima and Anton can handle securing the vans."

Max opened his mouth to argue further, then closed it with a shake of his head. He would have done the same in her position.

"Status on the rest of the team?" she asked. "Should we go help them?"

"Still engaged at the administrative building," he reported. "Jade's crew are almost done, and we will only be in the way." He grimaced. "You don't want to see the carnage they leave behind. It's gruesome."

They were making sure there would be no survivors to report what had happened and no one to alert other Brotherhood cells about the rescue operation.

She lowered her gaze to where blood was splattered all over his clothing. "You've been busy."

He cracked a smile. "The only way to ensure a Doomer is dead is by tearing his heart out or aiming a special bullet through his eye to shred his brain."

Kyra didn't even wince, and he loved her even more for that.

If he weren't so dirty and covered in enemy blood, he would have pulled her into his arms and kissed her senseless.

"They need to kill them all," she said. "If any escape, they'll go after my sisters immediately. The moment they realize we've taken Yasmin, they'll accelerate their timetable for abducting the others."

He nodded. "We need a complete sanitization of the site. No survivors to report back. Everyone on our team understands that."

"Max," Yamanu's voice sounded in his earpieces. "I sent Dima and Anton with Kyra's family to the safe house. And, Kyra, we will need to talk about your insubordination."

"Yes, sir." Kyra didn't sound or look remorseful in the slightest.

"You two move out. I'll follow with Jade and her crew."

15

KYRA

"I'm sorry that you trekked back to the compound for nothing," Max said to Kyra as they made their way to where the vans were waiting, hidden in a shallow ravine about half a mile from the compound.

She cast him a mock glare. "No, you're not. You're very happy that I missed all the fighting."

"Guilty," he admitted, taking her hand. "But not for the reason you think."

"Oh, yeah?" She lifted a brow. "So, you didn't want me to stay safe while you fought all the bad guys on your own?"

"Of course, I wanted that, but I also didn't want you to see me turn savage."

Her eyes softened. "I know how it gets in the heat of the battle. I wouldn't have held it against you."

He shook his head. "You don't understand. It's not just me doing what needs to be done. I relish doing it.

A monster stirs to life inside me, and it's eager to tear Doomers and other evildoers limb from limb."

Kyra considered that for a moment. "I get that. I don't turn into a total savage, or rather, I didn't, but that's only because I didn't know that Doomers regenerate from most injuries. I was sure that I killed them." She shivered. "I feel guilty for not finishing them off."

He squeezed her hand. "You had no way of knowing."

She nodded. "Because of the Doomers I left to regenerate, my people were not safe in Tahav. I'm glad that they moved to a different location."

As they crested the ridge, she could see that only two vans remained, the one with her family on board having left minutes ago.

"I'm also glad that Yasmin and her kids are on their way to the safe house." She looked at Max. "I feel like a big weight was lifted off me." She chuckled. "The truth is that I didn't believe you and Yamanu, along with Jade and half her team, could take on an entire compound of Doomers."

"Thankfully, they were not all Doomers," Max said as he opened the passenger door for her. "Most were Revolutionary Guard soldiers, and Yamanu took care of them with his blanket thralling. We only had to dispatch the Doomers."

He walked around the vehicle, his eyes scanning their surroundings before he slid into the driver's seat.

"Evil and eviler," Kyra murmured. "There is always a bigger fish."

He chuckled. "You have no idea."

"Really?" She tilted her head. "Then please enlighten me."

"It's a long story, and it has to do with the gods who created intelligent species all over the galaxy." He turned the engine on and started the slow and bumpy ride to the nearest road. "The ruler of the home planet of the gods is called the Eternal King, and he's the biggest fish of them all. The Doomers, with their delusional leader, are not even fleas to him. They are not even specks of dust."

Kyra sensed that there was an enormous story there, but right now, she couldn't concentrate on tales about alien gods and their galactic empire or whatever else the story was about. Her mind was on Yasmin and her children and their devastation over losing their father.

She'd seen enough children orphaned by the regime who had somehow found their way into her rebel camp. She'd given them purpose and helped channel their grief and anger toward taking revenge on the enemy and freeing as many of their people as they could, but none of them had ever become whole again.

They were forever broken.

As they reached a paved road, Max shifted gears and accelerated away from the compound, following a route they had mapped earlier that would avoid main roads and checkpoints.

In the rearview mirror, Kyra could see in the distance the compound burning brightly against the night sky, a beacon of destruction that would soon draw attention from the authorities.

"They'll think it's a terrorist attack," she said. "Or maybe an internal power struggle." She turned to the window.

With the adrenaline of combat wearing off, a melancholy settled in. "Yasmin's oldest boy asked about his father," she said quietly. "I had to tell him that he didn't make it."

Max tightened his grip on the steering wheel. "There's no good way to tell a child their parent is gone. But at least he has his mother and his siblings. Their future would have been a living hell if the Doomers had shipped them to the island, which they would have done now that Durhad is no longer around. They wouldn't have known what else to do with them."

If Yasmin was still fertile, she would have been sent to the Doomers breeding program, and so would her daughters. The sons would have been taken to the Doomers training program and turned immortal.

Max was right to call it a living hell.

"Nevertheless, they lost their father today, and I don't know how to make it better for them. When orphaned teenagers found their way to my rebel camp, we trained them to fight and take revenge on those who'd murdered their parents." She turned to look at Max. "Is that what I should do with my nieces and nephews? At what age can immortals join the Guardian Force?"

They hadn't had time to discuss all the intricacies of life in the immortals' village, and Kyra realized that she wouldn't even know how to answer her sisters' questions.

Max smiled. "Eighteen, but that's not the only path available to them. There are many paths that can lead to healing."

16

MAX

The parallels weren't lost on Max. Kyra's own life had been torn apart by a member of the Brotherhood, her memories of family erased, and her chance to watch her daughter grow up stolen. And now her sister's family also faced trauma, their lives forever altered by violence and loss.

But at the root of it all had been their father's fanaticism and political aspirations. If he hadn't torn Kyra from her family, shoved her into that mental institution, and asked Durhad to *hypnotize* her to forget her past, none of this would have happened.

Then again, Max would have never met Kyra, they wouldn't have fallen in love, and that would have been a great tragedy as well.

Should he be thankful to Kyra's hateful, abusive father?

Never.

One thing was for sure. Max didn't envy the Fates their job. He wouldn't have been able to stomach causing so much suffering just to match up two souls who were destined for each other.

After about twenty minutes of riding in silence, Max's comm unit crackled to life.

"We are withdrawing now," Yamanu reported. "Mission complete. Site sanitized."

The clinical terminology couldn't disguise what those words meant—every Doomer, every guard, every potential witness at the compound had been eliminated. It was brutal but necessary. The Brotherhood operated with similar ruthlessness, and showing mercy would only endanger more innocent lives.

"Copy that," Max acknowledged. "We are proceeding as planned."

He glanced at Kyra, finding her watching him with an expression he couldn't quite read.

"What?" he asked.

"Nothing," she said, looking away. "It's just that this isn't the kind of operation I'm used to. With the resistance, we were always outgunned and outmanned. We called it hit and run because that was usually the scope of our operations, either freeing prisoners or stealing supplies. We've never done anything like this."

"Does it bother you?" he asked carefully.

"No, of course not. I'm just awed at the efficiency and that it was all done with such a small team. The

Kra-ell are a great asset to the clan." She shifted, tucking one leg under her. "How did they find you? Or rather, how did you find them?"

He snorted. "That's such an amazingly convoluted story that it would take me a long time to tell it."

"Jasmine told me that they were sent by the gods, and something went wrong with their ship, so they arrived seven thousand years too late."

"What else did she tell you?"

"That Ell-rom is half Kra-ell and half god, and he's a double prince because both his parents were royal heirs."

Of course that was what Jasmine would focus on. Still, he couldn't blame her for reducing it down to the essence because there had been no time for more. Most of what Kyra had been told was on the plane after her rescue, and she'd still been confused from the drugs and the abuse she'd suffered.

Max couldn't believe that only days had passed since then. He felt as if he'd known her for months.

"Well?" Kyra prompted.

"I'll tell you the entire story later." He reached for her hand and clasped it. "Or maybe Jasmine will. She can probably do a better job of it than me. I'm not a good storyteller."

"Give it a try yourself when we are all settled down." Her other hand went to her pendant. "I need a good story to take my mind off the carnage. Don't get me wrong, I don't condemn it. I know it's necessary and that we can't fight evil with rainbows and unicorns. I just need to think about something else."

Max nodded, relieved that she understood. Too many people couldn't reconcile their moral frameworks with the realities of fighting an enemy that recognized no ethical boundaries.

Kyra was different. Her experiences had already prepared her for the harsh truths of their world. She didn't need to be sheltered from the uglier aspects of what they did, didn't need the comforting lies some required to sleep at night.

They drove in silence for a time, the rhythm of the road and the darkness surrounding them creating a strange bubble of calm after the chaos of the compound. Max kept checking the mirrors for signs of pursuit, but their escape appeared clean. The destruction they'd left behind had apparently consumed all available resources, leaving no one to follow.

Yamanu and the rest of the team had taken a different route, and he hoped they weren't being followed either.

As they approached the outskirts of Tehran, Yamanu came on the comm with updates. "Kyra's family is already at the safe house, and Nadim's network reports that there is no activity at the other locations."

That was a relief—the Doomers hadn't moved against Kyra's other sisters yet, and now that they'd eliminated the local Doomer cell, chances were that no more attempts would be made to abduct the rest of the family.

Max glanced at Kyra. "That's good news."

"I know."

Fatigue was beginning to show in the tightness around her eyes. They'd been operating at maximum intensity for hours now, with the emotional toll of the rescue compounding the physical demands.

"You should rest," he suggested. "We've got a little time before we reach the safe house."

She shook her head. "I'm fine."

"Kyra," he said, softer now. "You're no good to your sister or her children if you're running on empty. Take these fifteen minutes to recharge."

She hesitated, then relented with a small nod, letting her head rest against the window. Within minutes, her breathing deepened, though she wasn't fully asleep—just resting, her instincts keeping her partially alert.

His warrior queen.

Her repose didn't last long.

"My pendant failed me," she said. "I was sure that I needed to make contact with Soraya first and to approach the situation with diplomatic finesse rather than brute force. It didn't warn me that hours later we would conduct a full-scale assault on a military installation, leaving dozens dead, and a facility in flames."

Max nodded. "And yet we accomplished our

primary objective, which was rescuing Yasmin and her children. One family secured, three more to go."

17

KYRA

As they entered the city proper, Kyra removed the elastic holding the end of her braid, combed out her hair with her fingers, and then started braiding it again.

She was nervous about her upcoming talk with her sister. Did Yasmin remember having an older sister who had gone to study in America and was never heard from again?

Her original plan had been to tell her sisters that she was Kyra's daughter and show them the notes that the girls had given her, but that was to convince them to come with her. Now everything was different, and she didn't know whether she should stick to that plan or tell Yasmin the truth from the get-go.

As they neared the safe house, Kyra reflected on how unremarkable it appeared from the outside—just another middle-class residential apartment building in a neighborhood of similar houses. But she knew it had been carefully chosen for its strategic advantages. It was small, with two apartments on each of its three floors. There were balconies at the front and in the back, which could be alternative escape routes if the front and back entrances were compromised. The neighboring buildings had no side windows, and the backyards were too small for anyone to be spending time in them.

Max parked the vehicle in the covered carport behind the house and announced their arrival through the comm.

"Acknowledged," came Dima's response. "Perimeter secure."

The two apartments on the second floor had been combined into one large space, and that was where their team was staying. Kyra wondered where Nadim had housed her sister and the kids. Probably the third floor.

When they entered, the man greeted them warmly. "Welcome back. I'm glad to see you unharmed. The mother and children are upstairs, resting."

"Any issues?" Max asked.

Nadim sighed. "The youngest child cried herself to sleep. Fatima is preparing a meal for them now with some sweets for the children. Hopefully, it will help lift their spirits."

"We should shower and change clothes," Kyra suggested. "We are covered in dirt and blood."

"Yes, that's a good idea," Nadim agreed. "Dima has

already showered, and he's standing guard. Anton is showering right now."

They needed to get to her other sisters, but it was the middle of the night, and unlike a military extraction, this operation should be done during daylight hours. Then again, they didn't have the luxury of time. They needed to secure her remaining family members before the Brotherhood realized what was happening and moved against them.

"You go ahead," Max said. "I'll follow."

Kyra nodded and started removing her Kevlar vest on her way to their bedroom.

Their bedroom.

Everyone assumed that they were a couple, but all they had done was sleep in each other's arms. She glanced at the bed, and the image that flitted through her head was totally inappropriate, given what had happened earlier and what was still waiting ahead.

Perhaps the brush with mortality had made her want to celebrate life, and what better way to do that than to enjoy a night of passion with the man she loved?

Kyra shook her head. It would happen, but probably not tonight or the next. She had a sister to comfort and three more to save.

Showered and dressed in fresh clothing, she emerged from the bedroom to find that Yamanu and the rest of the team had arrived.

Jade, Asuka, and Rishba looked as bad as Max, or rather worse. In addition to dirt and blood, they were also covered in gore. They also looked so alien that there was no way Nadim hadn't noticed they weren't human. And yet, he hadn't asked or remarked on their appearance.

Yamanu, on the other hand, looked the same way as when he'd left the safe house earlier, with not a speck on him. How had he managed that?

"Do you need me to come talk to your family?" Max asked.

Her knee-jerk response was to tell him that she could do it alone and didn't need his help, but the truth was that she could use his solid presence even if he didn't utter a word.

"Yes, but you need to change first."

He smiled as if she'd given him a precious gift. "I'll be out in three minutes flat."

She doubted he could do that so fast but nodded anyway. He could take ten minutes or more if he wanted. She wasn't in a rush to have her heart cut into ribbons by her sister's grief.

Cowardly?

Yeah. But she was only human.

Well, not really. She wasn't even that.

Kyra sighed.

"What's the matter," Yamanu asked, "why the long sigh?"

"It's nothing." Kyra squared her shoulders. "I'm just not good with the soft stuff. I don't know how to comfort people, how to ease their fears and their pain. All I know is how to fight, fight, and fight some more."

Jade looked at her with approval. "You have a warrior's heart. That's nothing to feel bad about."

Perhaps out of everyone in the room, Jade was the one who could understand best what Kyra was feeling. Then again, who knew what these aliens felt?

They weren't very expressive.

But Jade was the leader of her people, and she must have encountered similar situations. Perhaps not with family members, but she sure had to deal with her community members going through hard times.

"How do you deal with grief?" Kyra blurted before she could think better of it. "I mean, not your own, but when you have to comfort others."

Something passed through Jade's enormous black eyes. "Grief and I are well acquainted, and I know that no words have the power to diminish the pain. For me, time took the edge off, and dreams of revenge kept me going. For others, my advice was not to give up on life because if you do, evil wins."

"Thank you." Kyra dipped her head toward the female. "Your pep talk resonates perfectly with me, but I doubt it would do any good to the woman upstairs who has just lost a husband she loved."

Jade shrugged. "She might surprise you. Yasmin gave birth to five children and raised them. That takes resilience. She can also draw strength from her children, you, and her other sisters."

18

MAX

When Max returned to the living room, Kyra looked a little less frazzled, and it seemed to be because of something Jade had said to her. He'd only heard the last bit of it, something about drawing strength from the children, but more must have been said before his arrival.

"Ready?" he asked.

Kyra nodded with a smile. "You clean up nicely." She lifted a hand to his wet hair. "I didn't like the dark color. I like you blond."

"Thanks." He wanted to say that he liked her dark beauty, but it wasn't something he was comfortable saying in front of an audience. Perhaps later, when they were alone in their room...

Yeah. Don't think about it now. The last thing Yasmin needed was to see a guy with an erection drooling after her sister or niece, depending on how Kyra was going to introduce herself.

"Let's go," she said, walking toward the front door of the apartment.

They took the stairs up to the third floor, and Kyra knocked on the door. "Can we come in?" She asked loudly enough for Yasmin to hear her.

The eldest son opened the door and dipped his head, motioning for them to come in.

Max activated the teardrop in case he needed to say something, even though he wasn't planning on doing much talking. This was Kyra's stage, and he was there for emotional support.

Yasmin sat on the couch with the little girl asleep next to her and another child, a little boy, on her other side.

In the kitchen, Nadim's cousin was busy preparing a meal, but snacks had already been served on the coffee table, along with tea and juice for the kids.

Except, it looked like nothing had been touched.

"Is it true?" Yasmin asked in a near whisper. "About my husband?"

Kyra knelt beside her but kept a respectful distance. "I'm sorry," she said softly. "There was nothing we could do. He fought bravely, but he was outnumbered and overpowered."

Yasmin closed her eyes, pain washing over her features, though it was clear she had already suspected the truth.

"Why?" she asked. "Why is it happening to our

family? First, they take Soraya and Rana's girls, and then they come for us. Why?"

It was the question they'd been expecting, but one they weren't prepared to answer fully—not yet, not until all the sisters were safe and the truth about their nature could be revealed in a controlled environment.

"You have something they want. A rare genetic trait you and your sisters inherited from your mother and passed on to your children."

Yasmin narrowed her eyes at Kyra. "Who are you really? The Kurdish resistance can't do what you did." Her gaze flickered to Max, standing silently in the doorway. "These people are not Kurds. Especially not the two with the Russian names that don't look Russian. They didn't speak Farsi or Kurdish either."

"Dima and Anton are not from here, and they also have a rare genetic trait."

It was a good way to say that they were also part alien, and for now, it was enough.

"Do you have that trait?" Yasmin asked.

"I do. And so does Max. It's very valuable, which is why these bad people want it. We are here to help you and your children and get you to safety. We will also protect your sisters. Those people might come for them as well."

"All of my sisters?"

Kyra nodded. "All of them and their children. We're going to get them out and bring them somewhere safe."

Yasmin seemed about to press further when Fatima intervened, placing a fresh cup of sweet tea in front of her.

"Drink," she urged. "Eat something. The children need to see you taking care of yourself." She looked at the frightened children. "They haven't touched anything. They are waiting for you to show them it's okay."

It was a masterful redirection, appealing to Yasmin's maternal instincts. The woman hesitated, then lifted the cup with a small nod of thanks.

Max remained standing by the door, watching Fatima continue her gentle ministrations, offering food to the children with soft encouragements. The oldest boy refused at first, but when Kyra spoke to him, he reluctantly took a piece of baklava and began to munch on it.

Fatima saw him looking at the delicacy and brought the plate to him. "Take one. I made them myself."

"Then I have to." He took the flaky pastry that was filled with finely ground pistachios and, by the smell of it, was drenched in a saffron-rosewater syrup.

As the decadent sweetness swept over his taste buds, his eyes rolled back in his head. "This is so good," he murmured.

Fatima beamed with pride. "Take another one," she encouraged.

He shook his head. "Give it to the kids. I'm saving my stomach for what's cooking in the kitchen."

"Lamb and Persian rice," she whispered conspiratorially. "You'll be licking your fingers."

"I bet."

She turned to Yasmin. "Should I serve the meal at the table, or should I bring you the plates here?"

"We'll eat at the table." Yasmin rose to her feet and glanced at her sleeping daughter. "She can eat later when she wakes up."

After they moved to the dining table and Fatima served up a large platter of lamb chucks over fragrant rice, she took another platter just as big and headed downstairs to feed the rest of the crew.

At first, the kids barely touched the food, their teary eyes and sad faces tearing Max's heart apart. He could only imagine how difficult it was for Kyra, and yet she managed to interact with them with respect rather than pity, encouraging them to eat.

It was, Max realized, the same quality he'd noticed in her interactions with her nieces at the penthouse in Los Angeles—a natural ability to meet them where they were, to offer strength without demanding they hide their vulnerability.

They were innocents, caught in a war they didn't even know existed, and targeted for a genetic quirk they didn't know they possessed.

1 9

FENELLA

enella collapsed onto the plush bed, groaning as she kicked off her shoes and watched them tumble across the expensive carpet. Her feet throbbed in protest at having walked miles around that bloody theme park all day.

It had been years since she'd subjected herself to this kind of voluntary torture.

"Stupid American tourist trap," she muttered, though there was no real heat behind the complaint.

She rolled onto her back and stared at the ceiling, surprised to find her lips curving into a smile as she recalled the girls' faces when they'd first caught sight of that ridiculous fantasy castle. The way Laleh had gripped her hand on the Transformers ride, screaming with joy. Even Arezoo had dropped her sophisticated act by the afternoon, joining her sisters and cousin in their fun and acting her age for a change.

"Christ, I'm going soft," Fenella murmured to the empty room, draping her arm over her eyes. "It's those bloody maternal hormones that should be long dead by now."

She placed a hand over her stomach, wondering if it felt queasy because of all the junk she'd consumed or because her hormones were staging a coup, demanding she did something about getting a baby in there.

"Dream on," she told them. "Not happening."

It was probably the fault of the sugary butterbeer. It had been sickeningly sweet, but she still couldn't stop drinking it, which was a metaphor for the entire experience. It had been over the top, fake and saccharine, but during the time she'd spent at the park, she'd actually managed to forget about the nightmares of the past few weeks. Or had it been months?

How long had she been in the clutches of that monster?

"Don't think about it," she commanded. "Time for some telly." She reached for the remote on the night-stand and flicked the television on.

"Ugh, news." She switched to another channel, but nothing caught her fancy.

She was just too tired. The sugar high was fading and exhaustion was creeping in, along with the nagging worry about Din's delayed arrival.

Fenella didn't believe in coincidences, and when the universe was shouting a warning, she listened.

A soft knock interrupted her brooding, and then the door opened a crack.

"Fenella? Are you awake?" Jasmine asked.

Fenella sighed, debating whether to pretend to be asleep, but there was nothing to watch, and she wasn't in the mood for a book, and chatting with Jasmine might help her relax. The woman had a positive, calming effect, maybe because she placed no demands on anyone and didn't argue about nonsense like so many people liked to do.

"Unfortunately, yes," she called back.

Jasmine poked her head in, her dark hair falling in waves around her face. "Would you like to join me and Ell-rom for some wine and snacks?"

That actually sounded lovely. Fenella could use something salty to wash down all the sugary sweetness.

"I'm coming." She rose to her feet but didn't bother with shoes.

She padded to the living room where Ell-rom sat on the couch with a tray of cheese, crackers, and fruit in front of him and a bottle of wine with three glasses.

It seemed like Jasmine hadn't expected her to refuse.

"Where are the girls?" Fenella asked as she sat on the floor next to the enormous coffee table so she could be close to the tray.

"They are all cuddled up in one room watching the first Harry Potter movie," Jasmine passed Fenella a generously filled glass. "I think today was a big success, and it was exactly what they needed."

Fenella took a sip, appreciating the rich cabernet. "I have to admit that it was fun. Even Arezoo enjoyed herself."

"She reminds me of my mother," Jasmine said, a fond smile touching her lips. "A born leader who thinks she needs to take responsibility for everyone around her."

The exact opposite of Fenella. She was a one-woman show, and she neither followed nor led anyone. She was a wanderer, a nomad, and staying in one place was not her thing.

"The girls are resilient," Ell-rom observed, holding a wine glass with his princely grace. "And they have each other's backs."

Something about his statement touched a nerve. Fenella had never had anyone she could rely on. Even when she'd still been a human, her baby brother relied on her and not the other way around, and then she'd had to abandon him to protect him.

Jasmine's phone rang, and as she glanced at the screen, her eyes narrowed. "Unknown Scottish number again. It must be Din."

Instead of the flutter Fenella had experienced before when Din had called, this time her gut clenched with dread.

"Here you go." She handed Fenella the phone. "It's him."

"Hello, Din," she said, aiming for nonchalance and missing by a mile.

"Fenella." His voice sounded tired but warm, that familiar Scottish burr wrapping around her name like a cashmere blanket. "I hope I'm not calling too late."

"It's nine in the evening. Barely past teatime," she said. "What's wrong now? Train derailment? Alien invasion? Biblical plague?"

There was a pause, and she could just envision his grimace.

"I just got notified that the flight was canceled. The next one available leaves tomorrow evening. It's not a huge delay, but I wanted you to know so you wouldn't worry."

The flutter in Fenella's chest transformed into a cold, heavy weight.

"Just don't," she said.

"Don't what?"

"Don't come. Cancel the whole thing and stay home." The words tumbled out before she could stop them. "I don't believe in coincidences, Din. These are warnings. It would seem that we are not meant to meet again."

Jasmine shot her a concerned look, which Fenella pointedly ignored.

Din's sigh crackled through the connection. "Fenella, love. It's just a bit of bad luck with the flights. It happens all the time, and there is nothing mystical about it."

"Two incidents in a row aren't luck, it's a bloody omen," she insisted, pacing now. "I haven't survived this long by ignoring my instincts, and right now, they are shouting that you should stay in Scotland, preferably in your room. Don't go anywhere until you get a sign that it's okay to leave it."

"Oh, sweetheart." His voice was like a warm blanket around her. "Your reappearance in my life is the sign I've been waiting for. Besides, I've survived much longer than you by not letting a wee bit of trouble dictate my life."

He had a point there, but she still felt uneasy about the whole thing. "At least tie a red ribbon around your luggage and in your socks to counteract the bad luck."

Jasmine and Ell-rom were looking at her like she was a lunatic, but she didn't care.

"Whatever you say, love. If you want me to tie red ribbons, I will do so. Anything else? Should I break a match because trouble comes in threes? That is supposed to end the cycle of bad luck."

Despite herself, Fenella felt a reluctant smile tugging at her lips. "That's a good idea, but a match is not enough. A pencil should do, though."

"Not a problem." She could hear the smile in his voice. "Listen, Fenella. If you truly don't want me to come, I won't push. But I don't think the universe is conspiring against us. The opposite is true. It's giving us a second chance."

Fenella hesitated, torn between the comfort of his

reasonable tone and the persistent warning bells in her mind.

"I don't know," she said finally, hating the uncertainty in her voice. "I just don't want anything bad to happen to you."

Damn. She hated caring about what happened to other people. Caring for herself was tough enough.

"I'll be fine. I'll call you tomorrow before boarding, aye?"

"Okay."

When she ended the call, Jasmine looked at her with concern. "You okay?"

"Peachy." Fenella handed her the phone. "Nothing like a couple of transportation mishaps to really boost one's confidence about a reunion fifty years in the making."

Jasmine sighed. "I wish I had my tarot cards to do a reading for you, but I gave them to my mother as a talisman for the mission."

"Tarot cards?" Fenella raised an eyebrow. "I wouldn't have pegged you for the superstitious type."

"I'm not, but I believe in the Goddess, the Mother of All Life, and I also believe that she guides those who seek her guidance. The cards were actually Kyra's. She left them with me before she was taken. I've kept them all these years."

Ell-rom placed a gentle hand on Jasmine's shoulder, the gesture sweet, reassuring, and making Fenella's heart squeeze with envy.

"Things happen, Fenella," Jasmine continued. "It

doesn't always mean something cosmic is trying to send a message."

"Perhaps," Fenella conceded, though she wasn't convinced. "Or perhaps I'm just looking for an excuse to avoid the whole situation."

"Are you?" Jasmine asked.

Fenella drained her wine rather than answer, and Jasmine had the good sense not to press further. Instead, she shifted the conversation to lighter topics, and they spent the next hour or so drinking wine, snacking on cheese and crackers, and talking about nothing of real importance.

By the time Jasmine and Ell-rom bid her goodnight and retired to their room, Fenella's mood had improved marginally, though the undercurrent of unease remained.

Not ready to hit the sack yet, she walked out to the terrace, drawn to the panoramic view of the city.

Leaning against the railing, Fenella's mind drifted to the last time she'd ignored her instincts.

Bucharest, 1989.

She'd felt the same crawling unease then, the same sense of wrongness that had preceded every disaster in her life. But she'd had a job to do, money to make, and she'd silenced the warning voice within.

The game had gone sideways almost immediately, and she found herself with three angry men with knives who had every intention of making her suffer.

Her strength and quick-healing body had saved her from carrying a big scar across her ribs, where one of the men had slashed her before she'd managed to break free.

If she hadn't been immortal, she would have bled out in that filthy shithole.

Following that logic, though, Din was just as resilient as she was, probably more so, and he was perfectly capable of handling himself.

He would be fine.

2 0

KYRA

The marketplace pulsed with life despite the early hour, with vendors arranging their wares while early customers examined the fresh produce with critical eyes and nimble fingers. Kyra waddled through the narrow aisles, the fat suit making her sweat even though it was still morning and the night's chill had not dispersed fully yet.

"The fruit stand at the northeast corner," Max said in her earpiece, his voice eliciting a different kind of warmth.

They had spent the night in each other's arms again, too exhausted to do anything more than a chaste goodnight kiss. They'd slept less than three hours when Yamanu knocked on their door announcing that Parisa had left Soraya's house and had returned to her apartment early this morning with her four guards. After her sons had gone to school accompanied by three of the guards, she left with the remaining guard, and they took a taxi to the market.

It was a great opportunity to corner her and have a talk with her rather than just showing up at her place while all four guards and her boys were there. Besides, the earlier, the better.

It had been a scramble to don the disguise and rush to the van. Thank God for Nadim, who'd made them coffee to go and a container with several pieces of Fatima's delicious baklava.

Kyra licked her lips and eyed a nearby stall that was selling it. The problem was that she didn't have any money with her. In her rush to leave the safe house, she hadn't thought to take a purse or stuff a few rials in her pocket. The lack of a purse was also a tactical mistake, as every woman in the market carried one regardless of her level of bodily concealment.

It made sense, as this was the only way the abaya- and hijab- or niqab-covered crowd could express some individuality and maybe even show off a little with a pricy handbag.

She spotted Parisa standing at a fruit stall, recognizing her face from the photographs Nadim's team had supplied. Kyra felt an unexpected pang of familiarity with the way she held up the fruit, turning it with just her fingertips and tilting her head to inspect it. That was exactly how Kyra shopped.

The lone guard stood several paces away, his

attention split between Parisa and the surrounding crowd, hand resting casually near his concealed weapon. He was clearly uneasy and vigilant with his task.

After the murder of Yasmin's guards and husband and the kidnapping of the family, the guards of the remaining sisters were on high alert.

Nevertheless, he wouldn't be concerned with a woman and stupidly wouldn't even consider that an abaya and niqab could hide a male assassin with ease.

Kyra moved closer, pretending to examine apricots at the neighboring stand. She timed her approach carefully, waiting until Parisa had moved slightly away from the guard before sliding into position beside her sister at the pomegranate display.

"These are much better than the ones at Masoud's stand," Kyra commented, keeping her voice pitched for Parisa's ears alone. "His are always overripe."

Parisa turned, her eyes narrowing slightly as she took in the traditionally dressed stranger. Caution flickered across her features, but good manners prevailed.

"I wouldn't know," she replied politely. "I usually shop at the Noori district."

"Of course," Kyra nodded, shifting her substantial bulk slightly to position herself between Parisa and the guard's line of sight. "This season's crop is excellent. Almost as good as the ones we had when I was a child in Shiraz."

Parisa's brow creased momentarily at the mention

of her childhood home. Kyra reached into her pocket, extracted the folded note, and slid it into Parisa's hand.

"Please read this," she murmured, her voice barely audible over the market's bustle. "Don't let your guard see it. It's from your niece."

Parisa stiffened, her other hand freezing over the pomegranate she'd been holding. "Who are you?" she whispered, not looking at Kyra but maintaining the pretense of examining fruit.

"I'm here to help," Kyra replied. "Your nieces are safe, but you, your sons, and your other sisters are in danger."

Parisa's eyes darted toward her guard, who was watching her intently. "I can't read it now. He's watching me."

"I'll block you from his view. I need the note back, or I would have told you to meet me at the women's bathroom and read it there." Kyra lifted two pomegranates and held them up to the sun, pretending to examine them in the light while effectively creating a screen with her voluminous clothing to hide her sister.

Behind her, she heard Parisa gasp and then exhale. "I read it. What now?"

Kyra put the pomegranates back down and turned to her sister. "Hand me the note and then meet me at the women's bathroom at the east entrance. I'll go ahead, and you should head there in ten minutes. Your guard can't follow you inside."

After Parisa slid the note into her hand, Kyra walked away, disappearing into the crowd.

She circled around, keeping Parisa in her peripheral vision while never looking directly at her. The fat suit made stealth challenging, but it also made her unremarkable—just another matron doing her morning shopping. The only things giving her away were her lack of purse and shopping bags.

"Do any of you have money?" she said quietly in her comm. "I need to buy something not to look suspicious."

"I do," Yamanu said. "I'm behind the scarf stand. The humans can't see me because I'm shrouding myself."

When Kyra saw Yamanu standing where he'd told her he would be, his hand extended with a wad of bills, she stifled a chuckle. "People will think that I'm plucking money out of thin air. Imagine the rumors it would spark."

She took the money from Yamanu's hand, quickly put it in her pocket, and proceeded to buy a colorful head covering, which she asked the vendor to put in a bag for her.

Feeling less conspicuous, Kyra headed toward the bathroom but didn't go in. Instead, she pretended to examine a display of copper pots.

"Parisa is on her way," Max reported in her ear. "The guard is with her."

Naturally.

Kyra considered staying outside the bathroom

and waiting until Parisa got in before following, but she was afraid the guard would recognize her from the fruit stand. She could pull out the head covering she'd bought and change her appearance a little, but there was no good place to do that without being noticed, and getting under Yamanu's shroud meant going back to where he was keeping watch.

"Go inside," Yamanu said in her earpiece. "They are almost there."

Kyra ducked into the bathroom. The place was packed with women waiting in line for the four available stalls, and there was no way she could talk with Parisa in there.

"Can you do something to give us privacy?" she asked quietly while pretending to adjust her clothing under the abaya. "It's packed in here."

Yamanu didn't answer, but the women around her started to scrunch their noses and twist their mouths, and some started complaining about the intolerable stench.

The place didn't smell great, but it wasn't particularly stinky either, or at least no more than it had been when she'd entered.

"Is the stench your doing?" Kyra asked quietly.

"I hope you can't smell it," came Yamanu's bemused answer. "Only the humans are supposed to be affected by my olfactory illusion."

"Oh, they definitely are."

One by one, the women started filing out of the

bathroom until only the most desperate remained, holding their noses with their fingers and shifting from foot to foot as they waited for a stall to become available.

When Parisa finally entered, the bathroom was practically empty, but the illusionary stench remained, and Parisa's face twisted.

"Can we do this somewhere else?"

Kyra shook her head. "Just don't breathe through your nose. The smell is harmless. Its purpose is to chase the other women away."

One day, they would talk about this encounter and have a good laugh, but for now, Kyra had to keep the lies coming.

"Her guard is staying in position by the entrance," Max said in her earpiece. "You're good, but don't take too long."

"The note was from Arezoo." Parisa's voice was tight with barely contained emotion, but she was trying to appear fierce, which Kyra appreciated. "Where is she?"

Instead of answering, Kyra opened the faucet, letting the water run to muffle their voices, then motioned with her chin at the stalls, which were still occupied. "They are all safe," she kept her voice at a near whisper. "Arezoo, Donya, Laleh, and Azadeh, as well as Yasmin and her children. My team and I rescued all of them."

Parisa's hand flew to her chest. "We were told that

Yasmin and her children were taken and that Javad was killed. Did you do that?"

"No. Those were the bad people. They killed Javad and took Yasmin and the children. We followed them, rescued Yasmin and her family, and eliminated the criminals, but there might be more of them, which is why I need you, your sons, Soraya, and Rana to come with me."

Parisa pressed a hand to her mouth, grief flashing across her features before being replaced by fear. "My sons are—"

"In danger," Kyra finished for her. "The same people who took your nieces and Yasmin's family will come for them next. They're after children with specific genetic traits that run in your family."

"What traits?" Parisa looked incredulous.

"I can't explain right now. What you need to know is that these people are part of a secret organization with ties to the Revolutionary Guard. That's why I couldn't just come to your house and talk to you. Soraya's husband is in the Guard, and he arranged for all the men guarding you. They all answer to him."

Parisa frowned. "But his own daughters were taken."

"He might not be affiliated with the people in the Guard who work with that secret organization, but by using Guard resources, he might be exposing you to more danger."

"Where would we go?" Parisa asked.

"I work with a resistance group that's been tracking their activities. We've already extracted your nieces to a safe location outside the country, and Yasmin's family is at our safe house now. I want to take you and your boys to the safe house as well, but it will require some cunning."

Parisa studied her, suspicion returning to her gaze. "Take off your face covering," she commanded suddenly. "I want to see who I'm talking to."

Kyra glanced at the stall before lifting the swath of fabric to reveal her face. This was a women-only space, and even the most pious and devout were allowed to reveal their faces to other women.

Recognition dawned in Parisa's eyes, followed by disbelief. "You look like..." she began, then stopped, studying Kyra's features intently. "You look a lot like my mother when she was young. Who are you?"

It was a question Kyra had been both expecting and dreading.

"I'm your eldest sister Kyra's daughter," she said, watching Parisa's reaction carefully.

Her sister gasped, taking an involuntary step back. "That's impossible. Kyra died childless in America."

Kyra shook her head. "She didn't die, and she had a daughter. Me." The half-truth felt bitter on her tongue, but now wasn't the time for the full revelation. The truth was too complicated and too loaded to explain in a few minutes in a public bathroom.

"Where is she then?" Parisa demanded, a fragile hope flickering in her eyes. "Where is my sister?"

Kyra chose her words carefully. "I can't tell you everything until our entire family is out of danger, minus the husbands, that is. Soraya and Rana are married to members of the Revolutionary Guard."

Parisa's eyes narrowed, studying Kyra with the intensity of someone trying to reconcile impossible facts. "How do I know that you are who you say you are? You could be with those horrible people who killed Javad, and you might be trying to trick me to get me and the rest of the family away from the guards Fareed got for us."

That was a valid question, and Kyra prayed that the proof she had would suffice.

She held up her hand, revealing the two rings Jasmine had given her—the rings Kyra had left in her jewelry box, not knowing she would never return for them. "These belong to Kyra, and she gave them to me. Do you recognize them? I know it was many years ago, and you were a little girl back then, but maybe you remember?"

Parisa stared at the rings, her composure cracking slightly. She reached out, her fingers hovering just above the gold bands as if afraid they might disappear if touched.

"This one was a present from our grandmother," she whispered, touching the one with intricate leaves. "The other one was from Mother, a present right before Kyra left for America. She said it was a loan and that she expected Kyra to return it in person." She looked up, conflict written across her features. "These could have been stolen." She narrowed her eyes at her. "Or pried from her dead fingers."

The door of one of the stalls opening startled them both, and Kyra let the swath of fabric she'd moved aside fall back into place, hiding her face. Parisa leaned over the sink and pretended to wash a stain out of her sleeve.

"It won't come off!" she said loudly. "You said to rub it hard. I'm rubbing!"

Kyra was stunned by how quickly and effortlessly Parisa had come up with a charade to explain why the two of them were loitering next to running water.

"Rub harder," Kyra said, demonstrating on her own sleeve.

"Are you okay in there?" the guard yelled from the entrance.

"Yes. I'm trying to get a stubborn stain out of my sleeve. That fruit stand was filthy!"

"Well, hurry up. Women are giving me dirty looks for standing out here."

"Two more minutes! It's almost out!"

Parisa's lips quirked up in a smile. "Amir is a good guy. Not all of them in the Revolutionary Guard are evil, you know."

Kyra nodded. "Of course not. People are rarely black and white. Most are shades of gray." She tilted her head. "What color is Fareed?"

Parisa's lips twisted in distaste. "I owe him a lot for helping me after my husband got killed, so I don't want to speak badly of him, but he's not a good husband to Soraya or a good father to the girls. There are worse men, but that doesn't make him good."

"Do you think Soraya will agree to go without him?" Kyra asked.

"That depends on what will await her on the other side. Where will you take her?"

Kyra smiled. "To her daughters." She leaned closer. "They are in America, and all of their expenses are paid. They lack for nothing. I promise you that you will receive no less. You will all be set for life, and it will be a very good life."

Something in her tone must have convinced Parisa, or maybe it was the hope of a better life, because she nodded. "Let's say I believe you. How are we going to get past the guards?"

"We'll get you out," Kyra said. "Talk to Rana and tell her to come stay with Soraya as well. It has to happen tonight, though. We are not concerned with the guards you have now, but if the others get to you, things might get ugly."

Hopefully, Fareed wasn't home and wouldn't mind two of his wife's sisters staying with her.

"Do we need passports?" Parisa asked. "I don't have a passport, and neither do my boys. We've never left Iran."

"We'll take care of everything. Take just what you can't part with. Clothing and everything else will be

170

supplied, so don't bother packing that. Meaningful jewelry, birth certificates, any family keepsakes you can't bear to leave behind, those are the kind of things you should take with you."

Parisa closed her eyes for a moment and then let out a breath. "What if this is some elaborate trap? How do I know I can trust you?"

Kyra met her sister's eyes through the narrow slit in her niqab. "Soraya's and Rana's daughters were taken, and then the same people attacked Yasmin's home and killed her husband and the guards who were trying to protect her. No one met them ahead of time and tried to convince them to leave. They were taken by force. If you don't get away, there is a very high chance that your sons will face the same fate that nearly befell your nieces. These people don't take no for an answer, Parisa, they wouldn't be here talking to you."

A long moment passed as Parisa made her decision. Finally, she nodded. "Tonight, then?"

"Yes."

"Can you spare the guards?" her sister asked. "I don't want their deaths on my conscience.

Since they were probably all human, Yamanu could thrall them to stand down, but they would face harsh punishments for failing.

"We will spare them. We have a special method of disabling guards without harming them."

"I hope you're telling the truth about my nieces."

"I am," Kyra assured her. "They miss you. Especially Arezoo—she talks about your cooking all the time."

A ghost of a smile crossed Parisa's face. "That child would eat nothing but my saffron rice pudding if allowed." The small moment of normalcy seemed to strengthen her resolve. "Very well. We will be ready."

MAX

Max adjusted his position on the rooftop, ignoring the bite of gravel digging into his elbows as he maintained his surveillance of Rana's modest, one-story home. Beside him, Anton lay flat on his stomach, his eyes focused on the windows of the residence across the street.

"These guards are not taking their job seriously," Anton said. "They are just sitting on the couch in the living room and eating the snacks Rana serves them."

Max chuckled. "If her baklava is as good as Fatima's, I don't blame them. After all, they are only human."

Rana and Soraya had both gotten an additional guard after what happened to Yasmin, but the question was whether the guards were there to protect them or merely to control their movements until the Doomers decided to move them. But even if they were there to protect, there wasn't much they would be able to do against Doomers, and that was why Max and Anton were guarding Rana from the roof while the rest of their team had split up to guard the other sisters.

Yamanu and Dima had taken position near Soraya's more heavily guarded residence while Jade and Kyra monitored Parisa's apartment building. Rishba and Asuka had stayed behind at the safe house with Nadim and Fatima, protecting Yasmin and her children.

Max wasn't happy with the arrangement. If it were up to him, he would have collected the sisters and the remaining kids right now and headed to the airport, but Kyra and Yamanu wanted to wait for nighttime so the extractions would attract as little notice as possible.

That was all fine and dandy if the Doomers never showed up to collect the rest of Kyra's family, but there was no guarantee of that despite the excellent cleanup job their team had done in the compound last night.

Yamanu believed that all the local Doomers had been dealt with, but Max seriously doubted it. Tehran's population exceeded ten million people, so chances were that more Doomers were scattered throughout the city, and they could be mobilized to complete the job.

Especially now when pride and revenge were involved.

"Vehicle approaching from the west," Anton said.

Max shifted his binoculars, catching sight of a black SUV turning onto the quiet residential street. Nothing about the vehicle stood out—no government plates, no identifiable markings—but it was clean and new, and it didn't match the profile of other vehicles they'd seen passing through this street throughout the morning.

The SUV slowed as it approached Rana's house, eventually coming to a stop at the curb. Two men in civilian clothing emerged from the vehicle, but their postures and synchronized movements screamed military or secret police.

"Shift change, perhaps?" Anton suggested, though his tone indicated he didn't really think that.

"Maybe," Max murmured, studying the newcomers.

The men knocked on the door, which was a good sign because Doomers were not usually that courteous. Perhaps the replacement guards were plainclothes cops. Still, something in the way they moved raised his hackles.

They were too smooth, too fluid, and that more than anything marked them as immortals.

One of the guards inside the house opened the door, and a moment later, he and the other uniformed guard left while the two newcomers walked in and closed the door behind them.

It all seemed suspicious, but Max wasn't sure that the newcomers were Doomers, not until he saw the original guards walking down the street like a couple of automatons.

"The old guards have been thralled," Max said. "There are Doomers inside Rana's house. We need to move in."

Anton swore softly in his native Kra-ell. "I thought we eliminated them all at the compound."

Unlike the Doomers who had taken Yasmin, these were careful and subtle—maintaining the appearance of normal security rotation, which was easier since Rana was alone in the house.

Max activated his comm link. "Yamanu, we have a situation at Rana's location. Two Doomers just replaced the human guards. They thralled them and sent them away. I expect them to march Rana out any moment now. We need to stop them before they disappear with her."

"Understood," Yamanu said. "We're seeing similar activity here. A vehicle just stopped a few houses down, but it looks suspicious."

"Jade, what's your status at Parisa's?" Max asked, switching channels.

"All quiet so far," Jade reported. "The one human guard is still with her, the other three with her sons at school. Doomers wouldn't want to attract attention by grabbing them there. They would wait for them to return home."

Max's mind raced through scenarios. If the Doomers were taking positions simultaneously at the homes of Rana and Soraya but not Parisa, whose sons were still at school, chances were that they were planning a simultaneous operation and were just waiting for the boys to return. That was what he would have done in their position.

Still, he wondered how many more Doomers were in the area. They'd eliminated all of those who had been at the compound, but clearly there were other cells operating in Tehran.

This was a puzzle to solve some other time, though. Right now, they needed to get what they'd come for, which was Kyra's family.

"We need to move now," Max said. "We shouldn't wait until Parisa's kids are back from school. We should take Soraya and Rana now, and Kyra should take Parisa to the boys' school and have them pulled out. "

It wouldn't be the smooth operation it could have been if they had everyone in one spot with just human guards. Yamanu could have thralled, but with Doomers changing the equation, different maneuvers were needed.

"Agreed," Yamanu replied. "All teams, prepare for immediate extraction."

Max turned to Anton. "We'll need a diversion to draw those Doomers away from the house. Something that won't put Rana at risk."

The Kra-ell warrior grinned, his eyes gleaming with anticipation. "I will knock on the door, and when they open, I'll disable them both with a knife to the head. You come in, and we finish them off together."

It was a crude plan, but it might work. The Doomers wouldn't expect anyone with Anton's speed and power. They would be taken by surprise.

"You have your Kevlar vest on, right?" Max asked the guy.

"Of course." Anton patted his chest. "I know what my vulnerabilities are."

The Kra-ell were not as immune to injuries as immortals, and they healed at a slower rate. That and their inability to enter unassisted stasis were their two main disadvantages compared to immortals, but they were superior warriors in every other way.

KYRA

Kyra crouched behind the row of parked cars. The fat suit and traditional clothing were gone now, replaced by tactical gear that allowed her the freedom of movement she'd need if things went sideways—which, based on Max's urgent communication, seemed increasingly likely. Her hair was covered by a scarf, though, to comply with the local modesty laws that were enforced brutally. Not because she feared the enforcers but because she didn't want to draw unnecessary attention. Many young Iranian women dressed in modern attire, which was allowed as long as they were not showing any skin, but covering their hair was mandatory.

Jade, on the other hand, looked so alien that she didn't need to bother. She would be assumed to be a tourist, and if anyone bothered her, they would realize their mistake pretty fast. The female was livid at the discrimination.

"At least it's not as bad as Afghanistan," Kyra said. "Women there are completely covered and are forced to look at the world through a mesh window."

"There are always worse hellholes." Jade's eyes were gleaming red, her blood lust evident. "I know what it's like to have no choice, and I'm angry at the Mother of All Life for allowing her proud daughters to be treated like that."

Kyra couldn't imagine the fierce warrior ever being subjugated, but she didn't know the female's history, and apparently, Jade had lived through some dark moments. After this mission, when they were all safely back in the village, she would invite Jade for a cup of coffee and hear her story if she was willing to share it.

It was no doubt fascinating.

Parisa's apartment building was across the street, a modest five-story structure with a single guard positioned at the entrance—the same one who had accompanied her to the market earlier. Through her binoculars, Kyra could see him checking his watch repeatedly, clearly anxious about something.

"He's been doing that for a while now," Kyra said. "I think he's expecting a shift change."

"Or he's received orders to prepare Parisa for transport," Jade suggested grimly. "Either way, we should move in. We have it easy with just one guard."

"Wrong." Kyra's hand went to her pendant, which

remained unnervingly cool against her skin. Its inconsistent warnings were becoming increasingly frustrating, but perhaps its silence now was itself a message—that direct action was necessary. "The boys are at school, and we need to get them. That makes our mission the most complicated one. I'm still trying to figure out how we are going to do that."

Her earpiece crackled with Yamanu's voice. "Jade, Kyra—status?"

"One guard at the entrance, Parisa inside," Kyra replied. "Her sons are still at school. No sign of Doomers yet, but the guard seems nervous. He appears to be looking for something."

"Get Parisa now, Kyra, and then go get the boys."

Kyra exchanged a look with Jade, who nodded her agreement. "Copy that," Kyra responded. "Moving now."

"Cause a distraction," Kyra told Jade. "Something to draw the guard from his post, but nothing that would put Parisa at risk or draw too much attention."

Jade's lips curved into a smile that showed just a hint of fang. "Leave it to me."

As the Kra-ell warrior slipped away, Kyra positioned herself closer to the building's side entrance. The layout was familiar to her now after hours of surveillance. Third floor, apartment 3C. Two potential escape routes—the main stairwell and a fire escape accessible from the kitchen window.

"Commencing distraction." Jade's voice came through the earpiece, followed almost immediately by the sound of a car alarm blaring from just around the corner.

The guard at the entrance hesitated, then walked to the edge of the building to see what was happening. It wasn't much of a distraction, but it created just enough of a gap for Kyra to slip inside the building's side entrance.

The stairwell was empty, the building quiet in the midday hours when most residents would be at work or in school.

Kyra took the stairs two at a time, and when she reached the third floor she paused, drawing her sidearm and checking that the silencer was securely attached. Hopefully, she wouldn't need it, but there was always a chance that Doomers could get into the apartment from the fire escape staircase or even from a neighboring apartment while Kyra was making her way to her sister.

Caution was a must, and as she stood in front of Parisa's door, she debated knocking or just walking in. Even if the door was locked, she could break the lock with one hard push.

In the end, she tapped lightly on the wood.

Silence stretched for several heartbeats, and Kyra was about to try again when she heard the soft sound of footsteps approaching the door.

"Who is it?" Parisa sounded tense.

"It's me, Kyra's daughter, Jasmine," Kyra responded. "Open the door, Parisa."

The door opened just enough for Kyra to slip

inside, then was quickly closed and locked behind her. Parisa stood with her back against the door. "What's happening?" she asked. "I thought we would get picked up from Soraya's home later tonight."

"Change of plans," Kyra said, holding her weapon by her thigh to appear less threatening. "The people hunting our family are moving faster than we anticipated. They've already replaced the guards at Rana's home, and our team over there is extracting her as we speak."

Parisa's breath caught. "My sons—"

"We will pick them up as soon as we leave here," Kyra assured her.

"I've packed the essentials." Parisa gestured to a small duffel bag sitting by the couch. "Documents, photographs, medications. I wasn't sure what else to bring. The boys have their essentials with them in their backpacks."

"That's perfect," Kyra said.

Her pendant suddenly flared warm against her skin, and Kyra's hand instinctively went to her weapon. "We've got company," she murmured at the same instant that Jade's voice crackled in her ear with the exact same message. Kyra moved to the window that overlooked the building entrance.

Below, two men in civilian clothing were speaking to the guard who had returned to his post. Even from this distance, she could tell that they weren't human. It was the sinuous fluidity of immortals that only select humans possessed, like classically trained dancers or gymnasts.

"They're earlier than expected," Kyra said grimly to both Parisa and Jade, who was still on the open channel. "We need a different exit strategy."

"There's a service corridor that connects to the building next door." Parisa offered. "This used to be a much fancier building back in the day. It was designed so service crews didn't need to disturb the residents when repairs were needed."

Nadim hadn't gotten ahold of this building's schematics, so Kyra hadn't known that. She'd only scoped out what was visible from the outside. "Show me where it is."

She took Parisa's duffel bag and then followed her sister through the apartment to a utility closet at the back.

Kyra made sure that Jade heard the last exchange. "We're using an alternate exit. Service corridor connecting to the adjacent building, and given what's happening, you need to head to the school now, while we still might have the advantage."

"Copy that," Jade replied. "I'll reposition the van at the secondary extraction point and steal a car to get the boys. Are you sure that you can get away unseen? Otherwise, there's no way I am leaving you here to deal with two Doomers on your own."

"I can handle this," Kyra replied. "The boys are a priority. Go."

Inside the utility closet, Parisa pushed aside a

stack of storage bins to reveal a narrow door. "This was designed as a fire escape connection," she explained. "Not many residents know about it." A fleeting smile touched Parisa's lips. "My late husband was very security conscious. He bought this apartment because of this alternative escape route."

The door opened to a narrow maintenance corridor lit by a single fluorescent bulb. Pipes and electrical conduits ran along the ceiling, and the air was heavy with the smell of dust and mold.

"This way," Parisa said, moving with surprising confidence through the dimly lit space.

MAX

As bullets rang past Max, he pressed himself against the wall of Rana's living room. The extraction that should have been relatively straightforward had devolved into a firefight within seconds of their entry. Rather than the two Doomers they'd observed entering earlier, they'd encountered four—with two more arriving as backup moments after Max and Anton breached the house.

It seemed the Brotherhood had been expecting them.

"Status on Rana?" Max called to Anton, who had positioned himself at the rear of the house, covering the kitchen and back door.

"Still in the bathroom," Anton said.

At least that was something. Max had immediately moved Rana to the home's single bathroom the moment the shooting started. It was the most defensible position with only one door and no windows. Now, they were pinned down, with Doomers at both the front and back of the place.

"Yamanu, we need backup," Max said into his comm unit. "Six hostiles, possibly more incoming. We're contained but unable to extract."

Static crackled through his earpiece before Yamanu's voice came through, broken and distorted. "—heavy resistance here too—Soraya secured but—reinforcements—"

"Your transmission's breaking up," Max replied. "Do you copy? We need immediate support."

More static, then Dima's voice cut through, clearer than Yamanu's. "We copy. Holding position with Soraya. Yamanu says they're jamming communications across the sector. Appears to be a coordinated Brotherhood response."

Max swore under his breath. If the Doomers were jamming comms and mounting simultaneous resistance at all extraction points, it meant they had far more resources in Tehran than anyone had anticipated. The compound they'd destroyed the previous night had clearly been just one cell of many. Max also suspected a breach in their organization.

Someone was feeding the Doomers information.

"Anton, we need to change tactics," Max called. "They're trying to contain us until reinforcements arrive. We need to break out now."

The Kra-ell nodded, his eyes gleaming with battle-light. "Frontal assault or break through the walls to create an alternative exit? I might be able to break through with a kick."

A frontal assault against six or more Doomers was not an option, and Anton, with all his superior strength, couldn't kick down block walls.

But an alternative exit was a good idea, and Max had just the thing.

"Good thinking about the alternative exit, but not by kicking the wall in. I'm going to make us a new door. Cover me." He pulled out a C4 packet, a remote detonator, and a timer.

As Anton laid down suppressive fire toward the front of the house, Max moved to the wall opposite the bathroom. If he remembered correctly, the exterior wall here backed onto a narrow alley between houses, which was perfect for their escape.

Max affixed the C4 to the wall, set the timer for thirty seconds, then moved back to the bathroom door.

"Rana," he called. "We're going to blow out an exit. I need you to stay down, back against the tub, head covered. Understand?"

"Yes."

"Twenty seconds," Max told Anton. "On my mark, we move Rana through the breach."

Anton nodded, adjusting his position to better cover the approaching corridor.

The seconds ticked down, and Max readied himself, adrenaline sharpening his senses to preternatural levels. He could hear the Doomers communicating in low voices, coordinating their own assault.

They were running out of time.

"Five seconds," he murmured. "Four, three, two, one—"

The explosive detonated with a sharp concussive blast, sending dust and debris flying as it cut an opening through the exterior wall.

"Move!" Max shouted, yanking open the bathroom door.

Rana emerged with remarkable composure, and Max guided her toward the newly created exit while Anton provided covering fire.

"Through here." Max helped Rana through the jagged opening. "Stay low and run straight to the gray van at the end of the alley."

Rana paused just briefly at the breach, looking back at her home with an expression that spoke volumes about what she was leaving behind. Then she nodded once and ran.

"Anton, go with her," Max ordered. "I'll cover your retreat."

The Kra-ell warrior shook his head. "I'm not leaving you to face six Doomers alone."

Max wanted to argue, but there wasn't time. The sound of boots pounding up the corridor told him the Doomers had abandoned caution in favor of overwhelming force.

"Fine. On three. One, two—"

He didn't make it to three before the first Doomer

rounded the corner, gun raised. Max fired immediately, catching the immortal in the shoulder and spinning him back. Not a kill shot, but enough to slow him down.

Anton moved with blinding speed, closing the distance to the stunned Doomer and driving his blade through the immortal's eye socket—one of the few ways to ensure an immortal kill.

"Go!" Max shouted, laying down suppressive fire as Anton pivoted and dove through the breach.

Max followed immediately after, bullets peppering the wall where he'd stood just seconds before. Outside, the narrow alley provided minimal cover—just a few trash bins and the uneven shadows of midday.

Rana was already halfway to the van, with Anton rushing her forward with one hand while the other held his weapon ready. Max sprinted after them, turning occasionally to fire at the Doomers now emerging from the breach.

They reached the van just as the first Doomer cleared the alley entrance. Max shoved Rana into the vehicle, and Anton jumped in behind the wheel.

"Drive!" Max ordered, diving into the van and slamming the door shut as bullets struck the exterior.

Anton didn't need to be told twice. The van lurched forward, tires screeching as it accelerated down the narrow back street. In the rear-view mirror, Max could see the Doomers already piling into their own vehicle to give chase.

"We've got pursuit. The black SUV."

Anton executed a sharp turn. "Don't worry. I'm going to lose them."

For someone who had just recently learned to drive using a simulator, the guy was a natural getaway driver.

KYRA

K yra and Parisa had progressed perhaps halfway down the corridor when Kyra's earpiece crackled urgently.

"Kyra, be advised," Max said. "More operatives showed up in Rana's place. Anton and I—" His voice cut off in what sounded like a burst of static or possibly gunfire.

"Max?" Kyra called, her heart rate spiking. "Max, come in."

Only silence greeted her, and her gut twisted painfully with worry.

He's immortal. Nothing is going to happen to him, she tried to calm her racing heart.

"What's wrong?" Parisa asked.

"My team has encountered more trouble than expected." Somehow, Kyra kept her voice steady despite the worry gnawing at her. "We need to keep moving."

Now Kyra understood the logic in Yamanu's team assignments and why he'd refused to pair her with Max. Their emotional involvement would have been an impediment, taking away from their focus on the mission.

Reaching the end of the corridor where another door was supposed to lead into the neighboring building, Parisa reached for the handle, and Kyra's pendant immediately burned hot against her skin in warning.

"Wait," she hissed, pulling Parisa back. "Something's wrong."

No sooner had she spoken than they heard footsteps approaching from the other side of the door. Heavy, measured steps—not the casual movements of a maintenance worker or a resident.

Kyra briefly considered alerting Jade to the appearance of more Doomers, but she knew that if she did that, Jade would immediately backtrack and they might then be too late to save the boys. Kyra decided to trust her training and her instincts, prompting her to handle the situation on her own.

"They've anticipated our escape route," Kyra whispered while backing away and pulling Parisa with her. "We need another way out." Parisa's eyes widened in alarm, but to her credit, she didn't panic. "There's a utility access to the roof halfway back," she whispered. "We passed it."

They retraced their steps, moving as silently as possible.

The utility access was a narrow ladder set into a shaft in the ceiling, covered by a hinged metal panel. Kyra helped Parisa up first, then followed, pulling the panel closed behind them just as the door to the service corridor burst open and footsteps rounded the corner below.

They emerged onto the flat roof of the apartment building, and Kyra pulled Parisa into the shadow of a large air conditioning unit, assessing their options.

"Four of the rooftops are connected," Parisa said, her voice remarkably calm given the circumstances. "We can move across them to the end of the block, then use the fire escape on the last building to get down." She smiled sadly. "My husband made sure to teach the kids and me all the possible ways we could escape our apartment if a bad situation ever developed."

The guy had been in the Revolutionary Guard, but Kyra was starting to suspect that he had also been a plant of the resistance of some other anti-regime forces.

"Smart man. I wish I had gotten to know him," Kyra said.

"Yeah, me too," Parisa said.

Kyra had a feeling that her sister was fighting tears, but now was not the time for a heart-to-heart comforting session. "Let's move. Stay low."

As they crossed to the edge of the first roof, Kyra's comm unit finally crackled back to life, and Max's voice came through, partially broken. "Extraction successful but—pursuing—regroup at—"

"Max, your transmission is breaking up," Kyra said. "We're currently on the roof, evading pursuit. Moving to the secondary extraction point."

Jade's voice came through more clearly. "I've secured another transport, and I'm on my way to the school. ETA ten minutes. The van is all yours. Can you make it to the rendezvous point?"

The female had stolen the other vehicle just as she'd said she would, and Kyra wondered how she'd managed that. It was a skill that she doubted Jade had picked up as part of her training back on the Kra-ell planet. She'd probably stopped a driver, pulled him out of the vehicle, knocked him out cold, and commandeered the car.

"Got it. Affirmative, we'll make it to the rendezvous point."

Kyra gauged the distance across the connected rooftops, then the drop to street level.

She guided Parisa across the first gap between buildings—a simple step across that posed no real challenge—and they continued their progress across the rooftops. The tactical part of Kyra's mind noted their exposed position, but the buildings' height and the blaring sunlight would make them difficult to spot from the street level.

"Your friends don't look like Kurds," Parisa said as they ducked behind a water-heating rooftop solar panel. "They're not really with the Kurdish resistance, are they?"

Kyra hesitated, then decided that partial truth was better than obvious lies at this point. "No, they're not. They're fighting the bad guys who want you for your special genetics. Some of us have unique capabilities."

"I thought as much," Parisa nodded. "No ordinary person moves the way you do."

"What do you mean?" Kyra asked, pausing to check if they were being pursued on the street below before crossing to the third building.

"My husband moved like that. He was in the special forces."

Kyra chuckled. "I was in the Kurdish resistance for many years before I joined the special team. My training was accumulated during that time."

Not a lie, not the entire truth either. She was good at that as well.

When they reached the edge of the fourth building, where the fire escape would take them to street level, Kyra peered over the edge, scanning for hostiles before gesturing Parisa forward.

"You're too young to have spent many years in the resistance."

The statement caught Kyra off guard. She hadn't thought the lie through, and Parisa was a sharp woman. She didn't miss much.

"I'm much older than I look," she said, then regretted the words immediately. She couldn't be much older if she wanted to pretend to be her own daughter.

Her sister didn't deserve the lies, but now wasn't the time for revelations, not with Doomers in pursuit and Parisa's sons still in danger.

"We need to keep moving," Kyra said instead of addressing the question further. "The fire escape looks clear."

25

MAX

"Are you hurt?" Max asked Rana.

She shook her head. "No. What's going on? Who is chasing us and why? And who are you?"

"My name is Max." He offered her his hand. "And I'm with an organization that saves people from those bad guys who want to abduct people with your specific genetic profile and use them in unsavory ways. There is more to it, but this is not the time to get into it."

"My genetic profile?" Rana repeated, confusion momentarily overriding her fear. "What are you talking about?"

Another sharp turn threw them against the van's side, cutting off Max's response. Outside, the sounds of pursuit continued, and Anton was still driving like a bat out of hell.

"Can you lose them?" Max asked him.

"Working on it," Anton replied without taking his eyes off the increasingly narrowing streets of the neighborhood they were flying through.

Max's comm unit crackled with static, and his heart accelerated, expecting to hear Kyra's voice. He was worried about her, and trying not to think about worst-case scenarios was taking a deliberate mental effort.

She was with Jade, who was on par with if not a superior warrior to him and Yamanu, and the female had promised him to protect Kyra. But now Kyra was alone with Parisa, and Jade was on her way to Parisa's sons.

"Max, what's your status?" Yamanu's voice broke through, clearer than before.

Max deactivated the teardrop so his speech wouldn't get automatically translated to Farsi, although it might be a futile effort if Rana spoke English.

"We have Rana with us in the van, but Doomers are in pursuit. We are implementing evasive maneuvers."

"Understood," Yamanu acknowledged. "Kyra and Jade have also encountered resistance. Appears to be a coordinated effort to secure all targets simultaneously, which is troubling, especially given that Durhad is no longer in the picture. But we'll discuss the implications later."

"Roger that."

It appeared that the Brotherhood had mobilized

significant resources across Tehran, likely in response to their raid on the compound the previous night. The strike had been unavoidable, given that the Doomers had taken Yasmin and her family, but it alerted the enemy to their presence.

"How many Doomers do they have in this city?" he muttered.

Anton didn't answer, executing another hard turn, then unexpectedly shifted into reverse, backing rapidly down an alleyway barely wide enough for the van to fit through.

Max checked the side mirror, noting with satisfaction that their pursuers had overshot the turn, buying them precious seconds. "Good move. Can you get us to the fallback point?"

"I'll do my best." Anton cut sharply down another side street.

The van lurched as they hit a pothole, causing Rana to bump her head against the van's ceiling.

Max reactivated the teardrop. "Put your seatbelt on, Rana."

She cast him a baleful look, then struggled with the seatbelt as the van kept lurching from side to side. Finally, Max leaned over and buckled it for her.

"Thank you," she gritted. "I think." She hesitated for a moment. "What about my husband? Does he also have any special genes?"

"No. Those genes were passed to you by your mother and from you to your daughter."

She narrowed her eyes at him. "What do you know about my daughter? Where is she?"

"She's safe. We rescued her and her cousins from these people, and that's how we learned about you. If everything goes according to plan, you will be reunited with her shortly."

For a long moment, she just gaped at him. "I want to believe you, but I don't know if I should."

"For now, you'll have to take my word for it." He gave her an apologetic look. "But once we get to the safe location, you will be provided with proof. Your daughter sent you a note."

Tears glistened in Rana's eyes. "I want to believe you so badly. My husband and Soraya's utilized all of their resources to find our girls, and they had no answers. I was losing hope of ever seeing them again." She swallowed. "I feared the worst."

"It could have been even worse than what you imagined if we weren't there to rescue someone else and got them out while we were at it."

Her eyes widened. "Thank you for taking them."

"No need to thank me. We wouldn't have left any women, let alone vulnerable young girls, in the clutches of those monsters."

Rana lifted shaking fingers to her mouth. "What was done to them?" she whispered. "To my Azadeh?"

He leaned over and placed a hand on her arm. "We got to them in time."

"Oh, thank God." Her shoulders slumped.

Anton took another series of rapid turns, the van

weaving through narrow streets and alleyways until they emerged into a more commercial district. The sudden transition from residential alleyways to a busy market street was jarring but effective—their pursuers would have a much harder time spotting them amid the increased traffic.

"I think we've lost them." Anton slowed down and checked the mirrors. "I'm switching the license plates."

It was a simple but effective modification that Nadim's people used. The van was a popular old model with no distinguishing feature, so switching the plates should do the trick to throw off their pursuers.

26

KYRA

yra descended first, with Parisa following
at a much slower pace, the metal structure
creaking under their combined weight but
holding steady. Once they were at the bottom, Kyra
led her sister into a narrow alley that would eventually connect to the street on which the van was
parked.

"My sons," Parisa said as they moved, her calm
façade finally showing cracks. "How will your people
be able to get them out safely? What about their
guards?"

Kyra wasn't sure what to tell her because she had
no idea how Jade was going to pull that off on her
own. The female had limited shrouding and thralling
ability that was nothing compared to what Yamanu
could do, but maybe it would be enough to get the
boys out without having to eliminate their guards.

"My partner Jade is extremely capable, and she'll

203

protect them with her life," Kyra assured her with more confidence than she felt, given the fractured communications coming from the other teams.

For all they knew, the boys had already been taken by Doomers.

Parisa nodded, though uncertainty lingered in her eyes. "The boys will be frightened. I wish I could be there to get them."

She shouldn't have sent them to school after what had happened to Yasmin and her family, but Kyra would never say that to her and add to the guilt her sister was most likely already feeling.

Parisa must have assumed that it was safe during the day and that the guards would protect them, which was a reasonable assumption for someone who didn't know the Doomers existed and what they could do.

"They'll be fine," she said instead. "Jade has a teenage daughter of her own, and she's also a very capable fighter. I trust her with my life."

Every word she'd said was true, but it still didn't guarantee successful extractions of the boys.

They emerged from the alley onto a busier street, and Kyra adjusted their pace to blend with the pedestrian traffic. Walking too fast would draw attention, but the sooner they got to the van, the better.

The café with a back exit to a parking garage where the van was parked was less than a block ahead.

Kyra's pendant remained warm against her skin,

not the burning heat of immediate danger but a steady reminder to remain vigilant. Her hand stayed close to her concealed weapon as they walked, her senses extended to their limits.

"Almost there," she murmured to Parisa, who was doing an admirable job of appearing casual despite the tension radiating from her body.

They were halfway to the café when Kyra spotted two men moving against the flow of pedestrian traffic, their eyes scanning the crowd with a predatory focus.

Doomers, without question.

"Don't look," Kyra instructed Parisa quietly. "But we have company at ten o'clock. Keep walking naturally."

To her credit, Parisa didn't so much as flinch, continuing her steady pace beside Kyra.

"Are they the ones from my building?" she asked, her voice barely audible.

"Possibly," Kyra replied.

The Doomers hadn't spotted them yet, but it was only a matter of time in the relatively sparse midday crowd.

Making a quick decision, Kyra guided Parisa toward a clothing store shop. "A quick change of appearance is in order."

Inside, she quickly selected two headscarves in different styles and colors than what they were currently wearing and two loose caftans to pull over her and Parisa's clothing. The shopkeeper seemed delighted by the quick sale that hadn't involved any haggling for the price, something that was uncommon for Persians.

"Put it on," Kyra instructed as they moved toward the back of the shop, using the racks of clothing as cover.

They donned the caftans and new headscarves. Kyra arranged hers to partially obscure her face and stuffed her other one inside her shirt to make her belly look more rounded. Parisa did the same, giggling as she stuffed her old scarf inside her bra, making her breasts look huge.

Kyra wasn't sure that it was a particularly good tactic for attracting less attention, but they didn't have time for anything more elaborate or less conspicuous.

"Through the back," Kyra said, nodding to a curtained doorway that likely led to storage or an employee area. "There should be an exit to the alley from there."

The shopkeeper called out in protest as they moved toward the restricted area, but Kyra ignored her, pulling Parisa through the curtain and into a cluttered storage room. As expected, a door at the back led to an alley.

"We can go through the restaurant next door," Kyra said as they emerged into the narrow passage.

They moved quickly now, no longer concerned with appearing casual since they were out of public view. The back door of the restaurant was propped open, kitchen staff moving in and out with supplies and trash.

Kyra guided Parisa through, ignoring the startled looks from the kitchen workers, who clearly weren't accustomed to customers entering this way. They passed through to the main dining area, then exited through the front door, rejoining the pedestrian flow on the street.

Kyra's comm unit activated again, Jade's voice coming through with unexpected urgency. "Situation at the school has evolved. Targets secured but facing pursuit. Diverting to fallback position."

"Copy that," Kyra replied. "We'll meet you there."

The fallback point was a small mosque three blocks east—chosen specifically because it offered multiple exits and the cultural protections that might give pursuers momentary pause.

"Change of plans," she told Parisa. "We're meeting your sons at a different location."

"Are they safe?" Parisa's voice was tight with worry.

"They're with Jade," Kyra replied, which wasn't quite an answer but was the best reassurance she could offer.

As they altered their route, Kyra's pendant suddenly flared with intense heat—a warning so urgent she instinctively pushed Parisa into the recessed doorway of a closed shop, her body shielding her sister as she scanned for the threat.

She spotted them almost immediately—four men

approaching from different directions, converging on their position.

"We're boxed in," Kyra murmured, her mind racing through diminishing options. "They must have anticipated our route."

The Doomers going to all that effort to catch them didn't make sense, even for the potential in their genes. It was probably revenge for last night and maybe for the Tahav operation as well. The Doomers must have connected the dots and realized that the same people had been involved in both.

They should have come to Tehran with a much larger team.

"What do we do?" Parisa whispered behind her.

Kyra assessed their surroundings, looking for any potential advantage or escape route. The doorway they stood in belonged to a shop that was closed for renovation, its windows covered with paper. Behind them, a construction tarp covered the entrance.

Making a split-second decision, Kyra pushed aside the tarp, finding the door beyond, which was locked as she'd expected. One strong shove and the lock splintered, the door swung inwards, and they slipped in quickly, the tarp falling back into place behind them.

The interior was dark, dusty, and filled with construction equipment and broken displays. It was perfect as a temporary hiding place but a potential trap if they didn't find another way out.

Kyra activated her comm unit. "Jade, we're

compromised. Four hostiles converging on our position. Currently concealed but pinned down at—" she checked their location quickly "—Ferdowsi Street, north side, vacant shop mid-block."

"Copy," Jade replied, her voice surprisingly calm. "Holding position with the boys at fallback point. Can you break contact and rendezvous?"

Kyra moved through the darkened shop, Parisa following close behind until they reached the rear, where a back door would likely lead to service corridors or an alley.

"Negative," she responded after trying to push it open like she'd done at the front, only to realize that it was cemented in place. "We're trapped. Need assistance."

There was a pause, and then Yamanu's voice came through. "Kyra, hold position. Diversion team inbound to your location, ETA less than five minutes."

"Acknowledged," Kyra replied, turning to Parisa, who was watching her with worry in her eyes. "Help is coming," she assured her. "We just need to stay hidden for a few more minutes."

"My sons?" Parisa asked, her voice barely above a whisper.

"Secured with Jade," Kyra confirmed. "They're safe for now."

Parisa nodded, some of the tension leaving her shoulders. "Then we wait." She looked around. "Should we find a place to hide?"

Outside, Kyra could hear the Doomers communicating, their voices just audible through the papered windows. They were checking each storefront, working their way toward their hiding place.

Five minutes suddenly seemed like an eternity.

"Over there." She pointed to a pile of construction debris. "We can get behind it."

It wasn't much, but at least it would keep them hidden from a cursory view.

They huddled on the floor for a couple of minutes before Parisa turned to her. "I need to know something," she whispered, "in case we don't make it out of here."

Kyra put a hand on her sister's bent knee. "We're going to make it."

"But if we don't," Parisa persisted. "I need to know the truth. You're not really Kyra's daughter, are you? You look the right age but that doesn't match your story about your years in the resistance."

Kyra opened her mouth, then closed it again, the mixture of hope and dread in Parisa's expression making the lie stick in her throat.

A noise at the front of the store saved her from having to answer.

Kyra turned around, crouching behind the pile of debris with her weapon drawn. Parisa remained where she was, her gaze still fixed on Kyra.

"We are related differently," Kyra whispered, the truth spilling out despite the dire situation—or perhaps because of it.

Parisa's breath caught. "Then who—"

The tarp covering the entrance rustled, and both women froze. A shadow moved across the papered window—someone peering inside, trying to see through the covering.

Kyra ducked lower behind the debris, keeping her weapon drawn.

Her pendant burned against her skin, the heat now almost painful. The broken door was pushed open, but then the sound of screeching tires and shouting erupted from the street outside. The shadow at the window disappeared as the Doomer turned toward the commotion.

"Diversion team has engaged," Yamanu's voice reported through the comm. "Kyra, now is your chance. Slip out and head to the service alley."

"Copy that," Kyra confirmed.

As they squeezed out through the door and used the tarp to inch toward the next store over, the commotion on the street continued with people yelling at each other and things getting thrown at cars by the sound of it.

Was the diversion team Nadim's?

It made sense since their team didn't have anyone to spare.

She and Parisa found a gap between stores that led to a narrow service alley, where a nondescript van idled, its side door open.

Dima sat in the driver's seat. "Get in," he called. "Quickly."

Kyra hurried Parisa into the van, then jumped in behind her, scanning the alley one last time before sliding the door closed.

"My sons?" Parisa asked immediately as Dima pulled away.

"Already secured," the Kra-ell warrior said. "Jade has them."

Kyra felt the tension drain from her body, but she remained alert, weapon ready, as Dima navigated through back streets and alleys, making sure that they weren't followed.

Her pendant had cooled somewhat, suggesting that the immediate danger had passed, but the lingering warmth indicated they weren't completely safe yet.

"What about my sisters?" Parisa asked. "Soraya and Rana?"

Dima's eyes remained fixed on the road as he made a series of rapid turns. "Soraya and Rana are secure."

27

MAX

ax's earpiece activated again, Kyra's voice coming through with beautiful clarity for a change. "Max?"

Relief washed over him at the sound of her voice.

"I'm here, and we have Rana with us. What's your status?"

"Dima and I have Parisa, and we are en route to the rendezvous point. Jade has the boys."

"Copy that. We are heading there as well." He paused, then added, "Are you okay?"

"I'm fine, but there were a few scary moments. Nadim's crew created a diversion in the nick of time. It made Parisa's and my escape possible and Dima was waiting and collected us from a back alley. Be careful. The Doomers seem to be everywhere."

Max was relieved that Yamanu had sent Dima to help Kyra and Parisa. He felt much better knowing that they were no longer on their own.

"I'm always careful, love. See you there."

When the comm went silent, he turned to Rana, who had been listening to his half of the conversation with evident interest because he hadn't deactivated the teardrop. "Your sister Parisa and her sons have been secured."

"Thank God." Something flickered across her features—relief mingled with suspicion. "You said that you found my nieces by chance when you went to rescue someone else from those bad people."

"That's correct."

"Who was that someone? And where were the girls held?"

Max had been expecting those questions, but it was Kyra's story to tell, and it would have to wait until they were safely on the plane heading home. Still, Rana deserved something more substantial than vague deflections.

"We were sent by a daughter to rescue her mother. I can't really tell you more than that at this point."

Rana didn't look satisfied with his answer, but she accepted it and leaned back in her seat.

Anton made another turn, this time onto a wider boulevard that would take them toward the industrial district where their fallback point was located. The van moved more smoothly now, blending with the flow of traffic.

"How far to the rendezvous?" Max asked.

"Ten minutes if traffic holds," Anton said. "I hope

Yamanu will be there with Soraya by the time we get there."

Max's earpieces crackled again. "All teams, be advised," Yamanu's voice came through. "We have a situation at the fallback point. Brotherhood forces have established a perimeter. They've somehow anticipated our extraction routes."

Max swore under his breath. "How did they know about that?"

"I don't know," Yamanu replied. "But we need to adapt. Divert to the secondary fallback point."

"Copy that," Max acknowledged. "Anton, change of plans. We need to head to the warehouse district instead."

The Kra-ell warrior nodded, already adjusting their route.

"What about Parisa and her boys?" Rana asked.

"They received the same instructions," Max said, though concern for Kyra gnawed at him. If the Brotherhood had somehow identified their fallback points, what other intelligence had they acquired?

What if the leak was Nadim? Or maybe Fatima?

Turner had vouched for Nadim and his team, but perhaps the guy had been compromised and betrayed them?

Even the best of people could be made to do the unthinkable when their loved ones were threatened, or some other leverage was used against them.

"These people are very well organized and very

determined," Rana said. "Those genetic traits you mentioned must be invaluable."

Smart woman.

"They are," Max confirmed. "Those fiends are part of a highly structured organization with specific objectives, and they are also motivated by vendetta. We killed their people and injured their pride."

"What are those special traits?" Rana asked, ignoring the second half of his answer. "What could we possibly have that would make them go to such lengths?"

Max hesitated, then decided on a partial version of the truth. "Your traits are hidden at this point, but when activated, they will make you stronger, faster, and a bunch of other qualities. At this point, though, it's gone beyond what they can benefit from your family's special traits. It's a matter of pride and revenge. We demolished their stronghold when we freed the mother and your daughter and nieces, and yesterday, we did the same to their stronghold on the outskirts of this city when we freed Yasmin and her children. We should have known that they wouldn't just lick their wounds and let us get away with it. We were banking on them not having a heavy presence in Tehran, but it was a bad gamble. Not that it would have changed anything. We would have still rescued Yasmin and her kids and demolished that place. We had no choice."

"Where is my daughter now? Is she with Yasmin and her kids?"

He shook his head. "She is in another secure location."

She nodded, accepting his explanation. "Thank you for taking such great risks for our family."

"As I said before, there is no need to thank me. It's what we do."

The van slowed as they reached a more congested area, and Anton navigated through the traffic with the confidence of someone who had driven around this city his entire life. They were entering the industrial zone now, a landscape of warehouses and manufacturing facilities that offered cover.

"Five minutes to secondary fallback point," Anton reported. "No signs of pursuit so far."

Max's comm unit activated once more, this time with Jade's voice. "We're being followed. Black SUV, three blocks back. Attempting evasive maneuvers."

"Do you need support?" Max asked.

"Negative," Jade replied. "Continue as planned. I'll handle this."

Max knew better than to argue with the Kra-ell leader. If she said she could handle it, she would.

The secondary fallback location was an abandoned textile factory on the outskirts of the industrial district. Its multiple entry points and maze-like interior made it ideal for a temporary gathering point. From there, they would change vehicles and make their way to the safe house where Yasmin and her children were already secured.

As they got nearer, Max scanned the perimeter

for any signs of Doomer activity. The factory seemed quiet, its broken windows and graffiti-covered walls giving it the appearance of long abandonment.

"Looks clear," he said. "But stay alert. They've anticipated too many of our moves already, and I don't know how they are getting their intel. I hope it's not a breach in our support team."

When Anton brought the van to a stop in a loading bay at the rear of the facility, positioning it for a quick exit if needed, Max turned to Rana. "Stay in the vehicle until I give the all-clear. If you hear gunfire or if I don't return within five minutes, Anton will get you out of here."

She cast the Kra-ell warrior an uneasy glance but then nodded.

KYRA

The industrial district loomed around them in gray metal and concrete, a stark contrast to the chaotic mixture of architectural styles of central Tehran.

As Dima navigated the van through the maze of warehouses and abandoned buildings, Kyra's hand remained on her weapon, eyes constantly scanning for threats.

Her pendant had cooled against her skin, but recent experience had taught her that its warnings were inconsistent at best. "Where are we going?" Parisa asked quietly, leaning forward in her seat.

"One of these buildings." Kyra caught her sister's gaze in the rearview mirror. The unfinished conversation from the shop lingered between them, questions suspended in the chaos of their escape. But this wasn't the time or place to address them. "This is just a meet-up point. Not our final destination."

Parisa nodded.

Dima slowed the van as they approached a dilapidated textile factory, its faded sign barely legible beneath years of dust and neglect. The loading bay door was partially open, and through the gap Kyra could make out other vehicles parked inside.

"Looks like Max and Rana beat us here," she said.

Her heart started beating a little faster as Dima pulled the van into the cavernous space, the hollow echo of their engine bouncing off concrete walls, and then it raced when she spotted Max standing beside a van, speaking with Rana.

Her sister looked remarkably composed, given the circumstances, and Kyra didn't know who she wanted to hug first, Max or Rana.

Another vehicle was parked deeper in the shadows, and she assumed it was the one Yamanu had used, arriving here first with Soraya.

When the van came to a stop, Kyra was out before Dima killed the engine, her eyes quickly finding Max's. The brief exchange of glances communicated everything words couldn't—relief, concern, the shared understanding of a mission in flux.

"Any trouble?" Max asked, moving toward her while trying to maintain a respectable distance, conscious of her sisters' gazes.

"It was scary, but Dima executed impeccable evasion techniques." She cast the Kra-ell a fond look. "He says that he learned to drive escape vehicles on a simulator in the village. He also insists that I have to do it too, and I'll become as good as he is."

"I might join you." Max reached for her hand. "I'll tell you all about it on the way back. There is much more than driving you can try on those simulators."

It reminded her of what Jasmine said about the Perfect Match technology and how it transcended entertainment and could be used as a training tool. That was probably what Dima had trained on.

"Hello." Parisa got out of the van. "Did anyone hear anything from Jade? I'm worried about my boys."

"She had to lose a tail," Yamanu said as he emerged from the shadows, his tall frame somehow blending with the darkness despite his height. "But she's confident they are no longer being followed." He offered Parisa his hand. "I'm Yamanu, and I'm in charge of this mission."

She took his hand, looking up at him with awe in her eyes. "Hello. I'm Parisa."

Kyra had to admit that he was quite striking, but he was happily mated, so her sister should cool her jets, as the saying went.

Yamanu turned to them. "Kyra, Max. We need to discuss our options."

Before Kyra could respond, a cry of recognition cut through the warehouse as Soraya stepped into the light, her eyes fixed on Parisa.

"Pary!" Soraya rushed forward, arms outstretched.

The two women collided in an embrace so fierce

it seemed they might never let go. Rana quickly joined them, the three sisters clinging to each other with tears gleaming in their eyes.

"You're alive," Soraya whispered, pulling back to examine Parisa's face as if to confirm she wasn't dreaming. "I was so worried. You should never have left my house. You and the boys should have stayed the night."

"I know." Parisa sighed. "They had school, but it wasn't as important as keeping them safe. I don't know what was going through my head."

Soraya kept her hands on Parisa's shoulders. "Never do that to me again, understand? I must have aged a decade since my girls were taken and then Yasmin and her kids."

Kyra stood apart, watching the reunion with a complicated twist of emotions. These were her sisters, her blood, yet she remained a stranger to them. The truth she carried inside her would change the dynamics between them but now wasn't the time to reveal it.

Yamanu cleared his throat. "I hate to interrupt, but we need to discuss the change in plans."

The sisters broke apart reluctantly, Soraya wiping tears from her cheeks as she turned to face him.

"What's happening?" Kyra asked after she and Max moved a few paces away from her sisters to talk with Yamanu.

"I believe our security has been compromised." Yamanu kept his voice low. "The Doomers have anticipated too many of our moves for it to be coincidence or just incredible guesswork on their part. They are not that good."

Max nodded in agreement. "The safe house may not be safe anymore. We should move Yasmin and her kids out of there as soon as possible."

"My thoughts precisely," Yamanu confirmed. "Instead of going there, we should head directly to the airport, and Yasmin and the children should meet us there."

"What about our belongings?" Kyra asked.

Everything she cared about was on her, so it wouldn't be a great loss if a few articles of clothing remained in the safe house, but perhaps Max and the others had items of personal value there.

"Rishba and Asuka can pack everyone's things and bring them along with Yasmin and her children to the airport," Yamanu said. "Eric has already arrived with the other plane, so we have enough room for everyone."

Kyra's instincts hummed in approval. The Doomers had proven more resourceful and numerous than they'd anticipated, and every minute they remained in Tehran increased their risk of capture or worse.

"I'll brief Rana and Soraya," Kyra said, turning toward her sisters.

"Tell them to get into the replacement vehicles." Yamanu pointed to where they were parked. "We need to be ready to move as soon as Jade arrives with Parisa's boys."

Kyra approached her sisters, who looked up with uncertainty and fear in their expressions.

"There's been a change of plans," she said. "We're not going to the safe house. We're heading straight to the airport and flying out."

"Out?" Soraya repeated. "Out where?"

"America," Kyra replied. "That's where your daughters are."

Soraya gasped, her hand flying to her mouth. "America? What are they doing there?"

"They saved them," Rana said. "They were saving someone else and found them."

"That's correct," Kyra confirmed, choosing not to mention that the other person rescued was her. "They're being very well cared for, I promise you. I have notes from all of them for you." She reached into her pocket and gave each mother the notes that were addressed to her. "You can read them on the way."

"But we don't have passports," Soraya said. "And the authorities will be looking for us. The moment my husband discovers that I'm missing, he will use every resource to find me."

"The paperwork has been taken care of in advance," Kyra assured them. "We have documentation for all of you. The important thing is to remember to keep your heads down and follow our instructions. You'll be traveling as Yamanu's wives."

Both women's gazes shifted to Yamanu, who stood conferring with Max by the vehicles. Soraya raised an eyebrow, studying him with a mixture of suspicion and curiosity.

"All of us? His wives?" she asked.

Despite the tension, Kyra chuckled. "It's just a cover, and he plays the part beautifully."

Yamanu probably wasn't going to change into the full disguise now because there was no time. He would just use shrouding.

Her sisters understood that in Iran, it raised fewer questions for women to be traveling with their husbands than alone.

Parisa, who had remained quiet during this exchange, looked toward the entrance. "Where are my sons? Shouldn't they have arrived yet?"

"Don't worry. Jade is on her way," Kyra assured her. "They will be here shortly." She hesitated, then addressed Soraya directly. "I need to ask you something. Do you mind leaving without your husband? I mean the real one. Not Yamanu."

The question hung in the air for a moment. Soraya's expression hardened, years of silent suffering briefly visible in the set of her jaw before she composed herself.

"No," she said firmly. "I don't mind at all. I longed for the day I would finally be free of him."

Kyra nodded. "Arezoo mentioned that things weren't good between you, but I needed to make sure. Sometimes kids see things differently."

Soraya laughed without mirth. "Arezoo told you the truth. He's been a tyrant from day one—controlling, cruel—but I had no choice. My father chose him and it was either marry Fareed or else." She let out a breath. "If my girls are in America, that's where I need to be."

Rana touched Soraya's arm in solidarity. "My situation is similar. My husband is not as bad as Fareed, but he doesn't love me. He has a mistress and spends more time with her than he ever spends with me. He blames me for not giving him more children, particularly a son." She looked away. "I think he's planning to divorce me anyway." She sighed. "My place is with my Azadeh. I have nothing keeping me here."

The naked vulnerability in their admissions struck Kyra deeply. After talking with their daughters, she'd known intellectually what her sisters had endured, but hearing it from their own lips made it viscerally real.

"You'll never have to see them again," she promised. "A new, joyous life awaits you in America."

KYRA

The sound of an approaching vehicle drew everyone's attention, and Kyra's hand instinctively moved to her weapon but relaxed when Max said, "That's Jade."

An old Saipa Tiba pulled into the warehouse, and a moment later, Jade opened the driver-side door and stepped out. Four boys of varying ages tumbled out after her, their eyes wide with fear and confusion until they spotted their mother.

"*Maman!*" the youngest cried, breaking into a run.

Parisa fell to her knees, arms wide, as all four boys crashed into her embrace. She held them fiercely, murmuring soothing words, her hands checking each of them as if ensuring they were whole and unharmed.

"We need to move, people," Yamanu announced, his voice cutting through the emotional reunion. "Everyone into the vehicles. Rana and Soraya with me and Dima. Parisa, the boys, and Kyra with Max and Jade."

The sisters exchanged looks, reluctant to separate after just finding each other again, but none of the vehicles were big enough to carry all of them along with someone who could shoot.

They must have realized that because no one argued, except for Soraya, who for a moment looked like she was about to protest but then seemed to think better of it. Instead, she turned to Kyra. "Thank you for coming for us. I don't understand everything that's happening, but I know you saved my daughters." She hesitated, studying Kyra's face with furrowed brows. "There's something familiar about you."

Kyra felt a hitch in her chest, a sudden longing to tell the truth. But now wasn't the time. "We can talk more once we're safely away," she promised.

Soraya nodded, but her expression suggested she wouldn't forget. With one last embrace for Parisa and a quick touch to each of the boys' heads, she followed Yamanu.

"Kyra," Max called, holding the new van door open. "We need to go."

She moved quickly, helping Parisa and the boys into the van before climbing in herself. Max took the driver's seat with Jade beside him, her weapon resting casually across her lap.

"Everyone secure with seatbelts on?" Max asked, glancing in the rearview mirror.

Kyra did a quick check. "Yes, sir."

As the vehicles pulled out of the warehouse, Kyra felt a touch of the surreal. She was sitting in the back with Parisa and the oldest boy, who was watching her with eyes that looked a lot like hers and Jasmine's.

"Jade said that you are taking us to America. Is that true?" he asked in carefully pronounced English.

"Yes." Kyra smiled. "You speak English well."

He shrugged. "Mom said we should learn a foreign language, and I chose English because all the good movies are in English."

Parisa smiled faintly, running a hand over her son's short hair. "I never imagined it would be useful quite like this."

"My mom is smart," the boy said with unexpected fierceness. "She knows things."

Kyra caught Parisa's eye over the boy's head, an understanding passing between them. The conversation they'd started in the shop remained unfinished, but Parisa's keen perception was evident.

"What's going to happen to us in America?" Parisa asked quietly. "Will we be refugees?"

"No," Kyra assured her. "You'll be well taken care of. Housing, education for the kids, everything you need."

"We don't have money," Parisa said. "Who will pay for all this?"

Kyra hesitated. "The organization of people with special genetic markers who is helping you right now takes care of its own, and it doesn't lack resources."

"What do they expect in return?" Parisa's voice held no accusation, just pragmatic caution.

"Nothing," Kyra replied honestly. "Your safety is all that matters. You will become members of their community the same way I did."

The skeptical look this earned reminded Kyra so much of herself that she nearly laughed. Parisa, like her, had learned the hard way that nothing in life came without a price.

"I know it's hard to believe," Kyra said, "but I promise you, there are no strings attached. The truth is obviously more complicated than the simple explanation I've just given you, and I promise to explain everything better once we're safely away from here."

Parisa studied her for a long moment, then nodded once. "I'll hold you to that."

After Max left the industrial district, he took a circuitous route to avoid main roads and potential checkpoints. Next to him, Jade remained vigilant, her eyes constantly darting to the rearview mirror.

"How far to the airport?" Kyra asked, leaning forward.

"About forty minutes," Max said. "Rishba reports they're already en route with Yasmin and her children, and Morris, our pilot, says that both planes are fueled and ready for departure."

The knowledge that they were so close to escape should have been comforting if Kyra thought that they were out of harm's way, but she'd learned that the final stretch of a mission was often the most dangerous.

The pendant remained cool against her skin, but since it was not always trustworthy, she relied on her training and instincts, remaining alert as the city gradually gave way to more open terrain.

She wanted to ask Jade how she'd dealt with the guards that had been assigned to the boys, but fearing an answer that would upset them, she decided to wait for a private moment.

The boys had fallen into an exhausted silence, the youngest two leaning against their older brother while the eldest, who sat next to Parisa, stared out the windows, trying to look brave despite the fear evident in his tense shoulders.

"When we get to the airport," Kyra told them, "stay close to me. Do exactly as I say, no questions and no talking. Can you do that?"

Four solemn nods answered her. These children had grown up in an authoritarian regime, and they understood the importance of following orders or suffering the consequences.

"Good," she said, offering a reassuring smile. "We will be on our way to see your cousins before you know it."

The mention of their cousins brightened their expressions. Even the eldest boy, who'd been working hard on maintaining a brave, stoic façade, looked hopeful.

"Are they okay?"

"Yes." She smiled at him. "In fact, they have just spent a fabulous day touring Universal Studios, visiting the Harry Potter World."

The stunned silence that followed was almost comical.

"Can we go?" asked one of the boys from the back.

"Of course. I'll take you there myself. I've never been to Universal Studios."

Maybe she had, but the memory was lost along with all the others that Durhad had stolen from her.

MAX

There were so many things Max wanted to do with Kyra, but even though he wasn't a fan of theme parks, he would take her to Universal Studios and make sure she had the time of her life.

"We need to go to the one in Florida," Max said. "The one in California sucks."

"Are we going to California?" Parisa asked.

Max watched in the rearview mirror as Kyra smiled and nodded.

"Will we all live together?" the boy sitting next to her asked.

The names of the boys had been in the dossier Onegus had prepared for their mission, but Max had forgotten what they were. The little one was Kavir, or was it Arman?

"Yes," Kyra said. "Maybe not in the same house, but right next to each other."

"That sounds lovely," Parisa said. "I've always wanted to live next to my sisters and raise our families together, but childhood dreams were replaced by the cold reality of our world, where our wishes didn't matter much."

"Think of it as an adventure," Kyra said, probably to take the sting out of her sister's words. "It's going to be a new beginning."

As the van hit a pothole, jolting them all, Max muttered an apology.

"Two vehicles approaching from the northeast," Jade said, her body tensing. "They're moving fast."

Max glanced in the side view mirror. "I see them. Could be nothing."

"Or it could be trouble," Jade countered. "Better safe than sorry. Take the next turn."

Max complied, steering the van down a narrow side road that hadn't been part of his planned route. Through the rearview mirror, he could see two black SUVs continuing along the main road.

Never a good sign.

Why governments, the military, and bad guys always chose black SUVs was something he had wondered about before. Why not white ones? Or why not vans, which were more versatile and gas-efficient?

Maybe it was meant to intimidate?

"False alarm?" Kyra asked.

"Maybe," Jade said, though she didn't sound convinced. She activated her comm unit. "Yamanu, be advised that we've taken a detour and might be a few minutes late. A possible tail that we need to lose."

"Acknowledged," came Yamanu's terse reply. "Proceed with caution."

Max kept looking at the rearview mirror, but when he confirmed that the vehicles weren't following them, he shifted his gaze to Kyra.

His warrior queen.

She looked serene, sitting quietly with Parisa and the boy, her gaze distant as if she was contemplating the mysteries of the universe. He knew what was on her mind, and he wished he could help her, but it was her story to tell, and she needed to figure out how to reveal her true identity to her sisters and when.

How would they react to learning that their long-lost sister hadn't died but instead remained virtually unchanged while decades passed?

Eventually, she would have to tell them about her immortality and their potential to become immortal as well, but it was anyone's guess how they would react to the revelation.

None of them seemed particularly pious or religious to him, and from what he'd seen so far, they all seemed like intelligent women. He wanted to believe that they wouldn't accuse Kyra of witchcraft, or being a demon, or some other superstitious nonsense. In the end, they would have to accept the truth of what she was and what they could be, but until then, they could cause Kyra lots of grief, and he sincerely hoped that wouldn't happen.

She deserved some peace in her life and the simple joy of a loving family.

"You've gone quiet," Parisa said.

"Just thinking," Kyra replied.

"About what you need to tell us?" Parisa guessed.

"Yes," Kyra said. "Later, though. Not now."

Max shifted his gaze from Kyra to Parisa, but there was no judgment in her expression, only curiosity.

Parisa nodded. "I can wait."

The airport appeared in the distance, its control tower rising above the surrounding structures like a sentinel, and as they got closer, Max slowed the van, motioning to Jade to make contact with the rest of their team.

"We are clear for approach," Jade said after a brief exchange. "Nadim's buddies created a diversion on the north side of the terminal to draw security attention away from our entry point."

"What kind of diversion?" Kyra asked.

Jade's lips curved in a rare smile. "A 'diplomatic incident' involving a fictional Russian oligarch and some misplaced caviar."

Kyra laughed. "Trust Nadim and his network to create something both effective and absurd."

"Yeah." Max grimaced. "After all the breaches in security, I'm not so sure I trust Nadim's team. Someone in there was compromised."

"I hope it wasn't Fatima," Kyra said. "She was so nice to us."

"And her baklava was delicious," Max said. "I need to get the recipe."

Parisa snorted. "If you get us safely to America, I'll make you so much baklava that you will get sick of it."

He smiled at her through the rearview mirror. "Challenge accepted."

The guard at the gate barely glanced at them as Jade showed him the fake documentation that had been prepared ahead of time, and within moments, they were through, driving across the tarmac toward a hangar where two private jets waited.

"Did you use your compulsion?" Max asked.

The Kra-ell had an ability that was a cross between thralling and compulsion, but only the strongest among them could use it effectively on humans.

She nodded. "It comes in handy from time to time."

"Everyone, remember the plan," Max said, looking at Parisa and the boys in the rearview mirror. "Stay close, keep your heads down, and don't talk. If anyone asks anything, let Kyra do the talking."

KYRA

Relief washed over Kyra when she saw Rana and Soraya standing with Yamanu, Yasmin, and her children spilling out from another van accompanied by Rishba and Asuka.

"We made it." She put a hand on Max's arm. "We actually made it."

"Don't celebrate yet," Max cautioned. "Not until we're airborne."

She frowned. "Can they attack us in the air? Do they have the capability to do that?"

"They can do anything." He gave her a sad smile. "With their mind control ability, they can infiltrate Air Force command and have us shot down. But luckily for us, it will take them too long to get to the Air Force command. Thralling has to be done face to face, not on the phone, and not even through a video call. By the time they locate the appropriate person to do their bidding, we will be long out of Iranian airspace."

"Then we should hurry up and get airborne." Especially since they were the most vulnerable here, exposed on the tarmac.

As soon as Max parked the van next to the others, Kyra got out and rushed Parisa and the boys toward the waiting planes.

The reunion between her sisters was swift but emotional, tears and embraces exchanged in a flurry before Yamanu urged them toward the aircraft.

Max, Kyra, and her family headed toward the larger plane while the rest of their team headed toward Eric's smaller jet.

The children were ushered up the stairs first, followed by their mothers.

Kyra waited her turn with Max, but as she started climbing the stairs behind Rana, she caught a flash of movement from the corner of her eye—a vehicle approaching from the direction of the main terminal, moving faster than should be allowed in an airport.

"Incoming," she alerted Max, her hand going to her weapon.

"I count four occupants," he said, reaching for his weapons as well.

"Doomers?" Kyra asked.

"I can't tell from this distance."

"Doesn't matter," Max said. "We can't let them delay our departure."

Kyra's pendant suddenly flared hot against her

skin—a warning that came too late to be useful. The approaching vehicle accelerated, clearly intending to intercept them before they could board.

"Go," Max told her. "Get on the plane with your sisters. We'll handle this."

"Max—"

"Go," he repeated, softer this time. "We've got it."

Kyra hesitated only a moment longer before nodding and going up the aircraft stairs. She trusted Max and the others to handle the threat just as they had done with all the others.

Before entering the cabin, she cast one last look at the tarmac, where Max, Yamanu, and the Kra-ell had spread out in a defensive formation. They looked formidable, otherworldly, and beautiful in their deadly focus.

Hopefully, the car contained only humans, and Yamanu could get rid of them with a simple thrall.

"Is everything alright?" Soraya asked as Kyra entered.

"It's probably just airport security." Kyra moved to a window where she could observe the confrontation.

The engines were already revving up, but the cabin door was still open, so Kyra hoped they wouldn't take off without Max.

Through the window, she could see Max and the others confronting the occupants of the vehicle, which had stopped several yards away.

She couldn't hear what was being said, but the

body language of the men emerging from the car was threatening. Then, suddenly, they relaxed, nodded in unison, and returned to their car.

It was the effect of Yamanu's thralling, which meant they were humans, not Doomers.

A moment later, Max entered the cabin and closed the door behind him. The plane began to taxi immediately.

"Everyone secure?" he asked.

When a chorus of voices answered in the affirmative, he smiled. "*Bon voyage*, everyone." He sat next to Kyra.

"Who were they?" she asked.

"Airport security. Something about lack of proper documentation. Yamanu convinced them they'd made a mistake."

She chuckled, more in relief than amusement. "I'm grateful for his particular brand of persuasion. He could be a world leader if he chose to be."

Max snorted. "When you get to know him better, you'd realize that he's the last person who would want such a position or be any good at it. Perhaps that's the reason the Fates bestowed such incredible power upon him. They knew he wouldn't abuse it."

"I wish those Fates of yours would be that discriminating with everyone they allow into a position of power."

Max nodded sagely. "True. Personally, I don't think that the Fates are all-powerful. They are limited in what they are allowed to do, and there are other forces in the universe that don't share their good intentions. Given all that's been going on in the world in the past two decades or so, I'd say that the forces of evil are rising rapidly, but I don't want to be a pessimist. Not today." He looked back to where her family was sitting. "Today, the forces of good won. We should celebrate the victory."

"Definitely." She took his hand and squeezed it. "Thank you for saving my family."

He leaned over and kissed her cheek. "You would have done the same for mine."

FENELLA

Out on the penthouse terrace, Fenella leaned against the railing and watched the sprawl of Los Angeles. There were no birds so high up, but for some reason, she imagined a hawk gliding through the air, riding the thermal currents, free to do as it pleased—a king of the sky. For half a century, she'd been drifting wherever instinct led her. Now, she was about to join a community of immortals in a secret location that she wasn't sure she could leave if she didn't like it.

"Thinking about Din?" Jasmine joined her at the railing.

"Not at all. Just enjoying the view."

In truth, Fenella hadn't thought about Din the entire morning. She'd been weighing her options. She could still walk away and disappear into the urban maze below like she'd done countless times before.

"The girls are nervous about going to the village," Jasmine said. "They feel safe here, and they don't want to leave."

"Can you blame them? They've been through hell, and this penthouse is their sanctuary. Of course they are wary about leaving it."

Jasmine tilted her head. "Are you nervous about going to the village too?"

"For different reasons," Fenella admitted. "I'm an independent spirit who hates being tied down, literally and figuratively, and commune-style living is not for me."

Jasmine pursed her lips. "I think you will like the village, but I get how someone who is used to a nomadic lifestyle can feel restricted in a small community. On the other hand, aren't you tired of constantly being on the move? You did it out of necessity, but now you have an alternative."

Fenella turned around, leaning her back against the railing and folding her arms over her chest. "That's why it's not an easy decision. I just hope that the decision is still mine. I have a feeling that they wouldn't let me go now that they know of my existence." She leaned closer to Jasmine. "I'm too valuable."

She hoped that Jasmine would argue that she was not a commodity and that no one would force her to stay, but instead, Jasmine just sighed. "I need to check on the girls. I didn't tell them to pack so they wouldn't be scared. I told them that we were just going to visit and check out some houses. That if they like it there, we would come back for their things."

"Everything we have was bought for us by the clan," Fenella said. "I'm sure that they expect something in return." She pushed away from the railing and headed for the sliding doors. "My stuff is packed."

Everything fit in a single duffel bag.

Inside, the four girls were clustered around the breakfast counter, picking at fruit and pastries. The excitement from the day before had evaporated, and they'd been subdued all morning, worrying for their mothers, aunts, and cousins.

Kyra had called Jasmine once with updates, but it had been a while ago, and they hadn't heard from her in nearly twenty-four hours. Fenella was sure that someone would have notified them if something had gone terribly wrong, so she wasn't as worried, but she picked up on the nervous energy emanating from the girls.

"Are you all ready to go visit the secret village?" Jasmine asked, a little too cheerfully.

"What's the village like?" Azadeh asked.

Jasmine had talked about it constantly, so Fenella doubted there was much to add to what she'd already said, but the girl's question was a plea for reassurance rather than new information.

Jasmine sat down beside them. "It's beautiful—

nestled in the mountains with views of the ocean. It's probably one of the safest places in the world. No one can get to you there, and you'll be among your own kind."

"We are not immortal yet," Arezoo said. "Are there other Dormants in the village?"

"Yes," Jasmine said. "Not many, though."

They hadn't told the girls how they would one day transition, and Fenella was glad it wasn't her job to educate them. These girls had led sheltered lives concerning anything and everything to do with sex, which was kind of paradoxical given how obsessed with it their male counterparts were and how entitled to it they felt.

Sexual assault victims could get executed in Iran if they reported the crime, while the violators got the equivalent of a slap on the wrist. In Iranian courts, it was always the woman's fault, no matter the circumstances. She wasn't even allowed to defend herself with something as small as a pocketknife because that, too, was an offense punishable by execution.

Talk about evil.

In the background, Fenella heard Jasmine selling the village to the girls. "We are going to eat lunch in the village café, visit the gym, the underground pool, and the movie theater, and then we are going to look at some houses. Or maybe we'll see the houses first and then check out the other stuff."

Jasmine was really good at this. She'd even convinced Fenella that life in the village would be wonderful and got her to voluntarily agree to join the merry band of immortals.

"When do we leave?" Laleh asked.

"In about half an hour," Jasmine said. "The big boss sent his butler to pick us up with a bus."

"A bus?" Donya wrinkled her nose.

"It's a very nice bus," Jasmine said. "It's like the kind they use for tours. Now, go put your shoes on, brush your hair, and whatever else you need to do to get ready."

Laleh chewed on her lower lip. "Can I wear the skirt you bought me in Universal Studios?"

Jasmine grinned. "Of course. You can wear whatever you want."

When the girls headed to their rooms, Jasmine walked over to the coffee carafe and poured three cups of coffee. "I should suggest a Harry Potter adventure for Perfect Match." She took the three cups and carried them to the living room, where Ell-rom was hunched over his laptop. "What do you think?" she asked as she put the cup in front of him.

"About what?"

"A Harry Potter Perfect Match adventure." She sat down next to Ell-rom.

"It's a good idea," he murmured while typing on the keyboard.

"How many kids do you have in the village?" Fenella asked.

"Not many, but adults also love Harry Potter." Jasmine took a sip of her coffee. "Besides, the adventures are designed for the general market, not just for those who live in the village. There is a whole generation of adults who grew up on those books and who are now in their prime earning years. I bet many would gladly part with their money to relive their childhood obsession."

33

MAX

Whi hen Max's phone vibrated in the pocket of his cargo pants, he had a good idea who was on the line. Yamanu was no doubt calling Kian to update him on the operation and wanted Max on the line.

"Max here," he answered quietly, moving to the cockpit where he wouldn't disturb the others. He could turn off his teardrop, but some of the kids seemed to know English, and there were things he couldn't say with them around.

Morris nodded his approval and gestured for him to take the copilot seat.

"Hello, Max," Kian said. "I'm here with Onegus, and I have Yamanu on the line. Which one of you wants to go first?"

"I don't mind going first," Max said. "Almost nothing worked according to our original plan, and we kept improvising, but we got Kyra's sisters and the kids out."

"That's good to hear," Kian said. "So, what went wrong?"

Max stifled a chuckle. "What didn't go wrong would be a better question. The Doomers have a much heavier presence in Iran than we suspected, and they were majorly pissed off after we demolished two of their bases. We were compromised at multiple points, which suggests a security breach within the local network. This is something that Turner needs to address with whoever is in charge there."

"What do you mean by compromised?" Onegus asked.

"The Doomers were waiting for us at nearly all extraction points," Yamanu said. "They anticipated our moves with disturbing precision. We were forced to accelerate the timeline and change extraction routes multiple times."

"They had a coordinated response across the entire city," Max added. "Frankly, I have no idea how they managed it. They are getting more sophisticated, which is troublesome on many levels."

"Any casualties?" Kian asked.

"One civilian," Yamanu said. "Yasmin's husband was killed defending his family before we arrived. The Doomers took Yasmin and her children, but we tracked them to a compound outside the city, got them out, and sacked the place after we disposed of all the Doomers."

"We sanitized it," Max added. "We left no survivors and no security footage behind, and we hoped that would do the trick and the rest of the extraction would be easy. Imagine our surprise when Doomers started popping up all over the place."

The pilot cast Max a worried glance. "How did you get the sisters and the kids out with such a small team and with Doomers coming at you from all directions?"

"I credit the Kra-ell," Max admitted. "They are a force of nature."

"I agree," Yamanu confirmed. "It's a pleasure to work with them. They learn incredibly fast, and they love fighting. The more desperate the odds, the more thrilled they are to be let loose on the enemy."

"That's good to know," Onegus said. "We need to work on recruiting more of them and giving them proper training. Your team of Kra-ell barely had any."

"They are naturals," Yamanu said. "It's like they were born to fight."

In a way, that was precisely what the Kra-ell had been bred to be over many generations of endless tribal wars. They were killing machines, and the clan was fortunate to have them fighting alongside them. Especially now that the Doomers were getting more sophisticated and better coordinated, the clan could use any help they could get.

"Can you estimate how many Doomers you've eliminated?" Kian asked. "Also, how many more have you encountered?"

Max frowned. "Between the compound in Tahav and this one, I'd estimate the Doomer death toll at about thirty, give or take a few. But we encountered many more today. They are deeply embedded in the Revolutionary Guard."

"That's concerning," Kian murmured.

"I wonder what they are cooking up there. It's obviously not about Durhad's little side project of collecting Dormants," Yamanu said. "I hope it's not connected to their nuclear ambitions, but I have a feeling that it is."

"Of course it is." Kian groaned. "Navuh is not stupid enough to start a nuclear war and annihilate most humans, but nuclear Iran is another destabilizing force that will throw the world into chaos. The more chaotic it gets, the more power the Brotherhood can wield, and the closer they get to achieving their ambitions of world domination."

There was a long silence on the line, and Max wondered if the others were imagining a world under the Brotherhood's rule like he was. All of Annani's and her clan's work would be destroyed, all the progress reversed, and a new Dark Age would ensue, worse than all the others preceding it combined. The savagery and suffering would be unimaginable, and women would bear the brunt of it.

"We will need to investigate what's going on there," Kian said. "But that's beyond the scope of this mission. What's the status with Kyra's sisters?"

"They're processing," Max said. "Kyra's older

sisters have just learned their daughters are alive, but the one who has lost her husband is obviously distressed, and so are her children. He was a good man, as opposed to the husbands of the other two. Soraya and Rana had no problem leaving their husbands behind."

"I'm sorry for her loss," Kian said. "I'll have Okidu waiting with the bus at the airstrip to deliver all of you straight to the village. Naturally, Julian will be there with the medical van to check all the newcomers for implants. Jasmine, Fenella, and Kyra's nieces are coming to the village later today to meet Ingrid. She will give them a tour of the available houses. Once they make their selection, she will put them to work to prepare them for their families' arrival."

Kyra would be thrilled to hear that. Having her daughter and nieces to welcome the rest of the family would make everything much smoother.

"Is Kyra planning to tell them about their genetics and what it means for their future?" Kian asked.

"She is, but she hasn't done so yet," Max said. "We have plenty of time. It's a long flight and we also need to stop for refueling."

"It needs to be done before they arrive at the airstrip," Kian said.

"It will be," Max promised. "Kyra will most likely tell the adults and leave it up to them when and how to tell the children."

Once the call ended, Max stood and stretched his

aching muscles. Looking toward the back of the plane, he caught Kyra looking at him and smiled.

He made his way back, sliding into the seat beside her. "Your sisters must be anxious to hear the story you promised them."

"I know." She leaned her head on his shoulder. "I needed a few minutes of rest before I tackle that talk."

"Do you want coffee? That always perks you up."

She lifted her head off his shoulder and kissed his cheek. "It's amazing how well you know me after such a short time."

He wrapped his arm around her. "You fascinate me. I pay attention to every move you make." He closed one eye and leaned away. "I hope that didn't sound as creepy to you as it sounded to me."

Kyra laughed. "Not at all. Well, for now, when we are still getting to know each other, that's not creepy. But it might get a little annoying if you are still doing it a year from now."

If she was talking about a year from now, they were good. "Let me know when I should stop, and I will."

"Deal." She let out a breath. "I should call Jasmine, but first, I need to talk to my sisters and tell them who I really am."

"Speaking of Jasmine," he said quietly, "She is taking Fenella and the girls to the village later today to look at houses, and once they choose the ones they like, they will prepare them for your sisters. We are heading straight there instead of going to the penthouse."

Kyra's eyes widened. "That's so exciting." She kept her voice down. "I hope Jasmine selects adjacent homes for us. I would love to live next door to my daughter and sisters." She glanced toward the back again. "Maybe I should text her."

"That's a good idea. Tell her to send you pictures once she gets there."

She lifted a brow. "Is that allowed? I mean, everything about the village is classified information, right?"

"Our phones are secure."

"That's good." She settled against him and slipped her hand into his.

Max felt the familiar connection surge between them. He'd known her for such a short time, yet it felt like they'd been partners for centuries.

"What about us?" she asked. "Are we going to move in together?"

"Nothing would make me happier, but it's up to you. I don't want you to feel pressured."

She chuckled. "Trust me, if I feel pressured, it's not because of our housing arrangement."

Max frowned. "Then what?"

She looked into his eyes. "I can't wait to be with you in every sense of the word."

Max swallowed, getting instantly hard. "I can't wait either, but—"

Kyra put a finger on his lips. "I know. It's up to

me, and you don't want me to feel pressured. You are not the one pressuring me, my love. The pressure comes from inside. It's everything I have bottled up and kept locked in for two and a half decades."

"Oh, boy." He pretended panic. "I'm not sure I will survive that."

Kyra laughed. "Don't worry. I'll make it good for you." She winked, pulled out her phone, and started texting as if she hadn't just detonated a massive explosive under his butt.

FENELLA

Fenella looked around the room that had been hers for a few days. The bed was made, the counter in the bathroom wiped clean, and the toilet scrubbed. She wasn't the type of guest who left a mess for the host to clean up, even if the host had a butler and a maid.

The truth was that it had probably been one of the nicest rooms she'd ever stayed in, but she had no regrets about leaving it and never coming back.

The fancy penthouse had been a pleasant interlude, but it was time to move on, either to the village or elsewhere.

"You don't have to take your stuff with you," Jasmine said from the doorway. "We are probably coming back for our things."

"I'm not. I like to make clean cuts. This beautiful penthouse was a nice place to stay for a few days, but it's not mine." She smiled. "I'm a nomad at heart. I don't put roots down."

Jasmine nodded. "The girls are ready to go. We should go down to the garage to wait for the bus."

"I'm ready." Fenella slung the strap of her duffel bag over her shoulder. "The beauty of not owning much is easy packing and light traveling. Frankly, I don't know why people are so obsessed with collecting possessions. They are just a burden."

Jasmine chuckled. "I'm guilty of never getting rid of anything. I still have clothing that I wore at sixteen and don't have the heart to part with."

Fenella patted her arm. "I feel for you. If you need help getting rid of stuff, I'll help you."

Down at the parking garage, the bus was already waiting for them when they got there, and as the doors hissed open, a squat man in a crisp suit stepped out. His whole appearance screamed 'butler' even though he wasn't wearing a uniform. It was in his fake smile and in the bow he executed with perfect flare.

"Mistress Jasmine. It's a pleasure to see you again." He shifted his gaze to Fenella, and his fake smile got even wider. "Mistress Fenella, I presume?"

She nodded and was about to say that it was just Fenella when he moved to the girls and correctly addressed each one by name. "Mistresses Arezoo, Donya, Laleh, and Azadeh."

"I'm impressed," Jasmine said. "How did you know who was who?"

"The village roster was already updated with the names of Kyra's family members."

"I see," Jasmine said as if it was self-explanatory for the butler to be updated on everyone's names.

"My name is Okidu," he said as he bowed again to Fenella and the girls. "I will be your driver today." He motioned toward the stairs leading to the bus. "Please, step aboard."

There was something off about the bloke, but Fenella couldn't put her finger on it. "Nice to meet you, Master Okidu," she said as she followed Laleh up the stairs.

Two could play the game of making the other feel uncomfortable.

"Just Okidu, mistress."

She turned around and offered him her best fake grin. "Well, in that case, call me Fenella without the prefix."

"Very well, M—" He stopped himself. "I mean miss."

Behind her, Jasmine chuckled. "Stop tormenting the poor guy, Fenella. He can't call you by your given name. It's not how he's programmed."

Fenella looked at Jasmine over her shoulder. "What do you mean it's not how he's programmed? He can't overcome his so-called programming?"

"Not easily." Jasmine put a hand on her back, giving her a light push. "I'll explain later."

These people were not as nice as she'd thought

they were if they forced their employees to call them masters and mistresses.

What was it, feudal Ireland?

The interior of the bus was much more impressive than its exterior. Plush leather seats were spaced out to provide plenty of legroom and there was an entertainment system built into each seat.

"Wow," Laleh said, checking out the system.

The others followed, their earlier wariness giving way to curiosity as they explored the vehicle. Ell-rom boarded last, ducking slightly to accommodate his height.

"This is bloody ridiculous," Fenella muttered as she settled into a seat. "Riding in a massive bus with just seven passengers. What happened to the van we took to Universal Studios?"

"It was a rental," Jasmine said. "Only approved vehicles can enter the village."

"How long is the journey?" Arezoo asked as the butler closed the door.

"It depends on the traffic," Jasmine said. "When it's light, it takes a little less than an hour; when it's congested, it can take up to two. Get comfortable, watch a movie, or listen to music."

"Very well." She watched as the vehicle went up the spiral driveway, climbing several levels before finally emerging on the street and into the bright California sunshine.

Fenella had never been to Los Angeles, so she preferred the view outside to whatever she could watch on the small screen attached to the seat in front of her.

The landscape gradually transformed, urban sprawl giving way to a more open terrain as they climbed into the foothills. She preferred the open nature and the freedom it represented.

Then, without warning, the windows of the bus started turning opaque, still letting the light through but nothing of the scenery.

"What's happening?" Donya asked.

"It's okay." Jasmine raised her hand to calm the girls. "It's just a security measure to protect the location of the village."

"By blocking the view?" Fenella asked.

"Precisely," Okidu said from the front, his first words since they'd departed. "The sanctity of the village's location is paramount to its security. The vehicle takes over, driving autonomously."

"So, no one knows how to get to the village?" Arezoo asked. "Not even the people who live there?"

"The villagers know they're in the Malibu mountains," Jasmine explained. "But the entrance to the road leading to the village remains hidden and is only known to a select few. It's for everyone's protection."

"Does everyone travel in and out of the village by bus?" Donya asked.

The same question occurred to Fenella, but she didn't want to be the one asking.

"Most residents have their own vehicles," Jasmine

said. "But all the cars in the village are equipped with these special windows and autonomous driving systems that take over a few miles before entering or exiting the village. That way, the residents can't betray the village's exact location, intentionally or otherwise."

Fenella's unease deepened. "Sounds a bit paranoid, doesn't it?"

"Not really," Jasmine said. "The clan's enemies are vicious and persistent."

The implication hit Fenella like a wrecking ball. If the clan's security measures were this extreme, the threat must be proportional. She'd been free for fifty years because she'd been beneath notice, just another woman drifting through the world. But joining the village would make her a target for those vicious enemies and having been at the mercy of one of those monsters, or rather his complete lack of mercy, she knew that it wasn't an idle threat.

"Are you all right?" Jasmine asked from across the aisle. "You look pale all of a sudden."

"Just thinking," Fenella replied, careful to keep her voice low so that the girls couldn't hear her. "Given who your enemies are, maybe I'm better off on my own. At least then, I'm not a target by association."

"Being an immortal female, you are a target wherever you are," Jasmine said bluntly. "But at least in the village, you are protected. Out there, on your own, you are exposed and defenseless."

"I've managed well enough on my own for half a century."

"You did until you didn't," Jasmine pointed out. "You got caught."

Fenella had no retort for that. The memory of her captivity was still raw—the drugs, the degradation, the abuse, the helplessness. She'd been lucky to escape with her sanity intact.

The bus slowed, the temperature noticeably dropped, the windows got darker, and the engine's hum bounced back at them in tight echoes.

They'd entered a tunnel.

"Are we underground?" Azadeh asked.

"Yes," Jasmine confirmed. "We're inside the mountain."

The bus moved slowly, propelled forward by the autonomous driving apparatus. Suddenly, there was a mechanical jerk, followed immediately by the distinct sensation of upward movement.

"What the bloody hell?" Fenella muttered.

"Vehicle lift," Ell-rom explained from across the aisle. "We are ascending to the parking garage level, which is only a couple of levels below the top where the village is."

The lift continued for what seemed an extraordinarily long time. Fenella counted silently, trying to gauge how many floors they might be rising. One, two, three... by the time they stopped, she'd estimated at least six levels, possibly more.

With a soft pneumatic hiss, the lift settled into

position. The windows gradually cleared, revealing an enormous underground garage filled with vehicles of every description—from practical sedans to exotic sports cars, all arranged in neat rows under artificial lighting.

Okidu guided the bus into an empty space and cut the engine. "Welcome to the village," he announced.

As the doors opened, Jasmine turned to address everyone. "This garage is just one of many underground levels that serve different purposes. The actual village is on top of the mountain, hidden from aerial view by sophisticated camouflage technology."

"How does no one see it?" Donya asked.

"Don't ask me." Jasmine chuckled. "It's no doubt some advanced cloaking technology. Supposedly, the village appears to be just another forested peak from above or below."

Fenella stepped off the bus, taking in the cavernous space with its perfectly maintained vehicles and gleaming floor.

These people liked to keep their spaces clean, which she appreciated. Over the years, she'd learned that the difference between good and bad neighborhoods was the level of cleanliness of their streets and their public spaces, and it didn't matter if the population was wealthy or poor. People who cared for their community didn't trash it.

35

KYRA

K yra watched Max walk toward the galley to make their coffees, his gait slightly unsteady as if her words had physically knocked him off balance. She bit her lower lip to keep from laughing. The mighty Guardian, who had fearlessly faced Doomers and torn out their hearts, was utterly flustered by her straightforward declaration that she was ready to take him to bed and unleash over two decades of stifled femininity on him.

She hadn't meant to be quite so blunt about it, but she wasn't a blushing virgin, and the guy deserved a forewarning. Life was too short, even for an immortal, to waste time waiting for what she wanted.

The stunned look on his face had been priceless. His blue eyes had widened, his lips parted in surprise, and he'd actually stammered before offering to get them both coffees.

Max stammering. It was adorable.

Kyra returned to the text she'd started and read it again.

We're airborne and safe. Everyone is on board and unharmed. Well, save for Parisa's husband, Javad, but she wasn't going to start with that. She pressed send and waited for Jasmine's response.

It came almost immediately: *Thank the Goddess! How are my aunts and cousins?*

Processing everything. Yasmin is grieving her husband, but having her children with her is helping. Soraya and Rana are eager to see their daughters. Kyra pressed send.

Are you in Iranian airspace still?

The question touched on Kyra's lingering fear. She glanced out the window at the vast expanse of clouds below. They were still flying over Iran, with its Revolutionary Guard and potentially Doomer-thralled military commanders.

Yes, she wrote. *Max says it's unlikely they'll pursue us by air, but I won't feel truly safe until we're clear of Iranian airspace.*

Three dots appeared as Jasmine typed her response: *I understand. We're on our way to the village now. The bus has these strange windows that turn opaque for security. The girls were startled at first.*

Kyra smiled, recalling what Max had told her after his call with Kian. *Max mentioned you're going to look at houses.*

That's the plan. The girls are going to help choose. They were nervous about leaving the penthouse, so I told them we were just visiting for now. I'm hoping once they see the village, they'll want to stay, and I'll just ask someone to bring their things over.

Kyra understood Jasmine's reasoning, but she wondered if that was the best way to handle it. *Maybe they need a proper goodbye to the penthouse first? It was their safe place after their ordeal. They might need closure.*

You're right. I didn't think of that. The three dots started dancing again, and then the message appeared: *Have you told your sisters who you really are yet?*

The question made Kyra's stomach tighten. *Not yet. They still think I'm Jasmine, Kyra's daughter.*

The girls will want to speak with their mothers when they find out they're safe, Jasmine wrote. *You need to tell them before that.*

I know. I'm just gathering my thoughts first. I'll let them talk with their mothers after I explain everything to my sisters.

The three dots appeared again. *Call me when you're ready. The girls are going to be over the moon.*

I will, Kyra promised. *Send me pictures of the houses you're considering. I can't believe I'm finally going to have a real home. Oh! And if possible, try to choose houses that are close together.*

She put her phone down just as Max returned with two steaming cups of coffee. He handed one to her, their fingers brushing in the exchange, and Kyra felt that familiar spark between them.

"Thank you," she said, taking a sip. It was perfect

—strong and black, just as she preferred. "You remembered."

Max settled into the seat beside her. "I remember everything about you."

He had mastered the art of delivering simple statements that somehow carried the weight of poetry.

"Jasmine says that the girls were nervous about leaving the penthouse," she told him, changing the subject.

Max nodded. "That's not surprising. They were clinging to the first place that offered them safety after what they'd been through."

"That's what I said." She smiled at their synchronicity. "Jasmine told them it's just a visit, hoping they'll fall in love with the village and want to stay."

"That's very possible," Max said. "The village is beautiful, and the community is great. They will feel at home right away."

Kyra wasn't sure about that. The girls had grown up in a very different society, but as the saying went, getting used to good things was easy. They would love to have a world of opportunities open to them with no gender-based discrimination and restrictions.

"I think you are right, but it's not going to happen overnight. It's a big change for them." She chuckled. "I can only imagine them putting on a swimming suit for the first time in their lives and jumping into the pool."

Max nodded. "I bet. I've seen those ridiculous photos of women getting into the water clothed from head to toe. It's like they want to erase women from existence." He let out a breath. "It's the teachings of Mortdh made manifest. He was the original misogynist."

What was he talking about? "Who's Mortdh?"

"Mortdh was a powerful god who had an arranged engagement to our clan mother. She chose to marry another, her truelove mate, and Mortdh felt scorned. He was insane to start with, but that must have pushed him over the edge. His son Navuh is the leader of the Doomers, and he carries on his father's legacy of rabid hatred for women." He snorted derisively. "Although truth be told, he's only pretending to believe in that crap because it serves his purposes. Apparently, he loves his mate, and although he has a harem full of concubines, he never touches any of them."

"The definition of insanity is that it doesn't make sense, so he can love his wife and hate all other women and somehow justify it to himself." Kyra took another sip of her coffee. "But how do you know that he loves her? Do you have spies in the Doomers' stronghold?"

"In a way, yes, we do." Max smiled. "I love how you always think like a warrior." He leaned over and kissed her cheek. "I love everything about you."

"Same here." She looked into his eyes and suddenly realized that they had started talking about loving each other as if it were a given.

It had just happened.

"I love everything about you. From your sarcastic humor to your enormous heart and everything in between."

His eyes were glowing as he stared back at her. "Fates, Kyra. I want to kiss you so badly. Do you think we can sneak into the bathroom together without your sisters noticing?"

And just like that, the serious moment was gone and she burst out laughing. "We could, if Yamanu was here and shrouded us. Regrettably, he's on the other plane."

Max groaned. "I don't think I ever missed the bastard as much as I miss him now."

"He's not a bastard." She playfully flicked his arm. "I like Yamanu." She smiled. "My sisters like him too. I need to tell them that he's taken."

"Among all the other things you need to tell them." Max leaned over and planted a quick kiss on her cheek. "For now, it will have to do. Anyway, back to your sisters, there are plenty of eligible bachelors in the village."

Nodding, Kyra sipped her coffee and thought how long it would take her sisters to shed the shackles of their oppressive past and embrace their newfound freedoms. The new houses were a good start.

"I've never had a real home, not that I can

remember anyway. The resistance camps were always temporary."

"You'll have one now." Max took her hand. "A place of your own, your family nearby. It's one of the best things about the village—the sense of belonging. The same is true for our castle in Scotland. It's a smaller community, but with most everyone living in the castle, it's like one big family."

"It sounds wonderful," Kyra said softly. Then, a thought struck her, and she felt a strange hollowness open in her chest. "I had a home and a family once. I just can't remember it."

Max's expression didn't change, but she caught the subtle tightening of his fingers around his coffee cup. "Yes, you did."

"I have—had—a husband." The notion was abstract, disconnected from any emotional reality she could access. "Should I go see him?"

Max set his cup down carefully. "We can't let Boris see you and keep his memories of that encounter, for obvious reasons, so what's the point? It will just cause him distress. And I'm not saying that because I'm jealous or anything like that."

"What if I wear a disguise to make myself look older? I'm sure Eva can do that for me. I feel like I need closure. Like he does. After all, we have a daughter together."

Max considered that for a moment. "That could be done. If Eva can make you look twenty years older, seeing you will be a great relief for Boris. He blames himself for your death."

She leaned over and rested her head on his shoulder. "You are incredible, you know that?"

"Of course." He puffed out his chest. "I'm Maximilian the Great."

"Would you come with me to see Boris?"

"Naturally. He is nearly bald and pudgy, but I'm still a little jealous of the history you two shared." He took a long breath. "I was in his head. I've seen the love he still has for you. And even though I feel sorry for him, I won't let him take you away from me."

She chuckled. "As if that could ever happen. I just want closure. Besides, he's married, right?"

"That never stopped any human from lusting after another woman, and I'm not about to let him lust after you. You are going to wear that fat suit when you meet him."

She cast him a glare that would have terrified most men. "Don't even joke about it. I come from a place where women are considered evil temptations and men place the burden of their own desires on them, forcing them to cover themselves from head to toe."

"I'm sorry," he said solemnly. "I keep forgetting you came from Iran and that you had to live with the restrictions and the oppression and fight for your rights."

She let out a breath. "I'm sorry for snapping at you

like that. I just hope to never even look at that fat suit again."

3 6

FENELLA

As the elevator doors slid open, they were greeted by an enthusiastic blonde woman with a body that looked like it had been specifically designed to make other women feel inadequate. She was dressed in a tailored skirt suit that hugged every curve, balanced on sky-high heels that should have been impossible to walk in, and her hair was styled into a perfectly sleek French twist.

"Welcome, welcome to the village!" she trilled, her voice carrying across the underground garage with theatrical projection. "I'm Ingrid, the clan's interior designer and housing coordinator."

Fenella instantly disliked her. Anyone that well put together and cheerful had to be hiding something sinister beneath their glossy exterior.

"I'm so sorry the full welcome committee couldn't be here," Ingrid continued, managing to sound both apologetic and thrilled at once. "We'll have a proper reception when the rest of the family arrives. So much excitement! New residents are such a treat!"

Jasmine stepped forward, extending her hand. "Thank you for meeting us, Ingrid. The girls are so excited to see the village and check out potential residences."

"Of course they are!" Ingrid took Jasmine's hand in both of hers. "And I have some absolutely perfect options for you. But first, introductions are in order." She turned to Fenella. "You must be Fenella." Ingrid offered her hand.

"Nice to meet you." Fenella shook it, surprised by the strength of Ingrid's grip, before reminding herself that everyone in the village was immortal and just as strong as she was.

The female moved to shake the girls' hands, addressing each one by name, which meant that she'd prepared ahead of time, and that made Fenella dislike her a little less.

People who were willing to put in the work deserved credit.

"Shall we begin with the tour?" Ingrid pressed the button for the elevator with a finger that was topped by a very long, elaborately decorated nail.

The designer noticed her looking, smiled and offered a better view of her fingernail. "I've had them done today." She cast a sidelong glance at Jasmine. "Angelica did them for me. Aren't they fabulous?"

"They are," Jasmine agreed just as the elevator doors opened.

Fenella detected a note of something there, wondering who Angelica was.

"This lift will take us directly to the glass pavilion," Ingrid explained as they stepped inside.

The elevator was spacious and silent, rising so smoothly that Fenella barely felt the movement. When the doors opened, they stepped into what could only be described as a glass jewel box perched on a mountaintop.

"Bloody hell," Fenella muttered under her breath.

The pavilion was made completely out of glass, offering views of the village beyond that were steeped in greenery. The morning sunlight streamed in, making the polished stone floor gleam like water.

"Wow," Laleh breathed. "It's beautiful!"

Along the perimeter of the space, illuminated glass cases displayed an array of artifacts—ancient-looking pottery, stone tools, fragments of what appeared to be clay tablets and several statues of different sizes.

Arezoo approached one of the displays, peering at a clay tablet covered in hieroglyphs. "What are these?"

Ingrid walked over to her in her impossible heels. "One of our residents is an amateur archaeologist. These are some of his finds from digs. He has so many of them and it would be a shame to keep this treasure in storage accumulating dust, so we've turned this space into a private museum for our village. The displays are changed every couple of months, so it never gets old." She chuckled. "Well, older than it already is."

"Are those real?" Donya asked, pressing her nose against the glass case containing a necklace made of lapis lazuli.

"Very real and very valuable," Ingrid confirmed. "Some pieces date back thousands of years."

Fenella wandered over to a case containing a small bronze figurine that reminded her of artifacts she'd seen in museums in Greece. "Seems risky to keep valuable artifacts in glass boxes."

Ingrid's perfect smile didn't falter. "No one in our village takes what doesn't belong to them." She frowned. "Well, except that whole episode with Drova, but that was just teenage rebellion." She turned to the girls. "Despite all the mischief, Drova is a good kid. You've met her. She was part of the rescue team that got you out of that horrible place."

"I don't remember much," Arezoo said. "Was she the one with the wounded shoulder?"

"Yes." Ingrid smiled. "That's the one."

"We owe her a big thank you," Arezoo said.

"Oh, well. I'm sure she will appreciate it." Ingrid headed toward a pair of sliding doors. "Let's continue our tour, shall we?"

As they stepped outside, Fenella was struck by the perfect temperature—warm without being hot, with a gentle breeze that carried the scent of pine and something floral.

"This way to the square." Ingrid led them along a path paved with natural stone.

The path opened onto a plaza surrounded by several buildings and meticulously landscaped gardens.

"This is our village square," Ingrid explained, performing a graceful turn that somehow incorporated a sweeping gesture toward the surrounding structures. "That two-story building over there houses our administrative offices. Next to it is our clinic. And that," she pointed to a charming outdoor café with wrought iron tables and chairs, "is where many gather for coffee, sandwiches, and pastries. When it is closed, you can still get all those things from the vending machines in the back." She motioned behind the small structure that was the service center of the café.

There, along a green wall, stood four vending machines. One for hot drinks, one for cold, one with sandwiches and pastries, and the fourth with an assortment of snacks.

Several people were seated at the café, sipping from steaming paper cups and engaged in conversation. They glanced up as the group passed, offering friendly nods and waves.

Ell-rom leaned over to whisper something to Jasmine, and when she nodded, he turned to the rest of them. "I'm going to leave you alone to continue your tour. I want to visit my twin sister."

Oh, that was sweet of him. He was such a nice guy.

"Perhaps you can invite Morelle over to the café later," Jasmine suggested.

He nodded. "I'll offer. Perhaps Brandon would like to join us as well."

"Of course." Jasmine kissed his cheek.

After he left, Ingrid kept walking. "We keep the village pedestrian friendly. Most of the time we just walk from place to place, but we use golf carts for transporting goods or luggage. They're quiet and don't disrupt the peaceful atmosphere."

As they continued past the square, Fenella noticed a playground where several children were playing.

"Most of the younger kids in the village are from recent arrivals," Ingrid said, following her gaze. "Aren't they marvelous?"

Several mothers were supervising the kids from nearby benches. There was something different about their appearance that was evident even from a distance. They too offered nods as the group passed, but no smiles.

Fenella remembered then where she'd seen people who looked like them. The warriors that had saved her, Kyra, and the girls had those enormous black eyes and willowy bodies.

Their kind didn't smile much, and she'd noticed that already.

"Are these mothers and children the same people as the warriors who rescued us?"

Smiling, Jasmine laid her hand on her forearm. "They are."

"Does everyone here know each other?" Fenella asked. "Seems like a fishbowl."

Jasmine nudged her. "The village is larger than it appears. There are several different sections."

"Precisely," Ingrid said. "But we do know each other despite having nearly five hundred residents at this time."

"That's not so many," Azadeh remarked.

"Quality over quantity, darling," Ingrid said with a wink. "Now, let me show you the residential area where we have homes available for your family."

They followed her down another winding path that led away from the village center. The surroundings became more wooded, with homes nestled tastefully among the trees. Unlike the cookie-cutter developments Fenella had seen in suburban areas, these houses had character while maintaining a cohesive aesthetic.

"All our homes are single-story," Ingrid explained as they walked. "There are several exterior designs that repeat throughout the village, but with slight changes of colors and different plants in the front yards, we ensured that each house has its individual flavor. Most have either two or three bedrooms, and some include a detached guest house."

The girls had grown increasingly animated as they progressed through the village, their initial wariness giving way to curiosity and excitement.

Even Arezoo, who typically maintained a stoic demeanor, looked impressed.

"Here we are," Ingrid announced, stopping before a cluster of houses. "These previously housed Guardians who have since relocated to another section of the village. They're in perfect condition— barely lived in at all."

The homes had a Mediterranean aesthetic— stucco walls in warm cream tones and wood doors with stone surrounds. They looked brand new to Fenella's eye, without a crack, peel, or discoloration in sight.

"Aren't they beautiful?" Jasmine asked. "Girls, what do you think?"

"Can we look inside?" Laleh asked.

"Of course!" Ingrid opened the door. "Let's start with this one. It's a three-bedroom."

"No locks?" Fenella asked.

"No need." Ingrid led them inside. "If you want, you can install a chain to lock it from the inside, but no one bothers. As I said, the village is very safe."

The interior was beautifully done. Earth tones, soft fabrics, and decorative pieces were perfectly coordinated without looking matchy-matchy. It required a real talent to put things together like that.

"This is beautiful," Donya breathed, running her hand along a smooth granite countertop. "It's like something from the movies."

"Ingrid did all the interiors," Jasmine said.

"You have excellent taste," Fenella admitted

grudgingly. "Very coordinated without looking too obvious. I could never accomplish something like this."

Ingrid beamed at the compliments. "Thank you. I strive for timeless elegance combined with modern comfort. Each home has its own character while maintaining cohesion with the village aesthetic."

As they moved through the bedrooms, the girls whispered excitedly.

The two smaller bedrooms each contained a queen-sized bed, while the master suite had a king.

"You two will share," Arezoo told Laleh and Donya, who nodded enthusiastically.

"We can replace the queen bed with two singles in whichever room the girls prefer," Ingrid offered.

After touring several more houses with similar layouts, some with only two bedrooms and others with three, the girls had reached a consensus on their favorites. Their excitement was palpable as they discussed which bedroom would belong to whom.

"What about me?" Fenella asked Ingrid. "Do I get my own place, or am I bunking with one of the happy families?"

"I can arrange a house for you alone, though most single residents share accommodations."

"I don't mind sharing," Fenella said. "I'm not even sure I'll stay long-term. Looks nice enough, but a bit too contained for my taste."

"You'll find there's more to village life than first

appears," Ingrid assured her with a knowing smile. "Would you like to see more housing options?"

Fenella considered it for a moment, then shook her head. "Everything looks great, and I'm not picky." There was no point getting attached to a place she probably wouldn't use for long.

Once the girls had decided not only on which houses would be theirs but also which would be perfect for the aunts and cousins, and Jasmine had snapped at least a hundred pictures with her phone, Ingrid led them to a different section of the village.

"Just to prove to you that the village isn't boring, I want to show you the bar and the restaurant." She showed them something that looked like a hobbit residence. "My partner runs the bar," Ingrid said with evident pride. "It's only open on weekends, but it's very popular. We have live music occasionally when the boys are up to entertaining us, and the cocktails are always excellent." She smiled at Jasmine. "Maybe you could sing for us sometime?"

"I would love to."

"Perhaps this place isn't completely hopeless after all," Fenella muttered.

Next, Ingrid showed them the village's only restaurant, an elegant space with both indoor and outdoor seating areas.

"Callie serves dinner only," she explained. "Perhaps if she can get more help in the kitchen, she could open for lunch as well."

"Don't look at me." Fenella raised her hands in the air. "I can't cook, and I'm a menace in the kitchen."

By the time they'd completed their circuit and returned to the café in the village square, Fenella's feet were aching, and her stomach was growling. The girls, however, seemed energized by everything they'd seen, chattering excitedly as they combined two tables into one and arranged chairs around them.

"I'll order for everyone," Jasmine offered. "Any special requests?"

As the others placed their orders, Fenella scanned the café's other patrons. Several males were sitting at nearby tables, and she didn't miss the appreciative glances sent her way. One particularly fit specimen with dark hair and impressive shoulders caught her eye and offered a friendly smile.

Fenella smiled back, enjoying the familiar dance of attraction. If all the village men looked like that, perhaps staying wouldn't be such a hardship after all.

"Oh!" Ingrid exclaimed suddenly, reaching into her handbag. "I nearly forgot. This is for you, Fenella."

She produced a white box and handed it over. "A phone courtesy of William."

"For me?"

"All clan members get one," Ingrid said. "It's secure, encrypted, and preloaded with essential contacts."

"I'll show you how to use it," Jasmine offered, seeing Fenella's overwhelmed expression.

"Thanks," Fenella muttered, examining the device. "It has been a while since I owned anything more complicated than a burner phone."

As Jasmine began sending pictures of the houses to Kyra, and the girls continued their excited conversation about their new homes, Fenella's thoughts returned to Din. With her own phone, she could surprise him with a call. If he had her new number, he could call her directly instead of going through Jasmine.

She glanced again at the attractive man who'd smiled at her earlier. He was still watching her with not-so-subtle interest. Fenella raised an eyebrow in acknowledgment, then deliberately turned her attention back to the phone in her hands.

Din deserved a fair chance, she decided. After all, he'd supposedly carried a torch for her for five decades. That kind of dedication deserved at least a phone call.

37

KYRA

Kyra tensed as she heard footsteps approaching from the back of the plane. She turned around to see Soraya making her way over.

Her sister stopped by her seat. "When are you going to tell us what's really going on?"

Kyra took a deep breath. "I'd like to wait until the children are asleep so we can talk freely. There is a lot to cover, and most of it is not for their ears."

Soraya studied her face for a long moment before finally nodding. "Makes sense. The children have been through enough today already." Then she squeezed Kyra's shoulder. "I'm not a patient woman, but I'll contain my curiosity until then."

Kyra smiled. "Thank you."

She watched her sister walk back to her seat. The confrontation had been briefer than Kyra had expected, but it was only a momentary reprieve, and the full reckoning still awaited her.

How was she going to even start? With the past that she couldn't remember? She'd reconstructed some of it from what Jasmine and Durhad had said, but it might be so full of mistakes and inconsistencies that it would sound like lies to her sisters.

"Are you okay?" Max asked. "You look frazzled. That's not an expression I'm used to seeing on you."

She smiled. "Navigating family dynamics is scarier to me than facing Doomers and dodging bullets."

He chuckled. "I hear you. I'd rather fight than listen to my mother's lectures."

"Is she that bad?"

He laughed. "Not at all. I like to exaggerate. But she's fierce and opinionated, and she's not happy about me returning to the Guardian Force. She liked it most when I was pursuing an acting and singing career."

"I can understand that," Kyra said. "She wants to see you safe and happy and not engaged in dangerous activities that expose you to the ugliness of this world instead of its beauty." She sighed. "The problem is that once you are exposed to it, you can't in good conscience do nothing about it. Not if you have the ability to make a positive change."

His eyes started blazing again. "I love you so much." He lifted her hand to his lips, turned it around, and kissed her palm. "The Fates made a perfect match by bringing us together. You get me, and I get you. It's so rare."

With her throat full with emotion, all she could do was nod. It hadn't even crossed her mind that Max's acceptance of her being a warrior was unique. Most men, especially the good ones, wouldn't want the woman they loved on the frontlines. It went against their instinctive need to protect. But Max appreciated and loved her enough to ignore the instinct and support her choices.

"I love you too. Not many men would be okay with what I do."

He was about to say something when her phone chimed, and a series of messages from Jasmine appeared on the screen, each accompanied by several photos.

"Jasmine is sending me pictures of the homes they toured." She lifted the phone so Max could see.

The first showed a Mediterranean-style house with warm stucco walls and flowering vines climbing over the decorative surround of the arched entrance. *This is the one Soraya's girls chose,* Jasmine's text read. *Three bedrooms with a lovely backyard.*

More images followed: a smaller but equally charming two-bedroom for Rana and Azadeh, two three-bedroom options for Yasmin and Parisa to choose from, and finally, two additional two-bedroom houses positioned across from a gravel path.

These last two would be for us, Jasmine had written.

One for me and Ell-rom, and the other for you and Max, or just you, if things between you don't go the way I think they will. They're all on the same street—or "path," I should say since there aren't actual roads in the village. Most people walk everywhere or use golf carts for longer distances or carrying things.

"Things are definitely going in that direction," Max murmured in her ear. "Text her back and tell her that we are madly in love."

Kyra turned to look at him, admiring how gorgeous he was, how perfect, how accommodating. "I might just do that."

She went back to scrolling through the images again, lingering on the last two. All were beautiful—a perfect blend of warmth and elegance.

"What do you think?" Max said. "Which one do you like best?"

"They're all beautiful." Kyra angled the phone so he could see better. "I never imagined that I would get to live in such luxury." She looked back at him. "With the man I love. It almost makes everything I've been through worth it."

"I wish you didn't have to suffer so much." Max lifted their conjoined hands and kissed her knuckles. "Let's just be thankful that this is over, and we are out of Iranian airspace."

"We are? When did that happen?" The pilot hadn't announced it.

"A while ago. We are flying over Europe, which,

for now, is still friendly territory. Give it a couple of decades, and the picture might change."

He wasn't wrong, but she didn't want to think about that right now. These were happy moments, and there weren't enough of those to go around for her to squander.

"I'm sorry," he said. "Let's talk about the house. The two-bedroom model means there is room for expansion. Maybe we will get lucky and make a little occupant for that spare room?"

Kyra's gut twisted with longing. "I would love that. Jasmine's childhood was stolen from me. I want to experience motherhood."

His expression turned serious. "After we get settled in, you will probably get a summons to see the Clan Mother. She needs your help to find her beloved. She also might be able to retrieve some of those memories you've lost."

In all the commotion of saving her family, she'd forgotten about Syssi's vision and her own part in helping the Clan Mother. "I hope I won't disappoint her, and as for my memories, I hope she can retrieve them selectively."

She'd had this conversation before with Jasmine, but it seemed like it had happened in another lifetime. So much had happened since.

"I don't know if that can be done," Max said. "But the Clan Mother is kind and merciful, and she will do her best to help you."

Kyra nodded. "That begs the question of what I'm

supposed to do after I help find her husband. I need a job, an occupation."

"First, you'll want time with your sisters, of course, getting to know them again. And when you're ready, there's always a place for you in the Guardian Force."

Kyra raised an eyebrow. "Do you think they'd accept me?"

"Are you kidding? With your experience? After what we encountered on this mission, it's clear that the Brotherhood has a much stronger presence in Iran than we realized. We'll need reconnaissance intelligence. Your knowledge and experience, not to mention your contacts with the resistance, would be invaluable."

The prospect sent a thrill of purpose through Kyra. Fighting alongside Max and using her skills to keep the darkness from consuming more and more of the light felt right.

"I'd like that a lot," she admitted.

"You'd be more than useful," Max said. "You'd be essential." He squeezed her hand. "But don't feel rushed. We are immortal and we think in immortal timelines. Take all the time you need to adjust."

Kyra nodded even though she didn't share his opinion about the timeline. To stop the world from spiraling in the wrong direction required all hands on deck, so to speak, and there was no time to waste.

MAX

K yra glanced back at where her family was sitting. "I think the kids are finally asleep. I should go talk to my sisters."

She seemed to be as enthusiastic about the upcoming discussion as Max would have been in her place. He would have done everything to avoid it and found someone else to do it for him.

Heck, maybe he could be that someone for Kyra?

Those weren't his sisters, he didn't have an emotional stake in this, not yet anyway, and he'd been immortal for much longer than Kyra. He could answer their questions better.

"I should come with you," he offered. "It will be easier coming from the both of us." He smiled. "After all, we need to even out the numbers for it to be fair. There are four of them and just one of you." He took her hand again. "You need me."

Kyra considered his offer for a moment, then

shook her head. "Maybe I can ask them to come here while you move back to watch over the kids."

"Me? A babysitter? You must be kidding."

Kyra pursed her lips. "You were good with the girls in the penthouse."

"That's because they are already young women. I know how to charm them. I'm clueless around younger kids, especially boys. I could be more helpful with providing proof and demonstrating abilities."

"You mean like when you showed my nieces, and it went so smoothly?"

Max winced at the memory. "Okay, that wasn't my best idea, but I doubt I will again encounter anyone as sharp and skeptical as Arezoo. That girl should become a prosecutor."

Kyra leaned closer to him. "If you haven't noticed, all my sisters are like that. They are smart and suspicious, and they don't take anything at face value."

"Oh, boy." He smoothed a hand over his hair. "I'm starting to think that I'm getting more than I bargained for. Four sisters-in-law with sharp minds and even sharper tongues were not part of the deal." He was teasing, of course, and given Kyra's amused expression, she knew that.

Could he love her any more?

"I'll protect you, big guy." She patted his shoulder. "You have nothing to fear with me by your side."

"That, I believe. So can I join in?"

Kyra nodded. "Let's do this."

As they started toward the back of the plane, Rana

rose to her feet and squeezed next to Soraya on one seat, vacating hers for them.

When Yasmin started to rise, Kyra put a hand on her shoulder. "Max and I can share one seat as well. They are very generously sized."

"I like sitting with Parisa." Yasmin stood up despite Kyra's hand on her shoulder. "Especially if what you are about to tell us is difficult to stomach."

So, Kyra hadn't exaggerated. Yasmin seemed the most mellow out of the four, and if she was so stubborn, Max could only imagine how difficult Soraya would be. She was the leader who the other sisters looked up to. If Kyra convinced her, the others would be easy.

"What I'm about to tell you is difficult to believe," Kyra said. "But some of it is hard to stomach as well. That's why I wanted to wait until the children were asleep."

Max waited for Kyra to sit in the chair Yasmin vacated before addressing the others. "Can I offer you ladies coffee?"

They seemed uncomfortable with his offer, all four turning their eyes to Kyra. In their culture, men didn't serve women, but that was precisely why he was offering to do it. The dismantling of oppression had started the moment these women had been whisked away.

"Thank you, Max. That would be lovely. Can you just bring the carafe here with cups for everyone? It will be easier that way."

"Great idea. And if anyone is hungry, the galley is stocked with prepared meals that just need warming up."

Soraya's eyes drifted to the teardrop hanging on a string around his neck. "This is a translation device, correct?"

Max nodded. They hadn't noticed it before in all the excitement of running away from the Doomers.

"I've never seen anything like that," Rana said. "Not even in movies."

"It's a newer invention." Max decided to hoof it out of there before they dragged him into revealing everything before Kyra had a chance.

"I'll be right back with that coffee," he said over his shoulder as he walked toward the galley.

"I've read the notes from my daughters," he heard Soraya say. "They said that they were rescued by the Kurdish resistance. Obviously, that's not true. You and your people are not Kurds."

"I was," he heard Kyra say softly. "For over two decades."

One of the sisters snorted. "What nonsense is this? You're too young."

"I'm much older than I look," Kyra said. "I'm about to turn fifty."

The long silence that followed was just enough time for Max to grab the coffee carafe that was still nearly full, put it on a tray along with a stack of paper cups, a bunch of sugar packets, and creamer, and head back.

KYRA

Coffee sloshed inside the carafe as Max made his way back, balancing it on a tray that also contained cups and various packets.

A smile tugged at her lips.

He moved slowly, not because there was turbulence or because he had difficulty balancing the tray. After all, immortals were very well coordinated, and especially a trained Guardian like Max. He was just being super careful and deliberate so as not to spook her sisters, treating them like a pack of wild animals that might bolt at any sudden movement.

She couldn't blame him. They were a little scary, but she appreciated that. Her sisters were not meek women, despite the way they had been raised and what had been expected from them in their stifling society.

Did they take after their mother?

A pang of sorrow pierced through Kyra's heart as she thought about the mother she couldn't remember and would never get to know. She'd passed away years ago, and Kyra wondered if it had been from sorrow over the daughter who had disappeared in America. She doubted very much that her father had shared with his wife what he had done. Her mother would have never agreed to that and would have found a way to get her out.

"Have I missed anything?" Max asked as he put the tray down on the pullout table between the seats.

"Not much." Kyra smiled at him. "I was just saying that I was with the Kurdish resistance for over two decades."

"That's impossible," Rana said, accepting a cup from Max with a nod of thanks. "You can't be older than twenty-five."

"I'm forty-nine," Kyra replied. "Soon to be fifty."

Parisa frowned, studying Kyra's face with that analytical gaze that seemed to be a family trait. "First, you said that you were Jasmine, Kyra's daughter. Then, when I challenged you about it, you said that we are related differently."

"I did say that." Kyra clasped her hands together. "The truth is too fantastic to reveal casually, and given the circumstances, I couldn't explain it at the time."

Soraya set her untouched coffee aside. "Just say whatever you need to say."

Kyra took a deep breath. This was it—the

moment she'd been rehearsing in her mind since they'd boarded the plane. "I am Kyra. Your eldest sister. Jasmine is my daughter, and she is with your daughters in America, taking care of them while I'm here, saving you from the same people who kidnapped them."

The silence that followed was suffocating. The four sisters exchanged glances—confusion, disbelief, and alarm passing between them like a current.

"If what you're saying is true, and you're Kyra, how can you look this young? Plastic surgery?"

It would have been so easy to say that, yes, plastic surgery made her look the same age as her daughter, but she needed to tell them all of it. "I don't age like other people."

"How come?" Rana asked, her eyes never leaving Kyra's face.

Yasmin leaned forward, her features still grief-stricken, but her gaze no less sharp. "Why would you make such an absurd claim? What do you want from us?"

"I want nothing from you except maybe rekindling the love we once had for each other," Kyra said. "Learn to know each other again. I know how it sounds, and frankly, if it hadn't happened to me, I wouldn't believe it either."

"Tell us something only Kyra would have known," Soraya challenged. "Something personal that she told me before leaving for the university."

Kyra's throat tightened. "I can't. I don't remember

anything from before I escaped the asylum. All my memories from my childhood and even my time in America are gone. I didn't even remember having a daughter until she found me in a military compound in Tahav."

"How convenient," Soraya said with a dismissive wave.

"No, not convenient at all," Kyra countered, heat rising in her voice. "You have no idea what I've been through, what was done to me. But the worst part was not knowing who I was and where I came from. I was fortunate to escape the asylum with rebel females who took me under their wings and led me to the resistance. If not for them, I would have been collected off the streets and brought back to that hell hole, that den of depravity and suffering."

The vehemence in her voice must have finally convinced her sisters of her sincerity, or maybe she'd just scared them into silence, but none of them said anything, and they all lowered their gazes.

"Perhaps I can help with some context," Max offered.

Kyra desperately needed to collect herself, so even though she had not planned on stopping at that point, she nodded. "Go ahead."

Her sisters turned their attention to him with varying degrees of wariness.

"Here is what we found out about Kyra when we investigated her disappearance on her daughter's behalf," Max began. "Kyra married an American while studying in the US and had a daughter with him. She changed her name, hoping to escape her father's detection. She told her husband that she feared her father would kill her when he discovered that she had married outside of the faith."

"Our father was strict, but he wasn't a fanatic," Yasmin protested.

Kyra's bitter laugh surprised even herself. "No? Then explain why he searched for me, dragged me away from my family, and committed me to an insane asylum."

The sisters fell silent again.

"According to what we've learned," Max continued, "your father somehow managed to get Kyra out of the US and into a mental institution in Tehran. He called in a favor from a very dark individual who was supposed to hypnotize and drug her until she forgot about her family in America."

"Is that even possible?" Rana asked, her voice barely above a whisper.

"I'm living proof that yes, it can be done. He wanted me to forget about my husband and daughter so I could be married off to someone of his choosing," Kyra said. "Someone who wouldn't mind marrying a woman who wasn't pure anymore but would pretend that she was, so our father's reputation wouldn't be tarnished. He probably found someone who owed him a favor."

Soraya's expression had grown increasingly troubled. "Our father was cold and ambitious. I can see him doing something like that."

"He was willing to erase me to preserve his honor," Kyra said. "He was a selfish monster."

Soraya nodded. "I'm prepared to suspend my disbelief and accept this part of your story. But what does it have to do with you staying young?"

"The man our father sent to erase my past took advantage of the situation," Kyra said. "He violated me repeatedly while I was drugged, and as an unexpected side effect, he induced my transition into immortality."

"Immortality?" Soraya shook her head, pushing herself to her feet. "Up until this point, I was willing to suspend disbelief, but this is absurd."

"Sit down, Soraya," Parisa said quietly. "Let's hear Kyra out."

"Why? So she can feed us more fairy tales about immortality and hypnotic amnesia?" Soraya remained standing, arms folded across her chest. "We've been through enough today without being subjected to these ridiculous claims."

Kyra turned to Max, desperation clawing at her chest. "Perhaps you can explain this part better than me."

Max nodded, setting his coffee aside and leaning forward, his expression earnest. "I know how this sounds. If I were in your position, I'd be equally skeptical. But the world is far stranger than you suspect, and humans share this planet with other intelligent beings. Some of them are good, and some are evil. Kyra has been unlucky enough to encounter the evil kind." He leaned over and wrapped his arm around Kyra's shoulders. "But she has been found by the good ones, and things are only going to get better from here."

40

MAX

Yasmin made a soft sound of incredulity. "You expect us to believe that you're what— vampires? Aliens?"

"Not vampires." Max chuckled. "But we do have enhanced strength, speed, and longevity. Aliens are closer to the truth, but you are just as alien as I am or as Kyra is. We are mostly human with some alien DNA mixed in." He took Kyra's hand and gave it a light squeeze. "The reason you and your kids were targeted by the bad players in this shadow world, which I'll explain in a moment, is that you are all dormant carriers of genes that can make you immortal."

He'd expected the gaping and the wide eyes, and he braced for having to keep explaining until the truth knocked them over the head. On the one hand, it was good that people were skeptical and didn't believe every piece of nonsense someone was trying to sell them, but on the other hand, he wished there was an easier way to do this.

He turned to Kyra. "I think Jasmine should make a movie explaining this so we wouldn't have to go through this over and over again. We need to come out with irrefutable proof."

"Immortality doesn't exist outside of religious texts and fantasy novels," Soraya insisted.

"I thought the same thing," Kyra said. "Until I realized that I'd gotten so strong that I could break through chains and tear down doors, and that I could eavesdrop on conversations I shouldn't be able to, given the distance. Then I joined the resistance, and despite years of fighting and constant exposure to danger, I wasn't dying, and I wasn't aging. Injuries that should have killed me healed in minutes. It was difficult to hide from my team, and they suspected that I was different. I didn't know why I was that way, and I suspected that I'd been subjected to some experimental drugs or genetic manipulation. I didn't know that I had always had that in me, and that the scumbag who my father asked to brainwash me into forgetting who I was and turning me into an empty vessel was an immortal who induced my transition to immortality. "

"Even if—and this is an enormous if—we were to believe this," Soraya said, "where is your proof? Where is your evidence that you're our sister Kyra? You look like her, but that's not proof either. Do you have birthmarks that you can show us?"

Max shook his head. "Even if she did have any blemishes like that before, they would have disappeared following her transition."

"How—" Soraya began.

"Convenient," Kyra finished for her. "I know." She slipped the two rings from her fingers—the ones Jasmine had given her. "Do you recognize these?"

Recognition flared in Parisa's eyes. "I forgot you showed them to me. One was our grandmother's and the other our mother's."

"These could have been stolen," Soraya argued, though with less conviction.

"What about this?" Kyra asked, pulling the small velvet pouch from her pocket. She opened it, spreading the tarot cards on the small table between them. "These were mine. I left them with my daughter when I disappeared."

Parisa leaned forward, examining the cards with a frown. "I don't remember you having tarot cards."

"I must have gotten them in America," Kyra said. "But I thought it was worth a try. I don't remember where and when I got them."

The youngest sister looked troubled, her gaze flicking between Kyra's face and the artifacts spread before them.

"Those things prove nothing," Soraya insisted. "Show us something that can prove you are immortal."

Max was ready to volunteer one of his tricks, but Kyra lifted her hand. "I'll do it." She pulled a dagger from one of the pockets of her cargo pants, and before anyone could even ask her what she was doing, she nicked the palm of her hand and held it out for her sisters to see. "Watch how fast it heals and then try to explain that."

The women were compelled to watch, and as the wound started closing before their eyes, Rana gasped. Yasmin murmured something that sounded like an incantation, and Soraya remained motionless, watching the wound until no trace of it remained.

"Convinced now?" Kyra asked.

"That shouldn't have been possible." Soraya lifted a pair of awed eyes to Kyra. "You really aren't human. Not anymore."

Kyra let out a relieved breath. "I'm not, and neither are you. You can all turn immortal, and so can your children. My Jasmine turned immortal just recently."

"How?" Rana asked. "You said that the bad guy from the asylum violated you and inadvertently induced you. Does that mean that the genes are activated through intercourse with an immortal?"

These women were really sharp. They didn't miss much.

"Yes," Kyra admitted, "but that's not the whole story. Adult female Dormants are activated by having unprotected sex with an immortal male and getting bitten by him. Males get activated by a bite alone, but they have to fight an immortal male to get him aggressive enough to bite them. Max's people have a special induction ceremony for that."

Yasmin's hand flew to her chest. "So, we will have to do it in front of people?"

"Hold on." Soraya lifted a hand to stop her sister, who sounded hysterical. "I think only the males have a special ceremony, am I right?"

"Correct," Max said.

"Now to the more important question," Soraya continued. "What do you mean by biting?"

"Oh, that." Kyra cast him a sidelong glance. "That's probably where the vampire stories come from. Immortal males have fangs and venom, and they bite during sex and while fighting other immortal males. Naturally, the venom produced is different depending on the trigger, and the one triggered by desire is much less potent than the one triggered by aggression. That's why a bite alone is not enough to induce a female."

That was actually one of the best explanations Max had heard, and he wanted to compliment Kyra on it, when he felt four sets of eyes drilling holes into his scalp.

"What?" he asked.

"I don't see fangs," Soraya said. "I assume that you are immortal, right?"

"Yes, of course." He rubbed the back of his neck, suddenly feeling like a bug under a microscope. "My fangs elongate in response to the triggers Kyra mentioned. Other times, they look like regular human teeth. Just slightly sharper."

"Then kiss her." Soraya waved a hand. "Get excited. I want to see those fangs."

Kyra's cheeks turned red. "You can't be serious. Max can't just kiss me here in front of you while you are all watching. It's indecent."

"Huh." Rana snorted. "We've seen you snuggling and kissing each other's cheeks for over an hour. We were joking about you acting like a couple of teenagers and not the adults you are."

"Your sisters are terrible," Max murmured. "Who would have ever suspected that they have such dirty minds?"

"Stop stalling," Parisa said. "Just kiss Kyra already."

"Not in front of you, you bunch of scoundrels." He rose to his feet and offered Kyra a hand up. "We can kiss in the galley and come back to show them my fangs."

41

KYRA

As Max took Kyra's hand, leading her toward the galley, she could feel her sisters' eyes on them and imagined the smirks on their faces.

Once they were alone, Max shook his head. "The last thing I expected was for your sisters to be a bunch of perverted ladies looking for cheap thrills."

Kyra giggled. "I know, right? Who would have thought." She stepped closer to him, looping her arms around his neck. "Maybe they were always like that, which makes me regret losing my memories of them even more."

"No wonder you turned out to be a rebel. They're a far cry from the meek, obedient, and submissive women I imagined them to be."

"The resistance is full of women like them. Women who have to pretend to be less than they are.

But let's not talk about that now." She smiled. "I don't mind giving them what they want this once."

"Oh really?" His eyes darkened. "And what do you want, Kyra?"

Her heart raced, the pendant warming against her skin—not in warning but in harmony with her rising body temperature. "Less talk and more kissing, big guy. Make it good for me."

"So bossy," he murmured, scooping her into his arms with effortless strength and lifting her until her feet no longer touched the floor. His lips landed on hers in a searing kiss that was hungry, demanding, possessive, almost desperate.

Kyra responded with equal fervor, decades of suppressed desire bubbling to the surface. She lifted her leg, wrapping it around his torso to pull him closer and rub her softening core against his hardness, her fingers threading through his hair. She felt something change—his teeth grazing her lower lip, longer, sharper.

It excited her.

Max groaned, or rather growled, a sound that was barely human, sending a shiver of anticipation down her spine.

She didn't remember being human and experiencing pleasure as one, but she was sure it wasn't as intense as the passion she was feeling now. Her immortal body magnified every sensation beyond what her human body could have ever been capable of.

She wanted to tear Max's clothes off his body, to have him do the same to her and take her right there on the floor or against the airplane door.

When a distant chorus of giggles penetrated their bubble of lust, Kyra pulled back, her breathing ragged.

"We must have been louder than we realized," she whispered.

Max's eyes were glowing with inner light, and his fangs were extended, sharp, and gleaming in the cabin's soft lighting. For a moment, Kyra forgot all about her sisters and was about to resume what they had interrupted, but Max broke the spell by chuckling. "At least I've got the proof they want." He glanced down at the very distinct outline in his pants. "But they are going to get more than they bargained for."

"They deserve it." Kyra couldn't take her eyes off him. He was magnificent in this state—dangerous and beautiful and all hers.

The thought sent another wave of heat through her body.

She suddenly felt shameless. Why should she be embarrassed about anything when her harpy sisters cornered her like that?

"And what do you deserve, Kyra?" Max asked.

"All of this." She smoothed her hands over his chest, going all the way down to where his erection was straining under his pants and giving it a light squeeze.

"Kyra," he groaned, gripping her wrists with his hands. "As much as I want to take you right here and now, we have to wait until we have actual privacy." He released her wrists.

"I know." She lifted her hands to his face and caressed the soft stubble. "I'm getting impatient."

He snorted. "Want to talk about it?" He took her hand. "I promise that it will be worth the wait. Now, let's show your sisters my fangs."

When they returned to where her sisters were waiting, Max bared his fangs with a wide grin. "Satisfied?" he asked, his glowing eyes and extended fangs on full display.

Yasmin gasped, a hand flying to her mouth. Rana leaned forward, her eyes wide with fascination, while Parisa simply stared, speechless for once.

"That's... that's not a trick," Soraya said, her voice faint. "You really are not human."

"Not entirely, no," Max agreed. "Neither is Kyra, nor are you, nor your daughters or your sons."

"So, we are in danger because of this potential?" Yasmin asked. "But why? Do those evil immortals want to kill others that are not part of their organization? Why do they seek us?"

Kyra turned to Max. "Do you want to answer that? You are better qualified than I am in Doomer matters."

Max's fangs had receded already, but his eyes were still slightly glowing, making him look other-worldly and even more beautiful than usual.

"There are two groups of immortals," Max said. "But we are all descendants of the mythical gods. I could say that they were just powerful aliens, exiles from another planet, but that wouldn't be the entire story because the gods really created humans. They combined their genetic material with that of primitive humanoid creatures and jumpstarted the modern, intelligent human. If not for them, it would have taken millions of years for evolution to do this."

Kyra listened to Max's story, fascinated by all the additional details she was learning, but eventually fatigue overtook her, and she dozed off. She awoke to hear him talking about the Brotherhood's breeding program.

"They want your sons to turn them into immortal warriors for their army and your daughters to remain in their dormant state and fortify their breeding program so they will give birth to as many children as possible, producing more warriors for the army and more breeders for the harem. When females turn immortal, their fertility rate drops significantly. That's why they don't let the girls transition."

"That's horrible," Soraya said. "Pure evil."

A collective shudder passed through her sisters as they processed the implications.

"That's why we had to get all of you out," Max added. "In the village, you'll be protected. They can't reach you there."

"What about Jade?" Yasmin said. "She looks different, and the other two female warriors that watched us look really alien. They were wearing dark sunglasses to hide their alien eyes, but Asuka forgot to put them on after she showered."

"They are fully alien," Kyra said. "The Kra-ell are a species from the same planet as the gods."

Rana gave a hysterical little laugh. "Aliens. Of course. Why not? We've already accepted vampires and immortality. Why not throw aliens into the mix?"

"I'm having a hard time believing it all," Parisa said. "But I'm trying. I just need time to internalize all of this."

"If what you say about the evil Brotherhood is true, we all need protection," Yasmin said.

"It's true," Kyra assured them. "Everything we've told you is the truth. I wish it weren't, but it is."

"So, what happens now?" Rana asked. "We go to this village, and then what? Do we become like you? Do our children?"

"Whether or not you do will be your choice," Max said. "And you don't need to make it right away. Regrettably, you can't take too long, though. The older you get, the more difficult the transition. It's not an easy process. As for the children, the boys can transition as soon as they are thirteen, but the girls need to wait until they are adults for obvious reasons."

Parisa chuckled. "I was seventeen when our father married me off. Your idea of maturity is different than ours."

Kyra gaped at her sister. "You're not suggesting the girls should attempt to transition at seventeen."

Parisa shrugged. "If they find a nice immortal boy they want to marry, then why not?"

Max shook his head. "The clan considers seventeen as the age of consent, but in America, it's eighteen, and I suggest that you stick to that."

Parisa regarded him with an amused expression on her face. "Let's leave it up to the girls. If they want to do this sooner, would you stop them?"

He swallowed. "No adult male member of the clan would ever seduce a young girl like that. If she chooses to have sex with someone her age or close to it, it's her decision, but our unattached male immortals are either too young or too old. We have several young Kra-ell, purebloods and hybrids, but they can't induce transition. Only immortals can do that."

Parisa frowned. "Why is that?"

"The Kra-ell venom is less potent, and as for the dearth of eligible immortals, the culprit is our low fertility rates. Children are rare."

The cabin fell silent as her sisters absorbed everything they'd been told.

"I have more questions," Parisa said. "Many more. But for now, I think we've all learned more than we can process, so let's keep the rest of our questions for later."

42

FENELLA

F enella sat on the edge of the bed in her new room, the white box containing her clan phone resting on her lap. After the tour of the village, she'd been escorted to a two-bedroom house that looked very much like the ones Ingrid had shown them earlier. The other occupant was a clan member who worked in the city, and she wouldn't be returning until much later.

Fenella hoped that Ingrid had remembered to notify the woman so she wouldn't be surprised to find a stranger in her house. What was her name? Shirley something? Or was it Shira?

She should have written it down. Now, she would have to call the woman darling and dear until she volunteered her name.

The house was absurdly nice—all clean lines and tasteful furnishings that probably cost more than Fenella had won gambling in the last decade. Even the sheets on the bed felt expensive, with a thread count that mocked every dingy hostel and fleabag motel she'd stayed in over the years.

This level of luxury made her uneasy. Nice things came with strings attached, and she'd learned long ago that the higher the quality of the accommodation, the steeper the eventual price.

Yet everyone here acted like this was normal. Just another day in their hidden paradise.

Fenella flipped open the box and removed the sleek phone, turning it over in her hands. It looked like the latest iPhone model but wasn't. It was a clan satellite phone that worked from anywhere and everywhere in the world and had the best security. Jasmine had shown her the list of contacts that had been pre-loaded, the map of the village that was tucked in the notes, and all the different applications that were similar to what was available on other phones but not quite the same. All the social apps were there, but they were funneled through security filters or something like that. Jasmine didn't know how to explain it, and even if she had, it would have flown right over Fenella's head. She barely knew how to use a computer and had never owned one.

She scrolled for Din's name and number among the contacts. Jasmine had found it for her and added a ridiculous heart emoji beside it so Fenella would have an easier time finding it.

Naturally, she'd immediately deleted the stupid heart.

Nevertheless, she needed to call him so he would stop bothering Jasmine every time he wanted to talk to her.

The phone rang only three times before he answered, but each ring stretched her nerves.

"Fenella?" Din's voice—deep and rich with that Scottish burr of his—transported her back to smoky pubs and rain-slicked streets. "You got your own phone now?"

"Yeah. It was waiting for me in the village." She winced at how stilted she sounded. "That's where I am now. I got a room in Shirley's or Shira's house or whatever. I don't remember what Ingrid said her name was. She's not here right now."

"I'm so glad you called." The warmth in his voice loosened something tight in her chest. "Are you settling in alright?"

Fenella leaned back against the headboard, kicking off her shoes and drawing her legs up onto the bed. "I suppose. Everything is so posh. It's like living in a luxury hotel, just without the obnoxious drunk tourists."

Din chuckled. "After a while, you'll miss the drunks. It gets pretty boring in the village. All those chirping birds and clean air are just too much."

Was he mocking her?

"You've been here before?" she asked.

"A few times," he confirmed. "Weddings, mostly. Some clan-wide celebrations that everyone was invited to, and I couldn't wiggle out of with a good excuse."

Fenella tried to picture Din at a wedding—brooding in the corner somewhere and being antisocial. The man she vaguely remembered from the pub fifty years ago had been quiet, serious, and lurked in the shadows.

Not really the friendly sort he sounded like on the phone.

"What's Scotland like these days?" she asked, changing the subject. "Still wet and miserable?"

"Gloriously so," he replied with a smile in his voice. "Though I've got a decent flat in Edinburgh now, not too far from the university. Bit different from the old days."

"The university? What do you do there? Are you studying something?"

"I teach archaeology."

That caught her by surprise. "Get out of here. Archaeology? I didn't peg you for a scholar."

"What did you peg me for, then?" There was an edge of amusement in his question.

Fenella considered it. "I don't know. Something more technical, perhaps? Security work, computers, or engineering."

"When you've got endless time, you can try out all kinds of things. Archeology has been my latest obsession. I fell into it by accident—I started taking night classes to pass the time and found I had a knack for it. There's something satisfying about piecing together the past." He paused. "Plus, teaching in the university has other benefits. Lots of pretty lasses who fancy a young-looking professor."

Fenella laughed. "Naughty, naughty, Din. You shouldn't play with your students."

"Never from my department. But others, well…"

Maybe that's how he'd become more friendly and confident.

"Speaking of archeology, there's this exhibition in the glass pavilion here—artifacts and such. Somebody's personal collection. Quite impressive, actually."

"Aye, I've seen it. Kalugal rotates the displays regularly. He's got a storage facility in the underground with countless items that he's collected over the years."

Fenella sat up straighter. "Is that the bloke who owns the plane that got us to California?"

"That's him."

"I didn't know that there was so much money in archeology."

Din chuckled. "There isn't unless you steal and sell artifacts. Kalugal steals them, but he never sells them. He's a collector. He makes his money from all kinds of shady businesses."

An idea occurred to her. "You should talk to him. If he has a lot of money to throw around, you could interest him in a dig, and he could finance it."

There was a pause long enough that Fenella wondered if the connection had dropped.

"I've never considered it," Din said finally. "I don't know Kalugal well, and he's... well, he's a former Doomer. Makes me uneasy, to be honest."

Fenella felt her brows shoot upward. "A Doomer? Here in the village?" Her hand instinctively went to her throat, the memory of Durhad still inducing a flare of panic. "I thought they were the clan's enemy."

"They are," Din said. "But Kalugal's different. He collected others like him, and they escaped from the Brotherhood. It was a long time ago, and he's been living a semi-legit life."

"What is he doing here, though? Why was he accepted?" Fenella couldn't keep the incredulity from her voice. "I understand maybe not going after him because he wasn't harming anyone. But this is too much."

"There's more to the story, and I don't want to get into details, but the bottom line is that none of Kalugal's men ever believed in Navuh's hateful ideology, which was why they escaped. They are immortal, they have military training, and they are bound by an unbreakable treaty to defend the village. The alliance makes us stronger."

Fenella digested this information. The world wasn't black and white, she knew that, but after what she'd been through, it was difficult to think about anyone and anything connected to the Brotherhood as not pure evil.

"I met a Doomer," she said. "He wasn't the redemption-worthy type."

"I know," Din said quietly. "I'm so sorry about what you've been through."

Fenella swallowed against the sudden tightness in her throat. "Yeah, well. I survived."

"You always do," Din said. "It's one of the things I admire about you."

Something in his tone made her uncomfortable —the weight of his regard, the implication that he had spent decades thinking about her, forming an image of who she was based on a handful of inter-actions.

"You don't know me, Din," she said. "You didn't know me then, and you know me even less now. I'm not the same girl you remember from that pub."

"I know that," he said, his voice steady. "I'm excited to get to know you as you are now."

She rolled her eyes. "Why carry a torch for fifty bloody years based on what—a few smiles across a bar?"

In fact, she couldn't remember if she'd ever smiled at him, or he at her.

There was a long pause before Din responded. "It wasn't just a few smiles, Fenella. You were full of life in a way that made everything else seem dull by comparison. But you're right—I don't truly know you. That's why I'm flying over. To find out if the woman you've become might be interested in the man I am now."

"Look," she said finally, softening her tone. "I think we should start afresh. No expectations based on the past. Just two people getting to know each other now."

"That's all I'm asking for," Din said. "A chance."

"Yeah, I get that." She tried to sound just the right amount of excited but mostly indifferent. "So, Professor Din, tell me about this animosity between you and Max. Was it really because of me?"

Din's laugh was short and without humor. "No, it was because of him and the insensitive, selfish ass he was."

"I take it you're still not fans of each other?"

"We made our peace after he called me with the good news," Din said. "But there was a time when I couldn't stand the sight of him."

"Because of me?" Fenella prompted.

"Because he was supposed to be my friend, but he pursued you, knowing how I felt about you. You didn't know, so it wasn't your fault, but he did, and he didn't care that he was crushing me."

"He left me the moment he realized how you felt, and then I became sick, and after that, I started noticing strange things about myself that I couldn't explain. The truth is that you both screwed me over with your stupid games."

"I'm sorry."

"Oh well, so is he. But this girl is the one who suffered."

He sighed. "I promise to make it up to you."

"You can't. There is no fixing everything that went wrong with my life, the family I had to leave behind, the nomadic life I had to live. While you and Max were indulging in your stupid grudge."

She didn't know why she was getting so angry all of a sudden. Up until Max had told her what had happened to her, she hadn't known who to blame for her transformation, and after, she didn't really have time to process it and get angry at the two idiots who'd ruined her life but had also given her immortality, so she couldn't be entirely pissed at them.

"Fifty years is nothing for an immortal," Din said. "I realize that it hasn't been easy for you, but you can live like a queen from now on."

"It was a lifetime to me," Fenella countered. "I've lived a dozen different lives since then. Been a dozen different people."

"And who are you now?" Din asked.

Fenella hesitated. "I'm still figuring that out. But I know who I don't want to be—a pawn in a stupid testosterone contest between you and Max."

"That's fair," Din conceded. "And for what it's worth, Max and I are okay with each other now. No more contests. He told me that he found his one and only."

"Yeah. That takes the fun out of the whole feud between you."

"What is she like?"

Fenella laughed. "Why? Do you want to fight over Kyra now?"

"Can you stop doing that? I'm just curious about

the female who's caught Max in her net. He's such a butterfly."

"Kyra is amazing. A strong woman. A warrior. He doesn't deserve her, but neither do you."

"Ouch."

"Yeah." She let out a breath. "Sorry about snapping at you. I don't know why I'm so irritable. Let's talk about archeology. It's safer."

"I love it," Din said, warming to the subject. "There's nothing quite like holding something in your hands that hasn't been touched by anyone else in thousands of years. Makes you feel connected to the sweep of history."

"I never thought about it that way," Fenella admitted. "I've spent so much time running from the past, I never considered digging it up on purpose."

"Perhaps it's time to stop running," Din suggested.

The comment hit closer to home than she liked. "Maybe," she allowed. "This place seems secure enough, if a bit boring for my taste. It's like a retirement community, you know? Do they have bingo night here?"

He laughed. "Is it really that bad? Was someone mean to you?"

"No. They are all disgustingly nice. It's just a big adjustment. Going from complete freedom to this gilded cage."

"Complete freedom," Din repeated. "Is that really what you had out there, Fenella? Living hand to mouth, always looking over your shoulder, never putting down roots?"

The question stung because it contained more truth than she wanted to admit. "Freedom is priceless, and I survived."

"Surviving isn't the same as living," Din said.

"God, you sound like one of those inspirational posters," Fenella groaned. "Next, you'll be telling me to 'live, laugh, love.'"

Din chuckled. "I wouldn't dare."

"When do you arrive?" she asked, changing the subject.

"Saturday evening your time."

"Another delay?"

He sighed. "Please don't start with the bad omen nonsense."

"Fine. Maybe we can get a drink at that hobbit bar Ingrid showed us."

"I'd like that," Din said.

An awkward silence fell between them, both seemingly unsure how to end the conversation.

"Well," Fenella said finally, "I should go. Jasmine mentioned dinner at Ell-rom's sister's, and I'm starving."

"Of course," Din said. "Thanks for the call."

"Don't make a big thing of it," she said, discomfort rising at the emotion in his voice. "It's just a phone call."

"Even so. I'll see you Saturday."

"Saturday," she confirmed and ended the call

before anything else uncomfortably sincere could be said.

Fenella set the phone aside and fell back onto the bed, staring at the ceiling. Talking to Din had been easier than she'd expected but also more disquieting. There was an intensity to his interest in her that both flattered and alarmed her. Fifty years was a long time to carry a torch for someone you barely knew.

When her phone rang, she was sure it was Din calling her back, but it was Jasmine.

"We're at your front door. Are you coming?"

"Yes. Give me a minute." She ended the call and pushed herself off the bed.

On her way out, Fenella caught her reflection in the entry mirror and groaned. Her hair was mussed, and a faint flush still colored her cheeks from the phone call.

"Oh, stop it, you fool." She brushed her hair with her fingers. "He's not worth getting excited over."

43

MAX

The wheels of the jet touched down with a gentle bump, and as Max lifted the window shade, he was momentarily blinded by the harsh California sunshine.

When they'd left, the weather was still clinging to winter, but it seemed that summer had suddenly descended while they were away.

He immediately closed the shade and turned to look at Kyra, who was still dozing off or just keeping her eyes closed. He wanted her to have these last moments of peace to relax because as soon as they disembarked, she would once again get consumed by caring for her sisters and their kids.

The truth was that he couldn't wait to be alone with her, and not just because he wanted to strip her naked and make love to her all day and night long until he erased every last bit of subconscious memory of all the horrible things that had been done to her. Logically, he knew that he couldn't do that, but emotionally, he was driven to give it his best shot. For now, though, he would just love a couple of hours without anyone else making demands on her time.

As they taxied toward the clan's private hangar, Kyra opened her eyes and looked at the closed shade. "Can you open it? I want to see where we are."

"Of course, but be ready for extreme sunshine in your eyes."

She shielded them with her hand. "I'm ready."

"Home sweet home," he said as he lifted the shade. "Or rather, home away from home. The village is about two hours from here, maybe more, depending on traffic."

Kyra nodded, scanning the airstrip. "It's nice to have a private airfield and a hangar. I didn't even know it was an option."

He chuckled. "We live in the land of the free, where everything is possible if you have the money to bribe local politicians or if you can thrall them to do what you want."

"And the clan can do both."

"Correct."

As the plane came to a complete stop, Max saw that the medical van was already parked by the hangar, with Julian and Gertrude standing beside it. The bus was a little farther away, parked next to Morris's car.

"Remind your sisters about the screening," Max

said. "Tell them it's nothing to be afraid of, and to prepare the kids."

Concern flashed across Kyra's face as she looked back at her sisters and their children. "Do you think the Doomers implanted Yasmin's kids with trackers? Or Parisa's? They could have done that while the boys were at school."

"It's possible," Max said. "With how sophisticated the Doomers suddenly appear to be, they might have gotten to the boys in school, given them a shot, and then made them forget about it. It's even more likely with Yasmin and her kids, who were held by the Doomers for several hours before we got them out. Then again, Yasmin and her children were in the safe house, and no one came for them while the Doomers came after the rest of us."

"So, can we skip Yasmin and her kids?" Kyra asked. "They are the most fragile right now."

"Of course not. It would be irresponsible of us to bring anyone to the village before verifying that they can't unknowingly bring the enemy to us."

"What's going to happen now?" Soraya asked.

"As I told you before, all of you need to be scanned for trackers," Kyra said. "Then we'll board the bus that will take us to the village. It's a two-hour ride from here."

"I hope the bus has a toilet," Parisa said, seemingly unconcerned with the scanner.

Parisa's youngest boy looked at him with big, rounded eyes. "Will it hurt?"

Max crouched down to the boy's level. "Not at all. It's just like taking a picture, only lying down. You will need to be very still while the machine takes lots of pictures."

The child didn't look entirely convinced but nodded anyway.

"Is it an X-ray machine?" Parisa's oldest asked.

"Similar," Max said.

As Morris opened the plane's exit door, Max extended the stairs and led the way down, with Kyra directly behind him and the rest of the family following in a tight cluster.

He welcomed the familiar dry and warm California air. It was wonderfully clean up here in the mountains.

"Welcome back," Julian said, extending his hand first to Kyra, then to Max. "I'm glad to see everyone made it out safely." He shifted his gaze to Kyra's sisters and their children. "Welcome to the United States of America," he said more formally, then looked at Kyra again. "Care to do the introductions?"

Gertrude joined them, and Kyra introduced her as well.

The children shook hands with the doctor and the nurse, and they in turn smiled and said all the right things, but the kids were still eyeing the medical van with trepidation. One of Parisa's sons was edging behind his mother, while Yasmin's youngest had buried her face in her mother's side and refused to shake hands with anyone or even show her face.

"Come on, Cyra," Yasmin tried. "It's rude to hide your face from the nice doctor."

Cyra shook her head while continuing to bury her face in her mother's skirt.

Gertrude crouched down next to the girl. "Hello there. I'm Nurse Gertrude, and I want to play a fun game with you."

The girl peeked at the nurse with just one eye, the other still hidden in the fabric. "What game?"

Gertrude smiled warmly. "Have any of you ever played spy games?"

The question caught the children off guard, confusion momentarily displacing their fear.

"Spies?" Parisa's youngest son repeated with a frown.

"Yes," Gertrude confirmed, her voice lowering conspiratorially. "Bad guys sometimes put little tracking devices on people without their knowledge so they can find those people later. We have a special spy-catcher machine. Would you like to see how it works?"

When Cyra nodded, Gertrude offered the child her hand, and to everyone's great surprise, the girl took it and went with her.

Max was sure that the nurse had used thralling to convince the child to come with her. That little girl had only let go of her mother's skirt when she'd fallen asleep, and from the moment she'd woken up, she'd gone back to clutching it like a lifeline.

"She's good with kids," Yasmin said. "Now that the

most scared one went first, the others will have to follow."

"Does Gertrude have children?" Kyra asked.

"No," Max said. "But she's been the clan's nurse for many years."

While Kyra and her sisters looked on, the children went through the scan one by one, each emerging with a small sticker badge that Gertrude had apparently prepared beforehand.

At some point, Kyra turned, smiled, and waved at Okidu, who was waiting patiently by the bus.

"Kian's butler is such a nice guy, but he's strange," she said.

"Of course he is." Max watched Gertrude escort Soraya to the van. "Didn't I tell you that he is not human?"

Kyra raised an eyebrow. "I thought immortals didn't age, and he looks to be in his mid to late forties. Did he transition at a later age? Which reminds me," she leaned closer to him, "Will my sisters look the same after their transition, or will they look more youthful?"

Chuckling, Max lifted his hands. "That's too many questions all at once. First, Okidu is neither human nor immortal. He's kind of a cyborg, although the term doesn't do him justice. He was created on the planet of the gods, and he's part machine and part biological being, but he's sentient, and he's constantly learning by mimicking and other means. That's how he can appear so human. There are only seven Odus on Earth, and all originally belonged to the Clan Mother. She gave one to each of her children, and three remained with her. Okidu takes care of Kian and his family."

Kyra stared at the Odu, then back at Max. "And you just have him driving buses and serving drinks?"

Max grinned. "He does a lot more than that. He also cleans Kian's house and some of the spaces at the keep, cooks, and even babysits. Kian treats him as a member of his family."

"Yet he calls him 'master' and behaves like a servant," Kyra said.

"That was his original programming, and he sees no need to change it. He enjoys what he does and gets greatly offended if anyone even suggests doing something that he considers his own domain. The more sentient he becomes, the more he clings to his role. I guess it gives him purpose and satisfaction in the same way that our occupations do for us."

Kyra grimaced. "I'm officially out of a job and need to rethink my career. But back to the butler. If he's part machine, he's probably very strong. How safe is it for him to babysit for Kian? I mean, as long as he's just a robot and does precisely what he's programmed to do, that's probably fine, but being sentient brings with it the good and the bad. You know what I mean?"

Max knew precisely what she meant, and he had no doubt that Kian had done some hard thinking before he felt comfortable leaving Allegra with Okidu.

"The Odus had thousands of years of the Clan Mother's positive influence, and she's always treated them as family, even when they weren't sentient, and more so after. Just as good parents produce good children because they set a good example, the Odus had the best possible example. They've learned kindness from the Clan Mother. Besides, they are programmed never to harm anyone unless they're protecting clan members."

"That's supposed to be comforting?" Kyra asked, keeping her voice low. "There are so many things that can go wrong within those parameters."

"Like what?" he asked.

Kyra pursed her lips. "I can't think of anything offhand, but I'm sure I'll come up with several ideas once I have some time to ponder this. In my experience, no matter how tightly you define the rules, there are always unforeseen consequences when it comes to dangerous tech or weaponry."

He found it fascinating that Kyra had picked up on the inherent danger the Odus represented without knowing anything about them and what they were capable of.

Was it instinct? Or was it her pendant sending her a warning?

It was under her shirt, and she hadn't reached for it like she did every time it warmed up or vibrated or whatever else it did to warn her, so her response probably hadn't been triggered by it.

"How did you get your pendant?" he asked.

She lifted a brow. "That's a random question. Where did it come from?"

He shrugged. "I was just thinking that if Okidu was dangerous, your pendant would have warned you."

Now her hand went to it, clutching it over her shirt. "It's not always reliable. I trusted it to give me a signal if my decision to get Soraya first was wrong, but it didn't warn me or prompt me to choose Yasmin instead."

Max tried to think of a rational explanation for that, but it was kind of an oxymoron to rationalize the behavior of a mystical object.

"I don't know what to tell you. Maybe it's not always on task." He wrapped his arm around her middle and drew her closer to him. "If you don't want to tell me how you got it, that's fine."

"I have no problem telling you. When I was escaping the asylum with the other women who helped me get to the resistance, we stayed the night at the house of an old relative of one of them. who also gave us clothing to hide who we were. I found the pendant in her backyard and brought it to her, thinking she'd lost it, but she said she threw it away and that I should keep it. I tried to refuse and offered to give it to Bahar, who was her sister's granddaughter, but the woman said that the pendant had found me and that I should keep it. I thought she was just rambling nonsense, but I didn't want to offend her by refusing, so I took it. I had no idea it would guide me from that day on."

"That's a fascinating story. Have you ever gone back to thank her for it?"

Kyra shook her head. "When I returned to Tehran several years later, she was gone."

44

KYRA

"All clear," the doctor said as he returned with Rana, who had been the last to get checked. "No tracking devices on anyone."

"That's a relief," Kyra said. "Thank you."

"My pleasure." The doctor glanced at the children, who were circling the plane.

The older boys were pretending to be knowledgeable about avionics, and the younger ones were pretending to believe them.

"Are we waiting for Yamanu and the rest of the team to arrive?" she asked. "Soraya and Rana are eager to reunite with their daughters."

Max nodded. "They should be here shortly, and we are all riding the bus back home. We should probably get everyone on board, so the kids are not running around when Eric lands."

"Good idea." Kyra turned to her sisters. "Everyone's clear, but we still need to wait for the rest of the team to arrive with the other plane. Once they get here, we will head to the village where Arezoo, Donya, Laleh, and Azadeh are waiting for you."

"How far is it?" Soraya asked.

"About two hours," Max replied, even though he'd told them before how long it would take. They were nervous and excited, and he was super understanding. "The bus has a toilet compartment, so no worries about that. I noticed that the kids have small bladders that need frequent emptying."

Parisa cast him a hard look as if she was insulted by his comment. "That's because they were drinking all those sugary drinks you had on board the plane."

"Do they have television on the bus?" one of Parisa's boys asked.

"Yes, they do," Max said. "You can start watching a movie right now if you want."

That was the magic word that got all the kids running for their backpacks and then rushing toward the bus.

Okidu bowed to each one of them, welcoming them by name, which was better than Kyra could do. She wondered if he'd talked with the girls to get the names of their cousins.

"How do you know my name?" Parisa's youngest boy asked.

Okidu's smile didn't look fake at all this time. In fact, Kyra had a feeling that he was about to say something mischievous.

"A little birdie whispered it in my ear, Arman." Okidu cupped his ear. "She whispered the names of your brothers too. Tyrus, Zaden, and Kavir."

The boy stretched on his toes, looking behind Okidu's ear, then frowned. "There is no bird."

"It flew away," Okidu said while flapping his hands to mimic a bird flying.

"I wonder if he saw that somewhere," Max murmured. "He must have seen it on one of those British soap operas he loves to watch."

Kyra certainly hoped so. Otherwise, it would mean that the Odu could lie, which was extremely disconcerting.

"Can you show us how to work the TV?" one of the older boys asked Okidu.

"Of course, master. I'm coming up." Okidu climbed into the bus.

"Such a strange man." Rana walked over to stand beside Kyra.

"He's not a man." Kyra motioned for her other sisters to come closer and explained what Okidu was.

"I want one," Parisa said. "It would be so lovely to have someone to help with the boys, clean the house, and cook. I might actually be able to read a book from time to time."

Kyra laughed. "There are only seven Odus in existence, and they all belong to the Clan Mother's family."

"That's a shame." Parisa let out a breath. "It would have been so nice."

As they climbed into the bus, they saw that the kids had commandeered the back seats, so the six of them chose the middle of the bus, leaving the front for the rest of the team.

"Perhaps this is as good a time as any to explain about this bus and its special features," Max said. "About twenty minutes before we reach our destination, the windows will turn opaque. Don't be alarmed. The windows will let in light but won't allow you to see out. It's a security measure designed to protect the location of the village. Every car that can enter the village is equipped with this feature."

"Why is it necessary?" Rana asked.

"You've been exposed to our enemies," Max pointed out. "They are relentless. Keeping the location of our village a secret is a necessity."

Rana was about to say something when the sound of an approaching aircraft drew everyone's attention. The jet appeared in the distance, making its final approach.

"That's Eric with the rest of the team," Max said. "Good timing."

The kids abandoned their movies to cluster on one side of the bus and watch the plane touch down smoothly and then taxi toward them.

It continued into the hangar and stopped next to the jet they had arrived on.

A few moments later, the door opened and Yamanu emerged, followed by Jade and the rest of her crew.

Kyra had gotten to know the five Kra-ell pretty well during this mission, and she liked them and appreciated their unparalleled fighting skills, but they still looked alien to her, with their unusual height and otherworldly features that were impossible to ignore.

"How's everyone doing?" Yamanu asked as he climbed into the bus.

"Julian cleared everyone," Max said. "You've just missed him and Gertrude. They left a few minutes ago."

Jade followed him into the bus, her large eyes scanning and her lips lifting in a ghost of a smile when her eyes landed on the kids.

"Hi, Jade," one of the boys called out. "Do you want to sit with us? We are watching a car race."

"Maybe later. I want to chat with Max and Kyra for a little bit."

"I thought her name was Jasmine," one of the girls said.

They hadn't told the children yet, but Jade didn't know that. Kyra turned around. "My name is Kyra. Jasmine was just a code name I used for the mission."

The explanation seemed to satisfy them, and they went back to watching the screens.

Jade stopped next to Kyra's seat. "You didn't tell them yet?"

"I told my sisters when the kids were sleeping."

Jade nodded, then swept her gaze over Kyra's sisters. "How did they take it?"

"Better than expected," Max said. "They are smart ladies." He lifted Kyra's hand to his lips and kissed the back of it. "Like their eldest sister."

Jade smirked. "You two should get a room, lock the door, and not come out until you both can barely walk."

Kyra was of the same opinion, but hearing it stated so bluntly brought heat to her cheeks. Her sisters' chuckles didn't help.

Thankfully, Jade continued down the aisle and sat next to Yamanu.

Max squeezed her hand. "Remind me to tell you later about the Kra-ell mating games."

"What about them?" Rana leaned between the seats.

Max rolled his eyes. "I said later, and I didn't promise to tell you anything, just Kyra."

When everyone had taken their seats, and Okidu pulled out of the parking spot and turned onto a narrow road, it suddenly occurred to Kyra that Max's fancy car wasn't parked where he'd left it.

"Where is your car?" she asked.

"Why, do you miss her?"

"No, but we left it here, and now it's not here."

"I asked my buddies to pick it up. It didn't feel right to leave my baby out in the open like that. She's used to me taking better care of her."

"What is he talking about?" Rana asked from behind them.

Kyra really needed to have a talk with her sisters

about boundaries, or things would start to get strained between them before they even got a chance to get to know each other.

"Max's car is very precious to him."

"Oh," Rana sounded disappointed.

"It will get a little bumpy," Max warned. "The section just before the main road is unpaved to make it look like there is nothing important up here. It's only a few minutes, though."

After the bumpy stretch, Okidu turned the bus onto the main road, heading toward the highway.

"Wait until you see the village," Max said. "It's like its own little world, nestled in the mountains with views of the ocean on clear days."

"I just hope my sisters are going to acclimate well," Kyra said. "It's a big adjustment—new country, new culture, new everything."

"They will," Max assured her. "They are a resilient bunch, and they've got each other and you."

Kyra fell silent, her thoughts turning to what would come next. "I've been thinking about what happens after," she murmured. "When we are all settled in, and after I help the Clan Mother find her beloved."

Max leaned closer, his lips nearly touching her earlobe. "You mean other than making love for days and nights until we both can't walk straight?"

His words and his warm breath on her ear delivered a rush of desire that made her so weak in the knees that she was glad she was sitting.

"I'm serious," she whispered back. "Don't give my sisters even more kindling for their needling."

He leaned away, his expression turning from playful to serious. "We talked about this. You could join the Guardian Force, and if that doesn't appeal to you, maybe you could ask Eva if she needs more agents for her undercover work."

The truth was that Kyra didn't like the idea of starting at the bottom again, which would be the case in the Guardian Force. She would need to train with the Guardians for a long time before she could be cleared for missions. Perhaps an undercover civilian job would be a nice change. At least she wouldn't be in mortal danger during her missions, and the chances of encountering Doomers would be negligible.

"I need to visit Eva, thank her for the disguise, and return it to her. I didn't check what Asuka and Rishba packed for me, and I hope they didn't forget it."

It would be very unfortunate if the borrowed disguise had been left behind. Especially if she hoped to discuss employment options with Eva and also ask for her help with another project she had in mind.

"I'm sure they didn't forget anything," Max said. "So, what will it be? A spy or a fighter?"

She chuckled. "I'm a fighter, and I also worked undercover. I'm keeping my options open."

"The Guardian Force would be lucky to have you, especially since we need someone with your knowledge of Iran if we decide to do something about the

Doomers there. But don't decide right away. Give yourself time to explore, to discover what other things you might be interested in. Maybe you have artistic talents like your daughter."

She leaned her head on his arm. "That reminds me that you haven't sung to me other than that one time."

"Do you want me to serenade you now?"

She chuckled. "Not now. But maybe later, when walking is a challenge."

MAX

About twenty minutes before the entrance to the tunnel, the windows turned opaque, still allowing light in but obscuring the view outside. The transition elicited a few nervous murmurs from the back of the bus, but not as much as Max had expected.

It was quite impressive how quickly the family was adjusting to the new world unfolding before them.

"The children still don't know," Max said. "Are you going to leave it to their cousins to fill them in?"

"I don't know. Perhaps their mothers should do that."

Max leaned closer to Kyra. "Children have a way of sharing secrets, especially ones as exciting as this. Their cousins might do a better job of it than the mothers."

"I'm not sure 'exciting' is the word I'd use," Kyra said.

"From a kid's perspective? Finding out you might eventually develop superpowers? That's the definition of exciting."

Kyra's expression softened into amusement. "When you put it that way, I suppose it is. I just hope they understand the serious parts, too, and I don't even want to think about explaining the sexual part of the induction to the girls. In that regard, they lived very sheltered lives in Iran."

"They had access to the internet, right?"

She nodded.

"Then they are not as innocent as you think they are," Max said. "I mean knowledge-wise. I hope they didn't get adventurous and risk their lives for a few thrills."

She smiled. "Since they weren't caught, it doesn't matter now if they did or not. I'm kind of hoping that the older girls got some thrills."

Max pretended shock. "Who are you, and what have you done with Kyra?"

She laughed. "I'm loosening up, reminding myself to live life and enjoy it because now I can."

As they approached the final stretch of road before the hidden entrance to the village, Max felt a familiar sense of homecoming. The village held a special place in his heart. It was where he'd found purpose after centuries of aimless wandering, where he'd returned to the Guardian Force and finally felt like he belonged.

Now, it would be even better with Kyra by his side.

"We are almost there," he said, giving her hand a gentle squeeze. "Excited?"

"Nervous," she admitted. "Not for myself. I know that I'm going to love it there because that's where my Jasmine lives and where you are. But I'm anxious about my sisters and their kids and whether they will fit in."

"They will, and you know that. You're just over-thinking everything."

Kyra let out a breath. "You are right." She leaned back in her seat.

"I'm always right." He did the same and closed his eyes as the bus entered the tunnel, and it got dark.

Kyra punched him lightly in the arm. "Overconfident much?"

"Always. It's my trademark."

"Yeah, and I kind of like that about you. I hope it sustains you while you take part in the family circus. Don't think you can just disappear into your Guardian training."

Max grinned. "I wouldn't dream of it."

"Are we underground?" Soraya asked.

"Just for a short while," Max assured her. "As I said before, the entrance to the village is through a tunnel."

The lift that took the bus up several levels was

349

another cause of gasps and children's frightened voices, but then they finally emerged into the underground garage, the windows cleared, and the audible gasps turned into the admiring type as the boys got a look at some of the fancy cars parked there.

"It's enormous!" one of Parisa's sons exclaimed, pressing his face against the glass.

"The village has several underground levels," Max explained. "This is just the parking area. The actual village is aboveground, on top of the mountain."

"We've arrived," Okidu announced as he parked the bus near the elevators. "Welcome to the village."

As the doors opened and the family began to gather their belongings, Max turned to Kyra. "You know," he said, "for all the chaos and danger, this mission ended well. Your family is safe, reunited, and starting a new life together. I really love happy endings."

"This is not an ending," she corrected him. "It's just the beginning."

KYRA

K yra stepped off the bus, scanning the parking garage for familiar faces. She'd half-expected to see Jasmine and her nieces waiting for them, and she couldn't help but feel a little disappointed that they weren't there—not for herself, but for Soraya and Rana.

"I thought Jasmine would be here," she said quietly to Max as her sisters and their children gathered behind them.

"She probably wanted to prepare a proper welcome in their homes." Max put his hand on the small of her back. "Jasmine is not the type who would let an opportunity for celebration go to waste."

Yamanu and the Kra-ell warriors filed out after them, their expressions relaxed now that they were safely back home.

"Where do we go now?" Soraya asked, herding her nephews and nieces together.

"This way." Max pointed toward the bank of elevators lined along the far wall. "The village is above us."

Kyra led her family across the garage, noting how they huddled together like a small flock of birds, their eyes darting around the cavernous space with mostly awe but also uncertainty.

"Is this America?" Arman asked.

Parisa smiled, ruffling his hair. "Yes, my sweet. This is a little tiny piece of America."

They divided into groups for the elevators, with Max, Kyra, and the family squeezing into the first one while Yamanu and the Kra-ell took the other.

Standing in silence they all faced the doors, waiting for them to open, and as they did so to reveal a magnificent glass pavilion, Kyra joined in her sisters' collective gasp. It wasn't just because of the unique structure or the beauty of the village beyond; it was because of the assembled crowd waiting for them in the pavilion.

A banner was attached to the opposite wall, its Farsi script declaring 'Welcome to the Village' in elegant calligraphy. Jasmine stood front and center, flanked by Ell-rom, Kian, and Syssi on one side and Arezoo, Donya, Laleh, and Azadeh on the other. Behind them was Fenella, who stood together with an immaculately dressed blonde woman, who Kyra guessed was Ingrid, the interior designer Jasmine had mentioned. The one in charge of housing in the village.

But Kyra barely had time to register the welcoming committee before a piercing cry cut through the momentary silence.

"*Maman!*"

Arezoo broke from the group, running toward them with Donya and Laleh hot on her heels. Soraya stumbled forward, her arms opening just in time to catch her daughters in a fierce embrace. The four of them collapsed together in a tangle of limbs and tears, clinging to each other as if afraid that a sudden wind might tear them apart.

Not to be outdone, Azadeh raced forward and launched herself at Rana with such force that her mother staggered, steadied only by Parisa's quick hand at her back. Mother and daughter held each other, sobbing openly, the weeks of separation and fear dissolving in an instant.

Kyra felt her own eyes burning as she watched mothers and daughters reunite, her heart so full it seemed to press against her ribs. She felt Max's arm settle around her shoulders, anchoring her as waves of emotion swept over her.

"You made this happen," he whispered against her hair.

"We did it together," she corrected.

The other kids hesitated for a couple of moments before also launching themselves at their cousins, and then their mothers joined the happy tangle as well.

The elevator chimed again behind them, and as

Yamanu, Jade, and her crew stepped out, they got a clapping ovation from the assembled crowd.

Yamanu bowed while Jade and her crew looked uncomfortable and used the first opportunity to slink away.

Jasmine approached through the commotion. "Mom," she said, embracing Kyra. "I knew you would get them. I just didn't know how much trouble it would be. I should have gone with you."

"Your cousins needed you here." Kyra hugged her daughter fiercely, and the surreal nature of the moment washed over her.

Here she was, surrounded by family she'd only recently discovered—a daughter grown to woman-hood without her, sisters she didn't remember, and nieces and nephews she was just getting to know. After decades of isolation, of belonging nowhere and to no one, she suddenly had family connections extending in all directions.

"I can't believe we're all here," she murmured against Jasmine's hair. "That we are all safe."

"Believe it." Jasmine pulled back to gaze at her with shining eyes. "Welcome home, Mom."

Kyra nodded and looked at Kian, who waited patiently until the sobs and sniffles subsided.

He then stepped forward, raising his hands for attention. The crowd gradually quieted, though the reunited families remained intertwined, reluctant to separate even briefly.

When he started speaking, it was through a translating device, but Kyra didn't see the bulky teardrop.

"On behalf of the Clan Mother and members of this community, I extend to you our warmest welcome." He paused, his gaze sweeping over the assembled group. "Here, you will find safety, and most importantly, you will find family—both the one you were born into and the larger one that embraces you."

Kyra was deeply touched by the warm welcome, her emotions overwhelming, and as she turned to look at her sisters, she was glad to see that they all looked appreciative and accepting without the snark they had exhibited before.

There was something about Kian that brooked no argument, a sincerity that permitted no doubt, not even from her skeptical sisters.

Syssi stepped forward, her multi-toned golden hair gleaming in the late afternoon sun. "Tomorrow, we'll have a proper celebration at the village square, but today is for rest as I'm sure you're all exhausted. Jasmine, Ingrid and Fenella have worked hard to prepare homes for each of your families," she said, her gentle voice a contrast to Kian's authoritative tone. "They're fully stocked with food and all the necessities. I know that you had to leave most of your possessions behind, but I don't want you to worry about a thing. Everything you need will be delivered." She turned to Jasmine. "I leave it to you to explain how things work around here."

"Thank you," Soraya said, speaking for the group. "For the rescue and for your hospitality. It is all a little overwhelming at the moment, and I don't know how we will ever be able to thank you properly, but I promise that my sisters and I will put our heads together and come up with something of value that we can contribute to this amazing community."

Syssi smiled, and even Kian gave Soraya an appreciative nod. "Kian and I will leave you in Jasmine's capable hands," Syssi said. "Your new homes are a short walk from here. Have a good night's rest, and we will see you tomorrow at noon for the celebration."

After Syssi and Kian left, Jasmine started herding their group toward the exit. "We should get everyone settled before they collapse," she said. "There's a golf cart outside for luggage, but maybe it's not needed, given how light you are all packed."

"The children don't even have pajamas," Kyra said.

Jasmine snorted. "You underestimate what can be done here in twelve hours or less. There is clothing for everyone, mothers and children. Just the basics for now, but they can order anything they need, and it will be delivered in less than twenty-four hours."

"I'm impressed," Kyra admitted.

Turning around, she saw Fenella, who was walking toward her.

"Quite the homecoming," Fenella said. "Your nieces haven't stopped talking about their mothers and cousins since we arrived here." She threaded her arm through Kyra's. "They were so scared of coming here that Jasmine didn't even tell them to pack their things, but they fell in love with the village at first sight, and they were very happy to have Okidu pack up their stuff and bring it over."

"I totally understand," Kyra said. "It's beautiful here."

Fenella nodded. "I have to admit that the place has its charms, but it's a little too much of a commune for me. I like my independence."

"Where's Din?" Kyra asked. "Wasn't he supposed to be here?"

"He'll get here Saturday evening," Fenella said. "First, he missed his flight because of an accident on the road, then his second flight got canceled, so I told him not to come because those were bad omens. Naturally, the bloke wouldn't listen to reason, so he's coming even though there was a third delay." She turned to look at Jasmine. "That reminds me. Did you bring the tarot cards back? I want Jasmine to do a reading for me regarding Din."

"Of course." Kyra patted her pocket. "I carried them with me for good luck." She pulled out the velvet pouch and handed it to her daughter. "As promised. I'm returning them to you in person, alive and well."

"Thank you." Jasmine took the pouch and held it to her chest. "I knew they would protect you."

Behind them, Kyra heard her sisters' murmurs of appreciation as they took in the carefully designed community, with its gravel and stone pathways winding between Mediterranean-style homes and manicured greenery.

"It's perfect," Yasmin said softly, the first words Kyra had heard from her since they'd exited the pavilion.

"It is, isn't it?" Soraya agreed, linking arms with her sister. "Hard to believe we will be living in this paradise."

"I keep expecting someone to hand us a bill," Parisa said.

"No bills," Max assured them from Kyra's other side. "Everything is provided free of charge, and you will get an allowance for personal expenses. The clan does expect everyone to contribute in their own way once they're settled, though. There's plenty of work for those who want it, and access to online education for you and the children."

"No school?" one of the boys asked.

"There is a school for those who want to attend, but given that you need to learn English first, home-schooling will probably work better until you have command of the language."

"So, what's that for?" One of the girls pointed at a two-story building.

"That's an office building," Jasmine said. "The one next to it is the clinic, and in front of both is the open-air café, which is the busiest spot in the village. It's closed now, but there are vending machines in the back that serve pretty good coffee, sandwiches, pastries, and snacks."

"Can we go there?" Cyra asked.

"Not now, sweetie." Yasmin put her hand on her daughter's head. "Aren't you curious to see our new home?"

The girl nodded. "Tomorrow then?"

"Yes," Yasmin said. "We can go there tomorrow."

The procession continued down a tree-lined path that led to the residential area. The warm Mediterranean architectural style was consistent throughout, yet each home had unique touches that prevented monotony.

"Here we are," Jasmine announced. "Soraya's girls chose this one."

As the three girls dragged their mother toward the entrance, Kyra watched as Arezoo opened the door and ushered her family inside with the air of someone who already considered it her home.

"No one locks their doors in the village," Jasmine said. "We don't even have keys."

It was nice. A little strange, but as someone who had lived most of her life in tents or half-ruined buildings with no doors. Kyra wasn't used to having keys anyway, so she wouldn't miss them.

They continued down the path, delivering each family to their new residence. Rana and Azadeh were next, then Parisa and her sons, and finally Yasmin and her children. Each home had been thoughtfully prepared with refrigerators stocked, beds made, meals waiting to be heated.

"The girls helped with everything," Jasmine said as they watched Yasmin and her children disappear into their new home. "They wanted everything to be perfect."

"This place is more perfect than I could have ever imagined," Kyra said, emotion catching in her throat again.

Only she, Max, Jasmine, and Ell-rom remained on the path now, the others having either entered their homes or departed for their own residences else-where in the village.

"Is there a home for us?" Kyra asked, turning to Jasmine. "Or am I just going to stay with Max at his house?"

She didn't really care where she was going to spend the night as long as it was with him.

Her daughter smiled, pointing to a house further away. "That one is Ell-rom's and mine," she said, then gestured to the property across the path. "And that one is for you and Max. If you don't like it, we can switch. I haven't gotten attached to mine yet."

The home was similar to her sisters' houses but with subtle differences—a slightly larger front porch and white rose bushes.

"I'm sure I'm going to love it," she said, then looked at Max. "Do you have a preference?"

He smiled. "Home is where you are, love."

47

MAX

J asmine beamed with happiness. "Well, I guess I'll see you tomorrow morning. If you need me, you know where to find me." She pointed at her house.

"I'll call first." Kyra pulled her daughter into a fierce hug. "Thank you."

"No need to thank me," Jasmine said with a slight tremor in her voice. "Nothing could make me happier than to have you here, living across the street from me, and my aunts and cousins a few houses down. For me, this is paradise."

"For me, too." Kyra kissed her cheek. "Goodnight, sweetheart. And say goodnight to Ell-rom from me."

Max hadn't even noticed that the guy had ducked out of sight, and it must have happened a while ago. Perhaps he'd gotten tired, or maybe the reunion had made him overly emotional. Despite his deadly abilities, the prince was a gentle soul.

"I will." Jasmine shifted her gaze to Max. "Treat my mother right, or I will put a hex on you."

He pretended to shiver in fright. "Your mother is my warrior queen, and I her humble servant."

Jasmine snorted. "Humble my ass. You don't have a humble bone in your body." She leaned over, kissed his cheek, and then leaned away. "Having you as my stepdad will be so weird."

He grimaced. "Ooh, yeah. You as my stepdaughter." He shook his head. "Let's just not go there."

Jasmine laughed, gave them a finger wave, and walked over to her house.

"What was that all about?" Kyra asked.

"You know the story. Amanda tried to play matchmaker and get Jasmine and me together. It was an automatic no-go because she reminded me of Fenella. I guess I owe Fenella a thank you for that. And before you ask, Jasmine didn't like me either."

"I don't know if I should be glad or sad about that. I want you two to like each other."

"We do. We made our peace when we investigated your disappearance."

Kyra let out a breath. "Good."

"Shall we?" He motioned at the house.

"Yes. Of course."

"Then let's do it properly." He swung her into his arms and walked over to the front door.

Kyra wrapped her arms around his neck. "Carrying the bride over the threshold?"

"Indeed." He opened the door with his foot and stepped inside. "Welcome home, Kyra."

"Welcome home, Max." She lifted her head and kissed his cheek. "Can you let me down now?"

"Yes, of course." He gently put her down and then laid their two duffle bags on the floor by the front door.

Kyra walked toward the kitchen, trailing her fingers over the granite countertops, the smooth surfaces of the polished appliances, even the gooseneck faucet, and then turned around.

"It's even nicer than the penthouse."

It wasn't, but it was theirs, and even though it was not much different than the house he'd been sharing with Thomas, it was the first time he was sharing a house with someone who truly mattered to him. That made it home.

"I love the open concept living area and the large windows that capture the golden evening light," she said.

"The automatic shutters are going to come down any moment now. The village is under a strict no-light rule at night to protect its location." Max frowned. "In fact, maybe we should alert your sisters before the shutters go down, as they may misinterpret what's going on."

"I'm on it," Kyra nodded as she texted Jasmine to split the sisters between them. A moment later, Jasmine replied, and Kyra smiled. "It's all good. Jasmine has already given my sisters the heads-up."

She started opening kitchen cabinets and drawers, finding them fully stocked with dishes, cookware, and utensils. "I can't believe they did all this."

Max watched her explorations with a warmth spreading through his chest. "Let's check out the rest," he suggested, taking her hand.

They checked out the guest bedroom next and then moved on to the master bedroom with its king-sized bed, seating area, generously sized bathroom, and walk-in closet. It was already filled with their clothing, with Kyra's meager wardrobe on one side and his own clothes on the other.

"Jasmine even had my things brought over from my house. I'm impressed."

Kyra laughed. "Presumptuous of her, wasn't it?"

"Perceptive," Max corrected with a grin. "Though I doubt she anticipated how quickly things would develop between us."

A folded piece of paper rested on top of a neat stack of T-shirts, and as Max picked it up and read it, his smile widened.

"What is it?" Kyra asked.

"A note from my roommate." He handed it to her.

Kyra took the paper and read it aloud: "Congratulations on finding your truelove mate. May your forever be filled with happiness. —Thomas." She looked up at Max with amusement dancing in her eyes. "That was nice of him."

"It was," he agreed, pulling out his phone. "I should

text him to say thanks and to apologize for the short notice. He wasn't expecting me to leave him quite so suddenly."

His fingers flew over the screen, composing a message: *Thanks for the note and for helping Jasmine with my things. Sorry about the abrupt move. Drinks on me next time we are at the Hobbit.*

The response came almost immediately, *No worries. Happy for you. Any chance you could introduce me to one of your girlfriend's sisters? I hear there are four of them, and they are all single.*

Max laughed, drawing a curious look from Kyra, who had moved to inspect the bathroom.

"What's so funny?" she asked.

"Thomas," Max said, showing her the message. "I should have warned you that gossip runs at the speed of light through the village. The hounds have heard about four new ladies in the village, so your sisters are going to become very popular very fast."

Kyra rolled her eyes. "My sisters need time to adjust first. I should talk to them about where they stand on faith and relationships. I have a feeling they're not particularly religious and would prefer a secular life, but I need to check with them to confirm." She smiled. "When I know their feelings on the matter, point me in the direction of the biggest gossip so I can have their wishes known."

"I know just the guy."

Max set the phone aside and pulled her into his

arms, relishing the way she fit against him. "But all of that can wait until tomorrow," he murmured, brushing his lips against her temple. "Right now, I believe you have a promise to deliver on."

Her amber eyes darkened with acknowledgement. "I do, don't I?"

"Mmm," he confirmed, his hands sliding down to her waist. "That's all I have been thinking of since you announced your plans for me."

"Me too," she admitted. "Well, it wasn't all I've been thinking about, but it did occupy a large chunk of my cognition."

"Perhaps we should start with a joint shower? It has been a long twenty-four hours."

"More like thirty-six," she whispered, her fingers playing with the hem of his shirt. "After so many days of travel and combat, I could use a thorough cleansing."

Max felt his body responding to her teasing tone, to the promise in her eyes. "Allow me," he said, reaching for the buttons of her shirt with deliberate slowness. Each one revealed another inch of skin that he wanted to worship, to memorize with his fingertips and lips.

Kyra stood perfectly still, only the quickening of her breath betraying her anticipation as he worked his way down. When the last button gave way, he pushed the fabric from her shoulders, letting it fall to the floor. She stood in front of him in her sports bra, lean and yet round in all the right places.

"Your turn," she whispered, tugging at his shirt until he raised his arms, allowing her to pull it over his head.

She placed her palms on his chest, her fingers tracing every ridge and valley. "You are like a golden god," she whispered.

He chuckled. "I'm a descendant of gods, so I guess the compliment's fitting."

Kyra laughed. "I love how modest you are."

"Modesty is overrated." He pulled her cargo pants down, and when all that covered her body was a bra and a pair of modest underwear, he took a moment to marvel at her strong, lithe warrior's body.

"You're gorgeous," he murmured.

Her eyes were glowing with inner light as she gave him another thorough once-over. "So are you. Now, lose the pants."

"So bossy." He did as she commanded, standing before her in his boxer shorts.

The stretchy cotton couldn't hide the massive erection he was sporting, and as her gaze lingered there a little longer than other parts of his body, he felt a stupid surge of male pride.

"Like what you see?"

"Very much so." Her voice was husky with desire. "Shouldn't you turn the water on?"

"Yeah, I should." Max didn't move, mesmerized by her body and wondering how to best divest her of what was still covering her.

He hadn't forgotten what Kyra had told him about

abstaining from physical pleasure for over two decades. The only times she'd been touched sexually hadn't been consensual, and it certainly hadn't been pleasurable.

Max forced the thought out of his mind because it had no place in this beautiful moment between them. Instead, he reached into the shower to turn the faucet on, adjusting the temperature until steam began to rise. Then he took her hand and guided her inside into the warm cascade that enveloped them both.

Water sluiced over them, dampening Kyra's hair and making the fabric of her bra and panties see-through.

It was doing the same to his boxer shorts.

"Can I peel this off you?" He pulled one strap down her shoulder.

She nodded, swallowing nervously.

Max took his time, pulling the other strap and tugging the garment down until her breasts popped free.

"Fates, Kyra." He knelt in front of her, reverently kissing each turgid peak while pulling the bra all the way down her toned legs.

When she stepped out of it, he tossed it aside, and it plopped down with a wet splash. Kissing down her flat belly, he pushed his thumbs into the elastic of her panties and pulled them down slowly, kissing every inch of tanned skin he exposed. When he discarded them, he was tempted to cup her bottom and sink his face in her mound, but he reminded himself that Kyra didn't remember ever being with a man before, and her reintroduction to the world of carnal pleasures should be slow.

48

KYRA

Kyra was losing her mind. The anticipation was killing her, but she didn't remember how to make love to a man, and she trusted Max to make it good for her.

When he lifted her into his arms and sat with her on the shower bench, she was a little surprised, and when he reached for the shampoo as if he was going to wash her hair instead of licking every inch of her body, she was a little disappointed.

But when he worked the shampoo gently into her hair, massaging her scalp, she sighed with pleasure and closed her eyes.

"That feels amazing," she murmured, leaning into his touch.

Perhaps going slow and relaxing first was better than moving straight into the ravaging part. Supposedly, the buildup was no less important than the act itself.

"I've never washed a woman's hair before," Max said when he rinsed the suds out with the handheld. "Did I do it right?"

Was he really asking her about her hair routine right now? Was he afraid of moving too fast?

She could feel his erection under her, and it was deliciously hard and velvety smooth.

Her core responded to the feel of him just as it should.

She wasn't broken, she hadn't shriveled and died sexually. She'd been waiting for him.

"I'm waiting for instructions," he reminded her.

"Conditioner," she murmured.

"Oh, that's right." He lifted his arm to reach for the conditioner. "How much should I use?"

If he kept this up, she was going to explode from frustration.

"Never mind." Rising, Kyra turned and looked into his eyes. "I want to kiss you." She cupped his cheeks.

Max leaned away as if he was the one who didn't remember how to do this. "Careful on my fangs," he murmured. "They might scrape you."

It was dark in the bathroom, but with both their eyes glowing, there was enough light for her to see his fangs clearly and they were as long and as sharp as they had been when he'd fought the Doomers.

Sexy and terrifying at the same time.

"I don't care if they scrape me." She kissed him lightly on the lips. "I heal fast. Remember?"

He groaned. "I've never made love to an immortal female before. This is all new to me."

His admission loosened the last tendril of tension within her. "I guess it's a virgin voyage for both of us since I don't remember ever making love to anyone."

Max chuckled nervously. "In a way, I guess." His speech was slurred because of his fangs, and that, too, was sexy. "I like it that you are not afraid of my fangs."

"Says who?" She flicked her tongue around one gleaming fang, then leaned away to look at him. "Will it hurt?"

"Only for a split second."

He squeezed conditioner into his palm, but instead of working it into her hair, he used it to massage her breasts while kissing her neck. "But then the venom will turn it into incredible pleasure, and you will climax, over and over again, until you black out."

She shivered. "If you keep doing that to my breasts, I might orgasm just from that."

"It would be the first one of many."

He took her lips gently, slipping his tongue inside her mouth, somehow making sure not to slice her lip with his sharp fangs.

When he retracted his tongue for a moment, she followed with hers, slipping it between his fangs.

He groaned, and his shaft twitched under her. Evidently, an immortal male's fangs were an erogenous zone, and swirling her tongue around them was turning him on, maybe too much because he cupped the back of her head and pulled her away.

"I don't want our first time to be in the shower," he hissed.

Kyra didn't see anything wrong with that, but given that she had no remembered experience, she let Max lead the way.

Lifting with her in his arms, he carried her out, wrapped her in a towel, and carried her to the bed.

"I love how strong you are," she said when he laid her down gently.

His smile was predatory as he yanked the towel off her and used it to dry himself off. He was a sight to behold, and she devoured him with her eyes as he tossed the towel aside and climbed onto the bed, all muscle and sinewy grace.

"I want a kiss." He put his hands on her knees and gave them a slight push. "Spread a little for me."

Kyra's eyes widened as she realized what kind of kiss he was planning.

The room was completely dark now that the automatic shutters had gone down, but Max could see her just as clearly as she saw him, and she had a moment of hesitation before doing as he asked.

Kyra had never thought of herself as submissive, but she felt a thrill at obeying Max's command and doing something she was slightly uncomfortable with. Maybe it was the primitive part of her, the cavewoman that lusted after the strongest male, and her arousal shot several notches up.

He dipped his head and rewarded her with a long lick that was followed by a probing finger, just a gentle circling before finally pushing it slowly inside of her.

It felt so good, and she wanted more, but she also wanted him to take it slow and treat her like a virgin. When he added his tongue to the play, pumping her with his fingers and circling her clitoris with his tongue, her moans turned into groans, and her hips shot up to get more of his fingers, more of his tongue.

He gave her what she wanted, devouring and pumping until the coil finally snapped, and she shouted his name, but somehow, no sound left her throat.

A moment later, he gripped her hips and plunged into her with one powerful thrust, and she came again, this time his name reverberating from the walls as she screamed it.

He drove in and out of her, going hard and fast, and she met him thrust for thrust, climbing up and up toward another climax. She was hovering over the edge when he draped himself over her, his big body enveloping hers as he licked the spot where he was going to bite her.

Kyra tensed, expecting him to sink his fangs into her neck, and when he did, there was a moment of searing pain, but then the venom entered her vein, and she orgasmed again, and then there was bliss, and she shot up to the sky and kept soaring.

49

KYRA

Sunlight streamed through the bedroom window, casting dappled patterns across the rumpled sheets. Kyra stretched, yawned, and then cuddled back into Max's warm body.

Memories of the night brought a smile to her lips.

She'd blacked out after his venom bite, soaring on the clouds of euphoria over psychedelic landscapes, but she didn't spend too long there and came back for more. They'd made love two more times before falling asleep.

Max's arm was draped over her, and his hand caressed her as she lay curled against him.

"We should get up," she murmured, even as she pressed a kiss to his chest. "The welcome party will be starting soon."

"Mmm." His hand slid lower to close over her bottom. "We have time."

His lips found hers again, and Kyra melted into

the kiss, savoring the warm, solid feel of him against her. She just couldn't get enough of him. He was like cool water after a lifetime of thirst.

"Max," she half-protested as his kisses trailed lower and his fingers feathered over her moist petals. "We don't have time for this. We're going to be late."

"They can't start without us," he reasoned, his voice muffled against her skin. "You're one of the guests of honor."

A glance at the bedside clock finally spurred her to action. "It's almost eleven-thirty, and we still need to shower and get dressed."

Suddenly remembering that she hadn't applied conditioner or combed her hair after washing it, Kyra gasped. "I'm a complete mess. How am I going to meet the Clan Mother for the first time with my hair sticking out in all directions?"

"You're beautiful." Max kept lazily stroking her back.

"Yeah, I can just imagine." She pulled out of his arms and rushed to the bathroom, completely unperturbed by her nudity.

After he'd kissed and licked every inch of her body, it would have been absurd to suddenly feel modest.

The mirror confirmed her suspicions, and she groaned, reaching for the hairbrush. "I look like a wild cavewoman who's never heard of a brush, let alone used one."

Max stood behind her, smiling at her through the

mirror. "I love cavewomen." He encircled her waist and pulled her back against him. "Just this one." He started kissing her neck.

"That's right." She waved the brush in mock threat.

"Give me one more kiss," he murmured, turning her around. "For good luck."

One kiss became several more before Kyra finally broke away. "You're incorrigible. Get the shower going. We have minutes to be out of here."

They managed to shower and dress in record time, though not without a couple more delays involving wandering hands and a few kisses.

By the time they stepped outside, Kyra's hair was gathered in a chignon because she hadn't had time to tame it, and the only makeup she'd bothered with was some mascara to curl her lashes.

"You look beautiful," Max said for the umpteenth time. "You don't need fancy dresses or makeup."

She shook her head. "Maybe I don't need that, but I sure would have liked to look more put together as I'm being introduced to every resident of this village."

Her sisters and their children were already waiting outside for them, together with Jasmine and Ell-rom.

"Sorry we're late," Kyra said. "We overslept."

"I bet." Soraya gave her a thorough once-over, her eyes sparkling with amusement. "You look good, Kyra. A good night's sleep did wonders for you."

"Aunt Kyra," one of the girls said. "Look at my new dress."

All the children were dressed in new clothing—nice button-down shirts and trousers for the boys, and pretty dresses for the girls.

"Jasmine has a good eye," Yasmin said.

She was also dressed in a new outfit, a long flowing skirt and a loose blouse that skimmed her plump body without clinging or making her look fuller than she was.

"Thank you," Jasmine said. "We should hurry up, or you will be late for your own party."

"Shall we?" Max suggested, offering Kyra his arm with exaggerated formality that made the younger children giggle.

As their family began walking toward the village center, Kyra felt the warm sun on her face and smiled, feeling contented in a way she had never felt before. It was a beautiful day, warm but not hot, with a gentle breeze carrying the scent of flowers and the distant ocean.

"This place is like paradise," Parisa remarked, her usual pragmatic manner softened by wonder. "I keep expecting to wake up and find we're still in Tehran."

"It's so strange," Rana said. "Having our big sister look younger than all of us. Though I suppose we'll get used to it, especially if we all transition at some point and turn back the clock." She chuckled. "I wouldn't mind losing the wrinkles and the gray hairs."

Kyra looked closer at her sister's head. "You don't have gray hair."

"They are there. I've been plucking them out."

It suddenly dawned on her that Rana had said those things in front of the children.

"Have you told the kids?" she asked quietly.

Yasmin nodded. "Arezoo prepared three different versions of the story according to their genders and ages. She made it much easier for us."

Kyra shot her niece an appreciative glance. "Thank you."

Arezoo nodded. "I figured Aunt Yasmin and Aunt Parisa would need help with that. It's much easier to explain it to the boys. I had more trouble making a good story for the girls."

"How did they take it?" Max asked.

Arezoo chuckled. "Kids are much more accepting of fantastic stories than adults. They are now convinced that all the superheroes are immortals and therefore real people."

That actually made sense.

As they neared the village center, the sounds of music and laughter grew louder, and when they turned a final corner, they found the village green transformed.

Tables draped in white cloths were arranged in rows, surrounding a large area that was clear save for a small podium. The music was coming from loud-speakers, and buffet tables laden with food were arranged on one side of the green.

"Wow," breathed one of Parisa's sons, his eyes wide at the spectacle. "Is this all for us?"

"It is," Jasmine said, resting a hand on his shoulder. "To welcome you and your family to the village."

"Awesome," said Parisa's eldest.

"This way, everyone." Jasmine led them toward the center.

When people rose to their feet and walked over to introduce themselves, Kyra rushed to translate, but Jasmine stopped her.

"They all got earpieces and the newly designed teardrop that is now a pin the size of a quarter. They were delivered this morning."

Kyra let out a breath. "That was very thoughtful. Who should I thank for that?"

Jasmine laughed. "William, of course. It could have been done by one of his teams, but he was the one who gave the instructions."

Kyra looked around the large assembly of people. "Point him out to me when you see him, will you?"

"I will," Jasmine promised.

As more people approached Kyra and introduced themselves, she could barely keep track of the names and faces, and she waited for a particular two. William and Eva. She needed to thank both of them, and she needed another favor from Eva.

Jasmine nudged her arm, drawing her attention to a striking couple. "I would like to introduce you to Morelle and Brandon."

Morelle was unmistakably Ell-rom's twin—the

same otherworldly beauty, the same towering height and striking blue eyes, and the same black hair. Morelle's was slightly longer, but not by much. The short hairstyle suited her well. She radiated a vibrant energy that seemed barely contained in her statuesque form. Beside her, Brandon appeared almost ordinary by comparison, although he was very handsome in his own right.

"Finally!" Morelle exclaimed, clasping Kyra's hands. "I've heard so much about you from Jasmine and Ell-rom."

Kyra returned the female's warm smile. "Thank you. It's a pleasure to meet you both."

"The pleasure is ours," Brandon assured her. "Having so many youngsters join our community at once is a boon from the Fates."

When a hush suddenly fell over the crowd, Kyra turned to see people parting to make way for a small, glowing figure.

There was no mistaking who she was.

Annani, the Clan Mother, the goddess, was a vision of ethereal beauty that was blinding in its perfection.

She looked so young and slight that one could mistake her for a teenage girl of seventeen or eighteen, with skin that was visibly glowing even in the bright light of day and fiery red hair that cascaded past her hips in big, luxurious waves. The goddess couldn't have been more than five feet tall, slim, and delicate, yet her presence was enormous, filling the space around her with a tangible energy.

"Breathe," Max whispered in her ear, his hand finding the small of her back to steady her.

Kyra realized she had indeed been holding her breath, and as she exhaled, she glanced at her sisters and saw the same stunned amazement on their faces. Even the children were silent, watching wide-eyed as the goddess glided up the steps to the podium.

The Clan Mother raised her hands. "I would like to extend my warmest welcome to Kyra and her beautiful family." Her voice was unexpectedly rich and resonant for such a small form, carrying effortlessly across the gathering without the need for amplification.

Her gaze swept over each of Kyra's sisters in turn and then the children. "You enrich our community with a new maternal line of strong, smart, and beautiful ladies and your equally strong, smart, and beautiful daughters and sons. Your journey to us has been marked by suffering, loss, and courage. Today, we celebrate not only your safe arrival but also the beginning of a new chapter in your lives—one of freedom rather than oppression, of choice rather than constraint."

Soraya was tearing up and dabbing at her eyes, Rana was clutching Azadeh's hand so tightly that her knuckles were white, and Yasmin had her arms wrapped around her five children, pressing them to her sides.

"In this village, you will find safety," the Clan Mother promised. "You will find purpose. You will find community. And most importantly, you will find the freedom to become your truest selves, without the artificial limitations imposed by those who fear feminine power."

The goddess's gaze found Kyra then, seeming to see through her to the core of her being. "Kyra, daughter of Shiraz, sister, and mother—you have traveled the longest road to return to your family. Your courage in the face of darkness has lit the way for others. Know that you are valued, you are seen, and you are home at last."

Tears flowed down Kyra's face now. Max's arm tightened around her waist, anchoring her as emotions threatened to overwhelm her defenses.

"The bonds of family—both blood and chosen— are sacred," the goddess continued, addressing the entire gathering. "When darkness comes, as it inevitably will, remember that together, we are stronger than the forces that seek to divide us."

With that, she stepped down from the podium, and the spell of silence that had held the crowd spellbound broke into enthusiastic applause.

"The Clan Mother is incredible," Kyra whispered to Max, hastily wiping away tears.

"She is," he agreed, his own voice rough with emotion.

This was everything Kyra could have hoped for— a beginning filled with promise and possibility. Yet amidst the joy, she felt a nagging sense of incompletion, a loose thread that needed tying before she could fully embrace this new chapter.

"Max," she said, turning to him. "I need to talk to Eva."

He frowned. "Now? Why?"

"I need closure with Boris," she explained. "He deserves to know that I'm alive, even if I can't tell him everything. But I can't see him looking like this." She gestured to her face. "I need Eva to make me look much older."

50

EPILOGUE

KYRA

The hunting cabin looked exactly as Max had described—rustic, isolated, nestled among tall pines that whispered in the mountain breeze. Kyra studied it through the windshield of their rental car with trepidation, suddenly reevaluating the wisdom of her decision to meet Boris.

She'd faced Doomers, gunfire, and torture with less anxiety than she felt now, facing a weathered wooden structure and a piece of her past that needed closure.

"Are you sure about this?" Max asked, his hand covering hers where it rested on her knee.

Kyra nodded, glancing at the small mirror in the rental's sun visor. Eva's handiwork was remarkable—fine lines etched around her eyes and mouth, subtle graying at her temples, a softening of her jawline, and a little padding but not as pronounced as the fat suit she'd worn on the mission.

The woman had aged her twenty years with such skill that even Kyra had been startled by her reflection.

"It needs to be done," she said. "For his sake and for mine."

It wasn't pure altruism on her part. Boris held missing pieces of her past she had no other way of reconstructing.

Max squeezed her hand. "Then let's do it."

They'd agreed on a cover story that contained as much truth as possible. Her father's dastardly deed, shock treatment, and drugs that robbed her of her memory, and finally being found in Kurdistan by chance. The rest she would improvise, though Max had assured her that Brundar's suggestion to Boris to accept that her disappearance wasn't his fault had taken root.

Nodding, Kyra opened her door before she could reconsider.

The air was cooler up here in the mountains, carrying the scent of pine and other vegetation. The cabin was not well kept—peeling paint, sagging gutters, and an accumulation of fallen branches on the roof.

Perhaps it was because Boris was getting older and didn't have the energy to do the upkeep, or maybe his finances were not allowing him to hire help.

Max knocked on the door, then moved aside.

The door swung open to reveal Boris, looking older and more worn than she'd expected given the pictures of him that Jasmine had shown her. His hair had thinned and grayed at the temples, his face was puffy and slightly lined, and his middle had thickened considerably. But his eyes were sharp, intelligent, and a beautiful shade of blue.

She had a feeling it had been his eyes that she'd fallen in love with.

They widened with shock as they fell on her.

"Hello, Boris," she said softly. The name felt strange on her tongue, divorced from any emotional context.

He staggered backward, one hand reaching for the doorframe to steady himself. "Kyra?" His voice cracked around her name. "My God... Kyra?"

He'd been expecting Jasmine, who had called ahead to make sure he was there, and at first, the plan was for her to come along, but in the end Kyra decided that she needed to do it alone. Max had to be there in case thralling was needed following their talk, but that was it.

"May we come in?" she asked.

Boris nodded mutely, stepping aside to allow them entry. The interior of the cabin was dimly lit and smelled strongly of whiskey and cigarette smoke. Empty bottles stood in haphazard formation on a coffee table littered with old magazines and an overflowing ashtray.

"I apologize for the mess," he said, hastily gathering some of the debris. "I wasn't expecting guests."

Evidently, he didn't count Jasmine as a guest, which made sense. He was her father after all.

His eyes shifted back to Kyra's face, drinking in every detail with desperate intensity. She felt a pang in her chest—not the rekindling of old feelings, but a profound sadness for what had been lost, for what this man had endured.

"Please, sit," he offered, gesturing to the sofa. "Can I get you anything? Coffee? Whiskey?"

"Nothing for me, thank you." Kyra lowered herself onto the sofa.

Max sat beside her, his presence steady and reassuring. Boris had met Max before when he'd come here with Jasmine, but from what Kyra understood, Max had been erased from Boris's memory with a thrall, so she should introduce him again.

"This is Max, my fiancé," she said.

Boris nodded and sank into an armchair across from them. "How are you here, Kyra?" he said, ignoring Max. "What happened to you? Why did you leave me?"

The questions were direct and poignant.

"I didn't leave voluntarily," Kyra said. "I was stolen from you, just as you've always suspected, but instead of killing me, they made me forget my family and who I was. Many parts of what I'm going to tell you are reconstructed because I have no recollections of them, but the information I've gathered is pretty reliable."

She told him how she'd been abducted by her family, taken back to Iran, subjected to drugs and shock treatments that had erased her memories, and how she'd eventually escaped with the help of the Kurdish rebels who had been imprisoned with her in the asylum and joined the Kurdish resistance, living as a rebel with no knowledge of her past.

"I don't remember our marriage, Boris," she said, watching pain flash across his features. "I don't remember anything from before I woke up in the asylum. Not meeting you or falling in love with you, not our wedding, not our life together, not even Jasmine's birth or her childhood."

His hands clenched into fists on his knees. "Nothing at all?"

She shook her head. "The damage is most likely permanent by now. I don't even have glimpses of the past."

The only clues she'd ever had were the dreams about Jasmine that she'd thought were about her own childhood.

Boris's eyes misted with tears. "I looked for you," he said, his voice ragged. "For months, I drove every-where and showed your picture to everyone. I called the police every day until they threatened me with arrest." He shook his head. "I knew it was your family. You said they would come for you. I thought your family had killed you, and then the divorce papers came, and I was angry but also hopeful that you were at least alive."

Jasmine had told her about that.

"I don't remember signing them. My father probably wanted a clean break. Or maybe I insisted on that to set you free."

He nodded. "That thought occurred to me. You were never cruel. You wouldn't have wanted me to suffer. To be alone. You loved me."

Kyra felt a deep ache for this man with whom she'd shared a life. "I believe I must have," she said.

It was the most honest answer she could give, and it seemed to comfort him somewhat. His shoulders sagged, and he reached for a half-empty whiskey bottle on the end table near his armchair.

"Every time I looked at Jasmine, I saw you, and it hurt."

"She understands," Kyra assured him, though the knowledge of his emotional abandonment of their daughter still stung. "She knows you were trying to protect yourself and, in your own way, to protect her too. It's not too late to make amends, though."

This was the other reason she was here. Boris and Jasmine had both been injured by her disappearance, and they needed to heal their wounds and become a father and daughter again.

Boris nodded. "She looks happy with that guy, what's his name?"

"Eli," Max supplied. "He adores her."

Boris looked at Kyra, studying her face as if

committing it to memory. "And you? Are you happy now?"

The question caught her off guard.

She glanced at Max and smiled. "Yes. I have my family back—Jasmine, my sisters,their children. And I have Max."

Boris's gaze shifted to Max, assessing him with the wariness of a rival. "Take good care of her, you hear?"

"Of course," Max said with a smile. "Kyra takes care of herself, though, and I just have the privilege of standing beside her and watching."

Boris seemed a little confused by his answer, but he nodded and then looked back to Kyra. "Thank you for doing this. I've carried the pain of your loss for all these years, and seeing you alive and well has lifted a weight off my chest."

"I know," Kyra said. "As soon as Jasmine told me about you, I knew I had to come and give us both closure. Neither of us deserved what happened to us, but you built a new life with a good woman, and now I'm building a new life with a good man."

A smile lifted Boris's lips. "A much younger man. Good for you, Kyra. You always went for what you wanted despite the way you were raised. You are a fighter. No wonder you ended up in the Kurdish resistance."

He sounded so much more upbeat now that Kyra felt the weight of her own guilt lift off her chest.

Even though she hadn't been the one who had caused his misery, she'd been at the center of it.

They talked for another hour—about Jasmine's childhood and Boris finally accepting her choice of becoming an actress instead of doing something more tangible with her good brain. He told her about his wife and his two stepsons and even about his insurance business woes.

She'd guessed correctly that finances had been tight as of late. Insurance companies were becoming stingier with paying their agents and brokers.

When it was time to leave, Boris walked them to the door, looking years younger than the man who had opened the door an hour ago.

"Will I see you again?" he asked, hope and hesitation warring in his expression.

"We have a daughter, Boris. Jasmine and I live in California now, but we will both make an effort to come visit you from time to time."

"I'd like that."

She would have to learn Eva's techniques of making herself look older.

"Goodbye, Boris," she said.

He hesitated for a long moment, his blue eyes boring into hers. "I never stopped loving you, you know. Not for a single day. That doesn't mean I don't love my second wife. I do." He put his hand over his chest. "But there will always be a place reserved for you in here, Kyra."

Her throat full, she nodded. "Take care of yourself, Boris."

He watched her and Max as they got into the rental, and as she looked in the rearview mirror, she saw him standing in the doorway until they turned onto the road.

They drove in silence for several miles, the mountains gradually giving way to gentler foothills. Kyra stared out the window, watching the landscape blur past as she processed the encounter.

"How are you doing?" Max asked.

"Sad and glad at the same time," she admitted. "I'm sad for what was, for Boris, for the pain he carried, for Jasmine, for her growing up with a distant father who was licking his wounds." She turned to look at Max. "But I'm glad I eased his burden and mine."

"He loved you very much," Max said. "Still does."

"He loved the woman I was," Kyra corrected. "That woman is gone. She died in that asylum in Tehran."

Max squeezed her hand. "You're still you, Kyra. Even without those memories. The core of who you are remained, even when everything else was stripped away. I could hear it in every word Boris said about you."

She considered this, feeling the truth of it settle in her heart. "You're right. And now I'm ready to move forward and build a life not defined by what I've lost or what was taken from me."

Max brought her hand to his lips, pressing a kiss to her knuckles. "We have eternity ahead of us, love."

Time stretched before her like an endless horizon, full of promise.

As the sun dipped toward the western sky, Kyra felt a profound sense of rightness settle over her. Her journey had been long, painful, and full of obstacles and detours, but it had led her here—to this moment, to Max, to her family, and to this new life.

And what a glorious beginning it promised to be.

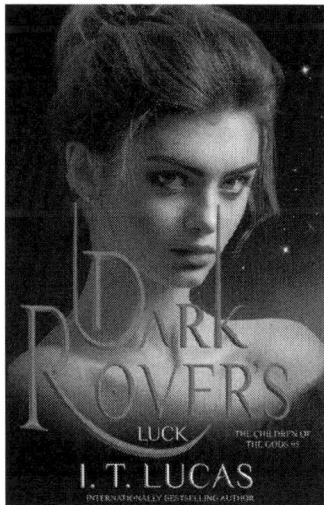

For five decades, Fenella has led the life of a ghost, wandering from place to place and relying solely on herself. Now, while seeking refuge in the immortals' hidden village, she uncovers an unexpected connection that may inspire her to stay longer than she planned.

Din has held a torch for Fenella for half a century. Yet, instead of the spirited bartender he fell for, he encounters a hardened, disillusioned nomad who struggles to remain in one place for long.

Some secrets are meant to remain buried, while others are destined to be revealed, and sometimes, luck is simply a matter of being in the right place at the right time.

NOTE

Dear reader,

I hope my stories have added a little joy to your day. If you have a moment to add some to mine, you can help spread the word about the Children Of The Gods series by telling your friends and penning a review. Your recommendations are the most powerful way to inspire new readers to explore the series.

Thank you,

Isabell

Also by I. T. Lucas

THE CHILDREN OF THE GODS ORIGINS

THE CHILDREN OF THE GODS

DARK STRANGER

DARK ENEMY

KRI & MICHAEL'S STORY

DARK WARRIOR

DARK GUARDIAN

PERFECT MATCH

THE DRAGON KING
MY WEREWOLF ROMEO
THE CHANNELER'S COMPANION
THE VALKYRIE & THE WITCH
ADINA AND THE MAGIC LAMP

TRANSLATIONS

DIE ERBEN DER GÖTTER
DARK STRANGER
1- DARK STRANGER DER TRAUM
2- DARK STRANGER DIE OFFENBARUNG
3- DARK STRANGER UNSTERBLICH

DARK ENEMY
4- DARK ENEMY ENTFÜHRT
5- DARK ENEMY GEFANGEN
6- DARK ENEMY ERLÖST

DARK WARRIOR
7- DARK WARRIOR MEINE SEHNSUCHT
8- DARK WARRIOR – DEIN VERSPRECHEN
9- Dark Warrior - Unser Schicksal
10-Dark Warrior-Unser Vermächtnis

LOS HIJOS DE LOS DIOSES

EL OSCURO DESCONOCIDO
1: EL OSCURO DESCONOCIDO EL
SUEÑO
2: EL OSCURO DESCONOCIDO
REVELADO
3: EL OSCURO DESCONOCIDO
INMORTAL
EL OSCURO ENEMIGO
4- EL OSCURO ENEMIGO CAPTURADO
5 - EL OSCURO ENEMIGO CAUTIVO
6- EL OSCURO ENEMIGO REDIMIDO

LES ENFANTS DES DIEUX
DARK STRANGER
1- DARK STRANGER LE RÊVE
2- DARK STRANGER LA RÉVÉLATION
3- DARK STRANGER L'IMMORTELLE

THE CHILDREN OF THE GODS SERIES SETS

BOOKS 1-3: DARK STRANGER TRILOGY—INCLUDES A
BONUS SHORT STORY: THE FATES TAKE A VACATION
BOOKS 4-6: DARK ENEMY TRILOGY —INCLUDES A
BONUS SHORT STORY—THE FATES' POST-WEDDING
CELEBRATION

BOOKS 7-10: DARK WARRIOR TETRALOGY
BOOKS 11-13: DARK GUARDIAN TRILOGY

MEGA SETS

THE CHILDREN OF THE GODS: BOOKS 1-6

INCLUDES CHARACTER LISTS

THE CHILDREN OF THE GODS: BOOKS 6.5-10

PERFECT MATCH BUNDLE 1

CHECK OUT THE SPECIALS ON
ITLUCAS.COM
(https://itlucas.com/specials)

FOR EXCLUSIVE PEEKS AT UPCOMING RELEASES &
A FREE I. T. LUCAS COMPANION BOOK

JOIN MY *VIP CLUB* AND GAIN ACCESS TO THE VIP
PORTAL AT ITLUCAS.COM

TO JOIN, GO TO:
http://eepurl.com/blMTpD

Find out more details about what's included with
your free membership on the book's last page.

TRY THE CHILDREN OF THE GODS
SERIES ON

AUDIBLE

2 FREE audiobooks with your new Audible subscription!

FOR EXCLUSIVE PEEKS AT UPCOMING RELEASES &
A FREE I. T. LUCAS COMPANION BOOK

JOIN MY *VIP CLUB* AND GAIN ACCESS TO THE VIP PORTAL AT ITLUCAS.COM

TO JOIN, GO TO:

http://eepurl.com/blMTpD

INCLUDED IN YOUR FREE MEMBERSHIP:

YOUR VIP PORTAL

- READ PREVIEW CHAPTERS OF UPCOMING RELEASES.
- LISTEN TO GODDESS'S CHOICE NARRATION BY CHARLES LAWRENCE
- EXCLUSIVE CONTENT OFFERED ONLY TO MY VIPS.

FREE I.T. LUCAS COMPANION INCLUDES:

- GODDESS'S CHOICE PART 1
- PERFECT MATCH: VAMPIRE'S CONSORT (A STANDALONE NOVELLA)
- INTERVIEW Q & A
- CHARACTER CHARTS

If you're already a subscriber and you are not getting my emails, your provider is sending them to your junk folder, and you are missing out on important updates. To fix that, add isabell@itlucas.com to your email contacts or your email VIP list.

Check out the specials at
https://www.itlucas.com/specials

Printed in Great Britain
by Amazon